A HEART WELL TRAVELED
VOLUME 1

A HEART WELL TRAVELED
VOLUME 1

EDITED BY SALLYANNE MONTI

SAPPHIRE BOOKS

SALINAS, CALIFORNIA

A Heart Well Traveled - Volume 1
Copyright © 2017 by Sapphire Books Publishing, LLC.
All rights reserved.

ISBN - 978-1-943353-89-7

This is a work of fiction - names, characters, places, and incidents are the product of the author's imagination or are used fictitiously. Any resemblance to actual persons living or dead, business, events or locales is entirely coincidental.

Editor - Sallyanne Monti
Cover design - TreeHouse Studio
Book design - LJ Reynolds

Sapphire Books Publishing, LLC
P.O. Box 8142
Salinas, CA 93912
www.sapphirebooks.com

Printed in the United States of America
First Edition – June 2017

This and other Sapphire Books titles can be found at
www.sapphirebooks.com

Preface

It's one of those defining moments, when in a split second, your world comes to a screeching halt. While the images of your life are played before you, a newfound love might appear, an existing love might be stressed beyond it's bounds, or a friendship might grow into unexpected romance. Amidst the intense connection and simultaneous longing to be together is the sinking reality that you and your love, are separated by too many miles and are deeply immersed in separate lives. As you ponder this in the cozy living room of your comfortable life you know to the depths of your soul that it's all about to change.

Can love really conquer all?
Sallyanne Monti

Acknowledgments

This unique anthology series comes to life through the heartfelt contributions of the many talented and acclaimed authors that are the women of our extended Sapphire Books family and our treasured lesbian literary community.

This is Volume One in the series.

It's an honor to collaborate with this ingenious group of lesbian romance writers and a privilege to preserve the essence of their words.

Sincere appreciation to all the Authors for entrusting their stories to us, Ann McMan and Treehouse Studios for brilliant cover design, and LJ Reynolds book designer extraordinaire.

Table of Contents

Just Like in the Movies

By N.R. Dunham

On being given this job, Cameron was also given two rules; don't screw the interns again, and don't let me hear of it if you do. She'd stuck to one of those at least, the most important in her opinion. What her father didn't know couldn't hurt either of them.

There were more than two rules, of course. There were endless rules, growing up a Morrison. The big one was to smile. Always be smiling, one never knew when the cameras were on. This rule Cameron did try to follow, so much so that she grinned through most of her parents' angry diatribes about how she was ruining the family name. It annoyed them immensely, her flashing the perfect teeth they'd financed when she was supposed to be acting contrite. Cameron thought more than once that Dad would've slapped the smile right off of her by now if he weren't concerned about the book she'd been threatening since she turned twelve.

Really, she wasn't breaking the rules. Emily wasn't an intern. Interns weren't paid. Emily was. Not very much, but paid. She was blonde haired and blue eyed, from Nebraska of all places. Her skin was pale and burned easily in the L.A. heat. She was, in short, a walking cliché, and it was fortunate that Cameron wasn't directly involved in her hiring. Emily was so boring on paper, small town girl, bright lights of Hollywood, big dreams, so utterly cliché that Cameron would've trashed her resume three seconds after picking it up. And what a stupid call that would've been, the next in a long line of stupid calls.

The production studio was the second child her parents never had, the last thing holding America's sweethearts together. It was also her last shot to make up for those rehab stints. And that semester at UCLA when she'd slept with half the students she was supposed to be teaching about film. Dad put her in charge of a small indie division of the company populated by upstart filmmakers. This was, Cameron knew, so she could inflict minimal damage and possibly, if the stars aligned and God was listening, do the occasional bit of quality work. She was on shithouse duty, the Hollywood royalty version of that anyway.

On reflection, saying most of this to her new employees five minutes into her first day on the job might not have been the best decision.

Emily though, Emily didn't care. As production assistants went she was perfect. Always on time, never complained, never argued. Which made her the polar opposite of Cameron. Also, she had an encyclopedic knowledge of Cameron's career. Cameron wasn't sure whether she was impressed or depressed when it became clear Emily had researched the whole company with that same thoroughness, not just her.

"Why do you want to work for me?" she'd asked once, after ten minutes spent drilling Emily on the details of the studio, budgets, and gross profit last year, upcoming projects. It was a very educational ten minutes.

"You're Cameron Morrison. Who wouldn't want

to work for you?"

Cameron shook her head, enjoying the way Emily's eyes widened. "You mean who wouldn't want to work for my parents," the Brangelina of the '80s that was the common comparison.

"I mean what I said," Emily informed her, holding her eyes with just the slightest hint of a tremor in her voice.

Cameron found her infinitely more interesting after that.

The sex, that still took awhile. Three weeks into shooting her first picture, Cameron was pulled aside by one of the other underlings, someone much less interesting than Emily. The movie featured an aging actor in a side role, someone her mother had a brief affair with twenty years before. That connection hadn't stopped him from hitting on Cameron during each of their sporadic meetings since she hit puberty and inherited her mother's boobs. He'd been mostly professional during the shoot though, no more perverted than usual. But the underling who wasn't Emily muttered and looked down as he explained that this C-list has-been had targeted Emily, the pretty in a Nebraska way, assistant who never argued.

Cameron entered his trailer without asking. Nothing was happening, thank God, but this unwanted relic from her childhood was sitting a bit too close to Emily, had his hand too high on her knee. Cameron sent him off to set and made it clear that if he wanted sex she would buy it for him. It was ultimately going on her parents' tab. He pretended not to know what she was talking about but wilted under her glare.

"You good?" Cameron asked, resisting the urge to smooth down Emily's skirt where the perv's hand had touched it.

"Of course. Miss Morrison," she added quickly. "I had it under control."

"I'm sure you did. You always do. You certainly know more about what's going on around here than I do at any given time. Not that that's saying much."

Emily smiled. "My mother gave me an emergency whistle and this thing on my keychain to stab people with." Emily showed her the keychain.

"Nice. My mother gave me birth control and a copy of the film with her first sex scene in it." Cameron paused. "I'm sure you can handle it. You shouldn't have to. If he tries something again, let me know. Before or after you use the keychain thing, that's your call."

A week later came the sex, on the couch in Cameron's office.

"You understand you don't have to do this," Cameron said, what she'd said to those students at UCLA. "You won't be penalized in any way. It won't affect your job. You don't have to sleep with my mother's leftovers and you certainly don't have to sleep with me."

"I understand."

"Good. And you also understand it goes both ways. You won't be getting a raise if the sex is good. Probably won't. It would have to be phenomenal sex, the kind you probably don't have in Nebraska."

Emily said she understood. Then proved Cameron had much to learn about Nebraska.

And so here they were, in Cameron's apartment, after weeks of truly phenomenal sex. Weeks that would've continued if life hadn't intervened.

"You sure you have to go?" Emily pouted from her place in Cameron's bed.

"Don't pull the sad face on me," Cameron warned. "I invented the sad face. Sad face was my bread and butter for five movies." She leaned over from where she stood by the nightstand, kissed the pout off Emily's lips.

"Was it weird, being a child star?"

Cameron shrugged as she dug through her bedside drawer. "Was it weird being a regular child, growing up in Nebraska? Don't answer that, it's Nebraska, of course it was."

"What are you even looking for? You know I packed your stuff already."

"Yes, and I told you not to do that. You're off the clock. You didn't have to do that."

"Like you're not too spoiled and lazy to pack your own bags."

Cameron gave her a look, eyebrows raised. "You're a mouthy little asshole off the clock, aren't you?"

"Since when has my mouth been a problem for you?"

Cameron shook her head and tried not to laugh.

"You sure you have to go?" Emily repeated.

"If we want this movie to make any money, yes. Promotion, darling, you know how it works."

"Promotion I get. Don't get why your parents have you doing it if they think you're such an embarrassment."

"I'm a hot embarrassment who gets press. Who do you think got more attention after they grew out of the cute kiddie phase, Shirley Temple or Lindsay Lohan?"

"I...I don't think that's a fair comparison for a multitude of reasons, the least of which—"

Cameron made a small noise of triumph as she held up the bottle of whiskey in her hand. "Found it!"

Emily sighed. "Seriously?"

"Yes seriously," Cameron said, unzipping the suitcase on the edge of the bed. "I'm going to be running the press gauntlet with my parents for a small eternity. I'm sure as hell not doing it sober." Cameron frowned as she looked into the bag. The clothes were balled up, thrown every which way. Something that bothered her even though most of them were hideous, things she either hadn't bought or hadn't bought in her right mind. The suitcase was packed sloppily and seemingly at random. One of her thongs was wrapped around a curling iron. Cameron was indeed spoiled and lazy, but even she would've done better than this.

"What the fuck, Emily?" She held up the curling iron.

"Oops?"

Cameron narrowed her eyes.

"Are you mad?" Emily lowered her head, worrying the comforter.

"I'm confused," Cameron said, measuring her words.

"Oh." Emily looked up at her. "Because if you were mad, you could punish me."

Cameron thought her eyebrows might be lifting off her face. "Seriously?"

Emily lowered her eyes again, slumped her shoulders. "Well. I'd deserve it. And it would give me something to remember you by for the next few days, until we get to really talk again."

"Uh-huh," Cameron said, abandoning the curling iron and the whiskey to crawl back up the bed. "You're just full of surprises, aren't you, Nebraska?"

⚘⚘⚘⚘

"Surprise!"

Cameron heard Emily chuckle into the phone. She'd just been texted photographic proof that Emily got her presents.

"I'd call it that, yeah. This stuffed bird barely fits in my apartment."

"That stuffed bird is a Western meadowlark. The—"

"State bird of Nebraska, yes, I figured that out."

"Of course you did. And of course it's big. Has to be big enough for you to cuddle with while I'm gone."

"You don't even like cuddling when you're here."

"You caught me," Cameron said, leaning back against perfectly fluffed hotel pillows. "It's a selfish gift. Birdie can take my place when you're clinging like an octopus and I need air."

"So romantic. And of course you couldn't just send roses."

"Roses are common, you're not. Besides, that goldenrod thing is the—"

"State flower of Nebraska, yeah. You do get that the goldenrod thing isn't typically a house kind of flower."

"You're not typical. Now shut up and let me get through this." Cameron cleared her throat, adapted a low, crooning voice. "Happy birthday to you, happy birthday to you, happy birthday Miss Personal Assistant, happy birthday to you."

Emily took long moments to stop giggling. "Miss PA doesn't have quite the ring of Mr. President, but thank you, you have a lovely voice."

"Mmm. My parents did almost name me Marilyn."

"Yeah? I saw those first baby pictures in *People*, you were never blonde."

"Yes well, Daddy gave serious consideration to having that surgically altered. Really though, I haven't sung sober in fifteen years. Are your ears hemorrhaging?"

"No. And that was sweet, all of it. Thank you."

"You're welcome. So, better than Jane?"

Jane was an acquaintance Emily openly admitted to fucking. Cameron had no room to complain, she liked things loose even when she was in the same state as her lover of the moment. Also, she sucked at monogamy. Sadly she also sucked at sharing.

"Wouldn't you like to know?"

"Of course I would. You're fraternizing with the enemy. I want to know about it."

"She works craft services, Cameron, she's not your enemy."

"She works craft services at another studio, Emily. She's serving sandwiches to the people who might crush us at the box office."

"Not if you do your job right. How's that going by the way?"

Cameron shrugged as if they were bantering in the same room. "Press stuff, interviews with my parents. The Morrison dynasty carried on behind the camera and all that. It's fine."

"You're miserable, aren't you?"

"Completely. But not anymore, because it's your birthday, and neither of us is allowed to be miserable on your birthday." Cameron smiled as she heard the faint sound of Emily's buzzer. "You should get that."

"Oh dear God, what did you do? I swear, if the governor of Nebraska is standing outside my door with a birthday cake…"

"Don't be absurd. If I were sending you a birthday cake it'd be delivered by someone much more interesting. Door, please."

She heard a huff of breath from Emily, closed her eyes to picture that cutely exasperated look. Heard Emily returning and the sounds of a package being opened.

"Did you send me a sex tape?"

"Why would I waste postage on something you can still find online somewhere? No, this is something else. I heard about you digging around the archives last week."

Emily sighed into the phone. "I thought you didn't care about this company, and yet you're still keeping an eye on things?"

"On the things that interest me. Including you. I intend to punish you for that one when I get back by the way."

"Promise?"

"Brat."

"What's on the DVD, Cameron?"

"Oh nothing. Just the blessedly unaired pilot to that Morrison variety hour my parents breathed unholy life into when I was eight. You'd think someone would've told them that musical skit shows weren't meant to exist in the early 90s."

There were a few silent moments before Emily answered. "No friggin' way."

"Way. Only because it's you're birthday. Now you can see why I don't sing sober anymore. And the next time you want something, baby, ask me."

"You would've said no."

"Yes I would've said no, but still."

"Oh God. I thought we were just going to have phone sex. This is so much better!"

"And on that depressing note, I'll leave you to your present."

"No, no, no. You're watching with me."

"No, I'm not. I lived it, Emily. Do you want to trigger my PTSD?"

"It's my birthday."

"The only reason I'm letting you set eyes on this without a signed nondisclosure agreement. By the way, the NDA is implied."

"Cameron…"

She was doing the pouty thing again, just as effective with her voice as it was with her mouth. "Fine."

Emily let out a noise that was absolutely ridiculous, a sort of gleeful scream. Cameron smiled and rolled her eyes.

"Happy birthday, Emily."

❧ ❧ ❧ ❧

"It's not my fault, I swear. My mother schedules these interviews one after the other after the other just to chip away at my already questionable sanity. Yesterday we played this game where we had sixty seconds to share our favorite memories from my childhood with the interviewer and see if they matched up."

Emily winced into the computer screen. "That sounds like it ended horrifically."

"I behaved. Relatively." Cameron smiled. "I'm sorry I haven't called. Been busy."

"Apparently."

"Okay, I know my Skype doesn't get the best reception, depressing considering how much the Wi-Fi costs here, but what's the tone?"

"No tone." Emily flashed a smile that didn't quite reach her eyes.

Cameron sat forward. "Hey. Seriously. Playing coy works better when we're in the same bedroom. Spill."

Emily was still a moment then shifted briefly out of frame. She came back holding a magazine with Cameron on the cover, dancing at a club. She wasn't alone.

Cameron sighed. "Did you spend money on that? I don't pay you enough to waste on that trash."

"Looks like you had fun."

"He's just a friend, an old friend. We worked together on that space movie."

"You explicitly told me he took half your virginity."

"Did I? I must've been feeling generous. He took a third, at most."

"Cameron."

"Nothing happened. We danced and played up to the cameras because they love it, and it gets us both publicity."

"Thought it was the movie you were supposed to be publicizing."

The tone was light enough, but it still made Cameron close her eyes. "They go hand in hand, the movie and I. I told you that before I left. Anyway..." Cameron added and instantly wished she hadn't, "you have Jane to take you dancing."

"And you have the luxury of not seeing what I do

with Jane plastered all over the media."

Cameron took a breath. She hadn't exactly thought ahead when she'd taken off last night, decided she couldn't pull off one more moment of aggressive civility with her mother. "I'm sorry. Really. But nothing happened. Here…" She reached up, undid the first two buttons of her blouse.

"Are you trying to distract me with video sex?"

"Partly. Mostly proving nothing happened. You know how I am about teeth, scratches. I think you know the signs by now."

"You don't have to prove anything to me."

"No?"

"No. But for the record, Jane's not the one I want to go dancing with."

Cameron's mouth quirked up. "No? I'll take you when I get back."

"Okay then. Meantime, lose the shirt."

"Thought I didn't have to prove anything?" Cameron was torn between annoyance at the initial implication this wasn't the case and a strange need to do it anyway, show she'd played against type for once, and behaved.

"You don't—Shirt's still messing with my view."

Emily's smirk was absolutely filthy and it shouldn't have surprised her at this point but still did, very pleasantly. "Oh. Okay then."

Cameron reached for her blouse with one hand, her jeans with the other.

❧❧❧❧

"Tag, you're it."

Cameron smiled at the sound of Emily's voice.

They'd been missing each other for days now. "Your voicemail message sucks."

"So change it. See how many of my friends actually believe I got Cameron Morrison to record a message for me."

"I did that once, you know. An auction thing, for charity."

"Yeah? Which charity? What did you say?"

"Something involving leopard endangerment, and I don't actually know, I was very drunk when I got around to recording it. Speaking of recording, did you watch Billy what's-his-name last night? I was very charming. I wore that dress you like."

"Recorded, not watched yet. Did you wear that dress because I like it or because your dad hates it?"

"Do I have to choose? You're a hard girl to reach lately. Jane keeping you up past curfew?"

"More like your company keeping me way past work hours. And I broke up with Jane."

Cameron was glad for the distance for once, glad Emily couldn't see her smile fade. Emily went on about the post-production hellhole she was trapped in, but Cameron missed most of what she said.

⁂

Emily's most recent communication wasn't actually much of one. Just pictures of Cameron, a media record of what she'd been up to lately, and with whom. Cameron waited twenty minutes after receiving them to attempt a call, though Emily would know her message had been seen.

"Jealous?" she asked when she heard the line pick up.

"Do you want me to be?"

It wasn't playful or flirty. "I told you to ignore that trash. It's for the press, not you."

"Really? Then why does it feel so much like you're trying to get my attention?"

"I've never had to try for your attention, sweetheart."

"Interesting timing, this spree of yours."

Her condescension had done the job, gotten under Emily's skin. Cameron tried to feel successful. "Is it? I don't follow."

"No, why would you, you don't have me there to map out every day of your life, keep it from imploding."

Cameron chuckled. "Someone grew up while I've been gone. Grew something anyway. You really think you're that indispensable?"

"Why would I when you're so intent to prove otherwise?"

"I don't follow," Cameron repeated.

"I split with Jane and suddenly you feel the need to fuck everything in sight?"

"Is that what you think I'm doing?"

"If you ever took your video calls anymore and I asked you to take your shirt off, would you?"

Cameron closed her eyes. "What do you want me to say, Emily?" She lost the battle with herself, didn't wait for an answer. "You knew the deal, why split with Jane?"

Emily swore in a loud whisper under her breath. Cameron imagined her shaking her head.

"And there it is. At the risk of shattering your world view forever, not everything is about you, Cameron."

"So you didn't do it because of me."

"For someone so desperate to show that she doesn't have to justify her actions, you sure seem interested in me justifying mine."

Cameron didn't answer, had no good answer to give. She heard Emily breathe against the receiver.

"I miss you, and I broke up with her," Emily said slowly. "Those things didn't cause each other, and they're not mutually exclusive either."

Cameron bit her lip. She'd have to fix her lipstick before meeting up with the industry snobs for dinner.

"Do you miss me?"

Still not playful or teasing Cameron should've teased, should've lied. "Yes. Too much."

"Oh."

Cameron swore Emily was nodding, had expected that answer. Swore she'd given away more than she wanted to without realizing. Emily was too good at her job, too good at most things. "I have to go."

"Of course you do."

"No, I really—"

"So go. I'm not stopping you. I'm not stopping you from anything."

Cameron pressed the phone hard against her ear, opened her mouth to speak, then did as she was told, ending the call.

❧ ❧ ❧

Their interactions over the next few weeks were fewer and farther between. Cameron continued courting the press in ways scheduled and unscheduled. Emily never commented on the unscheduled stuff, that landed in the tabloids, on the internet. Mostly they talked about work, and mostly that was via email.

Between interviews and partying Cameron kept up with the company as much as she could. It kept her busy, kept her mind off Emily.

The movie released with respectable numbers. Nothing to spawn an eight-film franchise, but it was an undoubted success. Her parents seemed pleasantly surprised. Cameron got a one-word text of congratulations from Emily when the numbers for the first weekend came in.

Emily was hired initially for just this one film. Cameron found reasons to keep her around, smaller projects, and pre-production stuff. She kept Emily around, kept apprised of the company, kept putting off her return to L.A., even after the press tour was finally done.

She sent Emily an email about one of the new projects, outlining responsibilities she already knew Emily could handle. Her phone buzzed with a text. Cameron checked the screen. Short, not necessarily sweet, a few words asking when she was coming back. Cameron started to type, made another questionable decision instead. Emily's phone rang three times before she picked up.

'Hey."

"Hey. Is there a problem? Rome burning without me?"

"Rome's fine." Emily paused. "Come home?"

Cameron closed her eyes, reached for the bourbon next to her on her desk. "Soon. My parents underestimated how much everyone would freak out over the Morrison's together again. Mom's talking about filming her trip to Paris next month and shopping it as a pilot for a reality show."

"And you're going with her. Is that something

you actually want?"

How could she answer when Emily already knew? "I'll be home soon."

"Will you?" Emily asked quietly.

"Is it that important? You said the company's fine."

"The company is fine. I'm just—I'm asking you to come home. You said if I wanted something I should ask. So, asking."

"I can't give you what you want," Cameron said, hands shaking too much to pour a proper drink.

"Do you even know what that is?"

Cameron breathed, clutched the cool glass. "I'll be home soon, Nebraska, we'll talk then."

❧❧❧❧

She went to Paris with her mother. They were shopping and Cameron was devising ways to kill herself with one of the clothes hangers when she got another email. She read it, ducked into a dressing room and threatened several cameramen in English and French when they tried to follow her. She got Emily maybe half a ring before voicemail would've picked up.

"What the fuck?" she said, her first words to Emily since informing her two weeks ago that the plane hadn't crashed getting in.

She heard Emily sigh into the phone. "Can you please try to be professional about this?"

"You can't just leave."

"I'm not under contract."

"This is what you call professional? You don't get your way on one thing so you quit?"

"I'm quitting because I'm unhappy and I can be

less unhappy for the same pay at five other studios, and me not getting my way? I changed one thing about my life, something that didn't even involve you, and you ran away."

"I did not—"

"You did. You ran away and you pushed me away and now you're having a tantrum because I reacted. I read about this, you child stars who end up with the emotional maturity of fourteen-year-olds."

"Oh did you, you read about us child stars. You're an expert then, aren't you, you know so much."

"I know enough."

"Yeah?"

"I know you're a fucking coward."

"I'm your fucking boss, Emily."

"Not for long."

"I don't want you to go."

"It's not always about what you want."

"Emily…"

"What?"

Cameron stared at herself in the dressing room mirror. "The last person I wanted, really wanted, sold pictures of us to one of the gossip rags, told them what a mess I was. She used that money to buy a house with her new girlfriend, used my secrets for that."

A long pause followed. "Is this the part of the script where I make sympathy noises? Pat your hand and tell you it's all okay?"

"Jesus Emily."

"What? You say I'm the one who can't leave, who's being stupid? I mean, sleeping with you in the first place was extremely stupid, that's on me. Big fuckup there."

"It wasn't a fuckup."

"Oh it was. And I'll live with it, but I won't use it as an excuse to be a coward the rest of my life."

"I didn't mean to hurt you."

"You did though and why, because some greedy idiot hurt you first a million years ago?"

"How much older than you do you think I am?"

"I can't do this anymore. Whatever this is or was…I can't. And that, that should make you happy."

"It doesn't."

"I can't help that. I'm sorry, Miss Morrison. Thanks for the opportunity."

Cameron was left with a silent phone, a reflection she hated, and her mother calling for her to get back out here, they were wasting film.

✤ ✤ ✤

Emily was running around between sets when Cameron found her. She carried a coffee tray and a satisfactorily stunned expression.

"Aren't you going to welcome the boss back? Two weeks notice has another week." When all Emily did was stare, Cameron took a breath and ordered her into her office.

"I can't…Robbie on the *Heavy Rains* shoot wants coffee."

"Robbie the sound guy or Robbie the stunt guy? Wait, I don't care because they both work for me, and so do you and I'm telling you to follow me. And bring the coffee."

Emily followed behind her, refused to walk next to her even when Cameron slowed her step. Emily shut the door behind them without being asked and set the tray on Cameron's desk.

"Aren't you going to ask how my flight was?" Cameron took one of the drinks, sniffed it, then set it down and drank from the other.

"How was your flight, Miss Morrison?"

The formal tone stung, especially since they were feet away from the couch they first fucked on. "Okay so, you don't care. Fair enough. But I do. Care."

Emily just looked at her.

"You want the truth?" Cameron shrugged out of the jacket she was wearing, undid the top buttons of her shirt so her bare neck was exposed. "The truth is that I've gotten tons of hickeys here since you stopped fucking the caterer girl. I've fucked my way around both coasts, I fucked my way through the whole second half of this press tour, and some of the fucking was actually really good."

"If you're trying to win me back I honestly can't tell. You're doing that awful of a job."

"I'm very aware. It went better in that rom com script I turned down last year. The point is yes, I did those things, those people, but I stopped." She pointed again at her neck. "Because the sex was good, but it wasn't great. It wasn't great because it wasn't you, Emily."

"And?"

"And I want you."

"Now, because I'm leaving."

"Always, because you're you, and I may have said your name while in bed with someone else. Can't tell you who legally, but she's shortlisted for the lead in a Bond remake."

Emily kept staring. "And you just came to this realization now."

"I'm stubborn and a slow learner. Literally, my

on-set tutoring was mostly remedial."

"So what, you want me to stay?"

"Yes, with me. I'd prefer if you stayed here too because you're too good for my competition, but it's your choice. And dating you would probably be easier without the possibility of a sexual harassment suit hanging over my head."

"Is that what you want, to date me?"

"Among other things. And you're right. I'm a spoiled, self-involved trust fund child with neglect and abandonment issues."

"Again. Not doing a great job selling yourself here."

"I know. But I miss you, and I'd like to take you dancing. Away from the cameras."

Emily only looked at her for the longest time, her expression unreadable. Then a slow smile curved her lips. "Pass me that coffee first."

Cameron reached for the other cup in the carrier and then carefully offered her drink instead. The lid's edge was stained with her lipstick.

Emily took it, her smile widening. "So. How was your flight?"

N.R. Dunham is a writer, a blogger, and a lover of Netflix. She's penned several short stories about sexy women and the women who love them, and hopes to get a longer, novel-length story written one of these days. She lives in Wisconsin, but dreams of traveling the world, taking selfies from exotic locales.
Facebook: https://www.facebook.com/NRDunham/

Trail Magic

By Michele M. Reynolds

Trail Journal: 4/29/1997-NOBO
I'm trying to keep the f-word in mind as I hike today.
Faith.
-Morning Dove

Nat smiled at the most recent Appalachian Trail journal entry. Something about the post resonated with her. The writing was messy and androgynous, and the date—today's—suggested that Morning Dove was an early riser, unlike Nat. It was only eight in the morning, and Nat was having a hard enough time staying awake as she copied the entry down into her notebook. NOBO. Northbound. Same direction she was going in, only Nat didn't have a trail nickname like so many of the entries she'd seen. Faith? She had faith that there was pizza with her name on it. Her feet couldn't carry her fast enough off this trail and to her car.

Nat slid the journal filled with brave, ambitious entries back into the ziplock bag and placed it on the shelf where she found it. She hoisted her pack over her shoulder and headed back north. It was a sunny, chirping birds and all the nature stuff people wrote poems about, spring day. Her blisters rubbed against her boots and she constantly slowed to readjust the straps on her pack. With every step, her footing was less stable.

That unsteadiness worsened as she eyed the steep hill before her. It was all that stood between her and the road where her car was parked. With considerable effort, she traipsed down the hill and to the road below. Angel harps should have been playing. Screw blue skies and fresh air, she'd take her '82 Honda Civic any day.

Hobbling on her blisters, she quickened her pace to the car, opened the trunk, threw in her damn pack and turned the car toward home. She rolled down the windows and cranked Tom Petty's *Long After Dark* CD. A hot shower was going to be amazing. After a few minutes the eerie synthesizer beginning of *You Got Lucky* filled her car. As she turned a corner, a figure was walking with a large pack.

It was a woman and she was holding out her thumb.

Petty sang, "Good love is hard to find."

Nat had never picked up a hitchhiker. She turned down the radio. Shrugging off the voice in her head warning her about the dangers of picking up strangers, Nat slowed to a stop.

"Thanks for stopping," the woman said, approaching the driver's side window. "I need a ride to the post office to pick up a resupply package."

Nat was greeted by the brightest blue eyes, that belonged on a cover of *Vogue* magazine. The woman's short, dirty blonde hair was pushed off her face by a folded purple bandanna, and she was covered in dirt.

"Sure, where's the post office?" Nat asked.

"In Elk Park, too far?"

"Hop in," Nat answered, trying to sound like

picking up a stranger was a daily occurrence.

"I'm Dove." The woman held out her hand as they drove.

Maybe she was Morning Dove from the trail journal. Dove isn't that common of a name.

"Nat." Nat shook her hand.

"You live around here, Nat?" Dove asked.

"Not so much around here but in Boone," Nat answered.

"The college town. I heard it's nice there," Dove said.

Dove had a lot of energy for someone who hiked mile after mile with a heavy pack on her back. There was an easiness about her that soothed Nat.

They pulled up to the post office and Dove extended her hand to Nat, "Thanks for the ride."

"You're welcome, and good luck," Nat answered and shook her hand.

Nat wasn't ready to part with this mysterious Dove yet. She had to find a way to spend more time with her while avoiding a restraining order.

A few minutes later Dove exited the post office holding a large box, and still sporting the huge pack. The combination made her look like a pack mule. It was admirable how such a small woman was so strong.

Dove eyed Nat and approached her car. "Something wrong?"

"No, just about to leave," Nat answered.

"Oh, okay then. Take care," Dove said. She walked over to a patch of grass, put down her pack and opened her package.

Nat's stomach growled. Nat's granola bar dinner and trail mix breakfast left a lot to be desired. The pizza she promised herself was taunting her.

Nat pulled down the car visor, and whispered to her reflection, "You can do this. You're a strong woman, dammit."

Palms sweating and heart racing, Nat walked over to Dove and asked, "Do you want to go to breakfast?"

Dove said, "Umm."

"My treat of course and then I'll drop you back at the trail if you want," Nat said.

She flirted with begging for her companionship.

"I never pass up breakfast," Dove said as she shoved the last item into her bag.

The two only had to drive a few miles before they reached a diner. It wasn't pizza but Nat wasn't sure pizza was respectable at this hour. After breakfast, Nat drove Dove back to the trailhead. Petty's *Deliver Me* piped through the radio. Nat internally chuckled at the interesting soundtrack of her trip today.

"I can't believe that you ate that entire Lumber Jack meal. I'm impressed," Dove said.

Nat boasted, "I can eat a whole pizza in one sitting."

"Impressive that someone like you could do that." Dove quickly averted her eyes.

Normally Nat would consider such a tone as flirtatious.

"I don't know how you're doing this whole AT thing."

"Why because I'm a woman and I'm hiking it alone?" Dove replied a little too quickly.

"No, because you're a person doing it at all. I don't like camping. I'm an embarrassment to the high percentage of Native American genes surging through my body," Nat confessed.

"Maybe your genes are tired of all the outdoor

time and they are choosing to take a break?" Dove offered.

Nat laughed and then answered, "I don't even like to exercise."

"You're a whole-pizza-eating-woman who doesn't exercise and you keep that body?"

Nat smiled back. "It's a curse."

"Well, throw that curse my way," Dove said.

She wasn't sure if she meant to throw her body or the curse her way. That was two comments that sounded like flirtation.

"I didn't even ask what you do for a living," Dove asked.

"I do nerdy stuff for the government," Nat answered.

"Come on, I bet it's more exciting than that," Dove pushed.

"I can't talk much about it. It has to do with coding and surveillance," Nat said. "That's all I can say."

"Wow, top secret?" Dove laughed.

"Something like that," Nat said.

"Here's the trailhead," Dove pointed to the side of the road.

They shook hands again.

"Thanks again. Good luck with all that top secret government stuff," Dove said.

"Good luck to you too."

Dove pulled her pack out of her car, hoisted it on her back and walked away from Nat.

Before Nat could stop herself she yelled, "Wait!" Nat jumped out of her car, opened her trunk and pulled out the backpack she had cursed just a few hours ago.

Dove turned around and walked back to the car.

"So…when I met you, I had just spent an awful night on the trail. I hiked what felt like twenty miles but was probably only five. I had parked my car right here and was heading home to a hot shower and pizza when I found you," Nat rambled.

Dove was listening but her face read confusion.

"I hated it. I hated the hiking, the camping, the soreness, the exercise but…"

"But?" Dove asked.

"But I want to try again. Would you consider letting a novice backpacker hike with you for a few days? I have enough food for a week and all my own supplies? And I—"

"Yes," Dove answered.

"Yes?"

"Sure, I'd love the company. I'd love your company," Dove said.

Nat smiled and hoisted the pack onto her back, making her stumble a bit.

"Wow! How much do you have in there?"

Nat shrugged.

"Lesson number one, don't overload your pack. We're exploding your pack before we go any further. It's no wonder why you were so miserable."

"Exploding?"

"Take off your pack and we'll go through it," Dove said and then laughed.

Dove removed two extra sweatshirts, a pair of sneakers, half of the food, three books, and a bag of quarters and bundle of fire starters. When she came to Nat's tent, she paused.

"We can sleep in my tent if you want," Dove said, holding up the bundle of poles and cloth.

Could she handle sleeping in a tent next to Dove?

Nat nodded and Dove placed the tent back in the car.

"Here try this," Dove said as she helped Nat slip into her lightened pack.

"Oh, this is much nicer." Nat said.

"Well, that's because you over packed. What are you going to do with your car?" Dove asked.

"Leave it here. Wherever I end up, I'll catch a ride back to it," Nat answered.

"Let's go then. You lead and set the pace."

Nat walked up the trail and only looked back at her car once. When she left it yesterday, she had felt worried and anxious about its fate, despite it being a Junker. Today it was freeing to leave her car behind.

She pushed up the hill and the pain of her feet surged with every twist and turn. Despite her feet, it was easier to hike with a lighter pack. She widened her gait assuming Dove was a fast hiker and she had no intention of holding her up. They walked until dusk, foregoing a lunch due to the big breakfast. When they found a campsite, Dove insisted on setting up a tent while she boiled water for dinner.

"Sit and relax. You have to be tired," Dove said.

Nat was tired. She sat on a log and leaned her back against a tree. She woke to the snapping of twigs and the warmth of fire on her feet. She frowned. She didn't remember taking off her boots.

"You've been asleep an hour," Dove said. "Hungry?"

"Starved."

The two shared a meal of macaroni and cheese with some dried fruit.

"Who's Jenny?" Dove asked.

"Who?"

Nat didn't have to ask. She knew all too well who Jenny was. She just needed time to come up with an answer that wouldn't involve tears.

"Jenny."

"My recent ex-girlfriend. Why, did I talk about her in my sleep?" Nat answered.

"No, her name was on the tag of your sleeping bag."

"Oh, I bought it for her," Nat said. "She never used it and left it—and me—behind."

"It's a shame."

Was Dove referring to the bag or Nat?

"You have some nasty blisters. I have stuff we can put on them tomorrow," Dove said.

"Did you remove my boots?"

"Yes, I hope you don't mind. I thought you would appreciate your feet getting some air. You didn't even wake up."

"That was sweet and dangerous. They must stink."

Dove laughed. Across the fire, Dove's blue eyes and beautiful face were perfectly lit. Her feet throbbed but she'd walk twice as far tomorrow on them if the night ended like this.

"How do your feet feel?" Dove asked.

"I think I'm fine, if I don't walk on them," Nat said.

Dove laughed again. "Such tender feet. What kind of Native American are you?"

"Penobscot."

Dove laughed again. When Dove laughed or smiled her eyes lit up.

"They're from Maine," Nat argued.

"It was rhetorical. I was referring to your tender feet."

After dinner, they both settled into the tent. There was just enough room for them both to lie on their backs, and Dove had fashioned a pile of clothes under Nat's feet to keep them up and the swelling down.

"Good night," Dove said as she turned on her side away from Nat.

"Good night."

After a few minutes Nat said, "Dove?"

"Yes."

"What if in the middle of the night I have to pee?"

"There's wipes in the pocket next to the door with my headlamp," Dove whispered.

"Okay, thanks."

That night Nat had to get up twice to empty her bladder. She fumbled out of her sleeping bag, elbowing Dove in the process. She felt around the door, trying to find the zipper to get out. She was to the point of almost peeing herself when Dove rescued her by sitting up and unzipping the tent. Her warm body brushed against Nat's. That was a lot of skin. Maybe she was sleeping topless or naked next to Nat.

Nat returned to the tent. "Sorry for waking you," Nat whispered.

"No problem," Dove answered.

Nat heard sincerity in her voice.

"Good night Penobscot," Dove whispered.

The two of them broke out into laughter.

"You know you're insinuating that all Native Americans are good at camping and hiking," Nat said.

"I think you insinuated it the first time you brought up your heritage," Dove responded.

"Point taken."

Nat hiked with Dove for three days and three

nights. Every morning Dove patched up Nat's feet and every night she set up camp, hung their packs and cooked dinner. Nat refrained from drinking any water after dinner and avoided the late-night zipper fumbling. Nat learned how to start a fire, pick a spot for a tent, and hang a backpack and to use a camping stove. Dove taught her how to distribute the weight in her pack and how to redistribute weight on hips and shoulders using her pack's straps.

More than learning how to camp and hike, Dove lent her a sense of peace. She had never got along so well and laughed as much as she did with Dove. She wished her time with her didn't have to end.

On the fourth morning, Nat woke to her feet throbbing. Dove wrapped them again and helped her push her swollen feet into her boots.

"Your feet are the most important thing to take care of on the trail," Dove said. "Yours are a mess and I think it's because of your boots. They aren't the best for this type of hiking."

"You sure it's not my tender Penobscot feet?" Nat laughed.

"No, I'm afraid not. I'd give you my boots but your feet are bigger," Dove said. "There's a road in four point three miles. I think you should hitch a ride back to your car from there."

Nat sighed and her eyes filled with tears.

"I'm sorry," Dove whispered.

"It's okay. You're right. I was enjoying the time out here. And my feet are so sore. I was trying to find a way to tell you that I wanted to go home without sounding like a wimp," Nat said.

"I thought you hated nature," Dove teased.

She didn't like nature but being close to Dove

made it easier. Her crush on Dove made her almost like it.

Nat answered, "I guess there's hope for me after all."

The two hiked in silence. Nat had enjoyed falling asleep next to Dove the way she tenderly tended to her feet and how she felt around Dove. She wanted to tell her about her feelings, to kiss her and to hold her. Fear of getting turned down and the awkwardness of being stuck in the wilderness together had stopped her. She wasn't sure if Dove was gay, but now she was leaving and had nothing to lose.

Not far from their camp they reached a rock outcropping that looked out to the green trees below. A river meandered through a distant field. All that was missing was a soaring hawk.

Nat turned to Dove and their eyes met and the air felt electric between them. Had Dove been reading her mind? They looked from each other's lips to eyes to lips. In that moment, the rest of the world didn't exist.

"Dove! Dove! Dove!"

Several voices called out.

Dove pulled away as a group of five men broke through the woods and to where Nat and Dove were standing.

"Who are they?" Nat whispered.

"They're known as the Frat Brothers," Dove said.

"Hey guys," Dove greeted as they reached Nat and her.

The short one answered, "Hey Dove, we're catching up with you. Told you all our partying wouldn't slow us much."

"I—" Dove started.

Nat interrupted, "I slowed her down."

"This must be Vivian," the tallest one said as he reached out his hand. "I'm Bean."

Dove was beginning to blush.

"No, this is Nat," Dove said and then bit her lip.

"Hi Nat," they said in unison and looked her up and down.

"Sorry boys, she's playing for my team," Dove said.

"Well, we better get going. We have resupplies to pick up. Happy trails," Bean said as he pushed his Frat Brothers on. "Nice meeting you, Nat."

The men walked away as rambunctiously as they had approached them.

Nat was the first to speak, "Are all guys on the trail like them?"

"Oh, some, most hike alone or just in as duos or trios. A lot of the guys are really granola, you know crunchy and Earthy, Vegan types and—"

Nat blurted, "Who's Vivian?"

"My ex-girlfriend."

"Was she on the trail with you?" Nat asked.

"Umm," Dove said as sat on a nearby boulder and motioned for Nat to sit next to her. "The last time I saw them was a month ago. I was still pining after Vivian then. She lives in Montana now and I had sent her a letter professing what I thought was my love. Since then, I got a letter back and it wasn't the answer I wanted."

"I'm sorry."

"I'm not. This is what this hike is about for me. You know the whole finding myself."

Nat admired the beauty before them and answered, "I certainly do."

The two sat there in silence soaking in the sun.

"And you probably don't need a girl who you met in North Carolina messing up that process," Nat said.

"I—"

"No, it's okay. Really, I get it. You're doing something amazing here. Let's go get me a ride so I can get a hot shower and eat an entire pizza," Nat said as she stood and pulled Dove off the boulder.

They hiked in silence again and then reached the road. Dove insisted on waiting until Nat caught a ride and while they waited Dove handed her a piece of paper. It had a list of addresses on it and the last one was Maine.

"It's a list of all the post offices that I'll be resupplying from now and until Maine. In case you'd like to write to me. You don't have to," Dove said.

"I will."

Their eyes locked again. Energy surged through Nat's body. She wasn't waiting another second. She surged forward and kissed Dove hard. Dove met her with the same hunger. Desire rose from Nat's chest and she grabbed the straps of Dove's pack and pulled her closer. Dove smiled into the kiss and continued to move her lips against Nat's. Nat pulled away, breathless.

"I wanted to do that back on the mountain," Nat confessed.

Dove smiled. "I know."

That smile drove Nat crazy. Squeaky brakes stopped them from kissing again. A minivan driven by a woman pulled over. The two jogged to the car and noticed the baby seats in the back.

"She looks safe enough," Dove whispered, then turned to the woman. "She needs to get back to her car at Mountain Road near Elk Park. Can you take her?"

"Sure, it's on my way. Hop in, honey. You need a ride too, sweetie?" the woman answered in a North Carolina accent.

Dove answered, "No, I'm still hiking. Thank you."

Nat threw her pack in the car and hugged Dove. They held tightly for a few seconds as the woman driving patiently looked on.

"Be careful," Nat said as she stole a kiss from Dove's neck.

"Always. You enjoy your shower and eating a whole pizza."

That night Dove opened her sleeping bag to find a note from Nat on top.

"She's sneaky," Dove whispered as she rested back in her sleeping bag to read the letter.

Dear Morning Dove,

I don't even know your real name. That's kind of mysterious, don't you think? We haven't talked about it yet, but I'm leaving tomorrow. My feet have been in too much pain and I've pushed myself hard enough.

Thank you for the time you've allowed me to spend with you on the trail. I've not only learned how to be a better hiker and camper but it's given me time to clear my head. You have a peaceful way about you that allows me to just be, me.

It's late and I'm sure it'll be late by the time you read this. So, I'll keep this short. I hope you find what you are looking for on the trail.

I also hope you find time to write me back. Call me if you need anything. I especially hope that I'll see you again.

Good night. Don't let the tent bugs bite!

-*Nat*

Dove smiled and drifted off to sleep holding the letter.

Dove read the letter every morning and every night. While she hiked through fields, through forests and over mountains she mentally constructed her letter back. When she finally settled in her tent at night to write, all the hiking brilliance had disappeared and she was too tired to conjure witty thoughts.

On the night before her next resupply, she put pen to paper and wrote.

Nat,
(Is that short for Natalie? I guess it's only fair that I don't know your real name either). Thank you for taking the time to hike with me.

I've read your letter twice a day since I received it, some days, three times. I enjoyed my time on the trail with you too. Every day I fight my heart that wants to turn back to you. Thank you for understanding that I need to do this.

There is not a doubt in my mind that I will see you after the hike. (But if I meet a Penobscot who is as kind, funny, smart and as beautiful as you, who also knows how to unzip a tent in the middle of the night, all bets are off).

I'm looking forward to going to the post office tomorrow and getting my resupply. Even though I'm excited to get clean socks and underwear, I'm more excited to get a letter from you. (Now if that's not romantic, I don't know what is).

Good night from a NOBO on the AT,
Morning Dove

At every resupply there was a letter from Nat and at each resupply Dove mailed a letter back to her. Nat talked about her family, books she was reading about the AT and funny things going on in the media. Dove's body stayed strong and she continued north. Most days she met a half dozen people and some days she saw and talked to nobody.

By her fifth letter, Nat wrote:

I know we only spent a few days together and traded a few letters over the last two months but I think I'm in love with you. I'm sorry to say this after such a short time and after just one kiss. I feel a lightness and easiness when I'm with you.

Nat wrote about trivial day-to-day things and ended the letter with *I love you (and I'm not sorry anymore).*

Nat's letters made Dove laugh aloud and smile the entire time she read them. Dove wrote back:

Thank you for your amazing letter. As I'm not ready to say I love you, I will say that I definitely feel something strong between us. I hope that you are okay with me not being ready to profess my love. Your letters make me laugh, smile and keep me company on the trail. I have no idea how in April I was strong enough and crazy enough to leave you. I must have faith that I can finish this and that I will figure out where to go next in life.

Nat wrote back:

I'm fine with you not saying you love me back as long as you're okay with me saying it so quickly. I'm glad you have faith that you're going to finish the trail and figure out your life. It reminds me of a trail journal entry I read: "4/29/1997-NOBO. I'm trying to keep the f-word in mind as I hike today. Faith"

That was the entry I met just before I picked up this gorgeous, thru-hiker.

On a rainy day in August, Dove crossed over into Maine and picked up her last resupply package and the last letter she would receive from Nat on the trail. She looked at the letter in her hand and wondered how many days she could wait to open it. She had two hundred and fifty-six miles and about twelve days before she reached Katahdin. She mailed her last letter from the trail to Nat. Dove had taken more care and thought writing that letter then anything she had ever written.

Dove continued halfway through Maine to Bigelow Preserve. Despite Maine's steep terrain, she was clocking seventeen plus mile days and would reach Katahdin in ten days. She camped a night in the preserve and managed again to hold back on reading Nat's letter.

That night, Dove set up camp later than usual. She slid her tired body, feet that had clocked hundreds of miles these last few months, and her full heart into her sleeping bag. She was determined not to read Nat's letter until the end of the trail at the top of Mount Katahdin. She stared up at her orange and blue tent ceiling and imagined the pines and stars above her. She thought of the letter she had written Nat. After a dozen drafts, she had it memorized.

8/30/97

Nat,

Thank you for the letters. They have kept me company since North Carolina. I made it. I'm in Maine with two hundred and fifty-six miles to go. This is my last letter from the trail, because in less than two weeks I'll reach Katahdin. My body is stronger than it's ever been and my mind is clear. My heart, on the other hand, has decided it's too far from you.

I haven't decided what I'm going to do with my life. All I know is I'd like to spend some more time with you. I, also, want to get a chance to revisit our kiss. So, after Katahdin, I'll make my way back to you (but not on foot this time).

I will see you soon.

Love, Dove

Michele M. Reynolds writes fiction with a mix of adventure, humor and romance. She's a self-published author and is best known for her second book Love's Autograph. She creates mostly contemporary romance but has written paranormal, post-apocalyptic and a YA book. She's a member of the Golden Crown Literary Society.

Written Range

By T.L. Hayes

No, Sarah, no I...I just...if you'll just let me. Goddammit, Sarah, will you let me finish? I just asked if you're coming home this weekend like you said you would, that's all. I didn't say anything about..." Robbi paused to listen again to Sarah angrily defend her reasons for staying in Seattle.

"I know you have a job to do and I appreciate how hard you work. That's why one would think that you would want to take some time off every now and then." Robbi sighed, knowing she was about to give in. She always gave in. That's why she hadn't seen her girlfriend in four months. And there was never a good reason. Despite Sarah's constant insistence that she was doing important things that just couldn't wait for her to go out of town for two or three days.

Finally, Sarah paused and Robbi said, "Okay, you're right. I'm sorry if I sounded bitchy. I just miss you and hate that we haven't seen each other in so long. Please, say you'll keep our plans next month. It's kind of important." Robbi listened again then, "I know your job is important, I know. But...okay, fine, I'll talk to you later. I love you too."

Robbi hung up and sighed, then almost threw her phone across the room. The only thing that kept her from it was that her friend Kris was sitting across the room on the couch, with her feet propped up on the coffee table, trying to pretend that she was really interested in her water bottle. Because of this, Robbi squelched her urge to toss her phone and instead set it gently on the bar that separated the kitchen from the living room.

Kris capped her water bottle and sat it on the coffee table, then stood up and walked up to Robbi and put her hand on Robbi's sleeve and looked at her with kind eyes. "I'm sorry."

Robbi put her hand over Kris' and tried to give her a reassuring smile. "It's okay, I'm used to it."

"Well, I wish you weren't. Why does she keep doing this to you?"

"Don't start." Robbi patted Kris' hand again, then walked away from her into the kitchen and to the cabinet next to the fridge and took down a tumbler then took the bottle of whiskey off the top of the fridge and poured herself a good three fingers worth.

Kris put her hands on the bar and said angrily, "You're right, I shouldn't start. You should. I'm tired of listening to you continue to give in, continue to get stepped on and hurt."

Robbi said nothing, just stood with her back to the counter and sipped her whiskey.

"And I'm tired of seeing you drink so much. Look at what she's doing to you."

Robbi said quietly into her drink, "Then go home."

"What did you just say?"

Louder, "I said go home if you can't watch me drink. Although, a real friend would sit and drink with me."

Kris came around the bar and said, "No, a real friend would do this," then she reached for the glass and a trusting Robbi let her take it. Kris poured the rest of the contents into the sink, then turned and faced Robbi with her arms crossed over her chest and stared Robbi down defiantly.

Robbi said tiredly, "I have more."

Kris fought a smirk. "The only thing stopping me from dumping that whole bottle is because I have a deep respect for eighteen year old Scotch. I'm trusting you to leave it alone."

"Why do you have to be such a grown up sometimes?" Robbi grinned at her.

"Because someone has to be in order to keep you out of trouble." They grinned at each other and Kris put her hand on Robbi's arm. "You need to have a real conversation with her. One where you get to actually talk and Sarah has to listen. Tell her how this is making you feel. If you don't, I will."

Robbi snorted. "Yeah, that'll go over well, as if she couldn't hate you enough as it is."

"Aww, she hates me? Good. Though, I'd rather she be afraid of me."

Robbi let out a surprised laugh and put her arms around Kris in a hug. "My little badass." Robbi pulled away from the hug and kissed Kris on the cheek before letting her go.

"When I have to be. Someone needs to stick up for you since you don't seem inclined to do it."

"I stick up for myself! But, I know the pressure she's under with her new job and how hard she's working and..."

Kris cut her off. "Don't you fucking do that, don't make excuses for her! She's being inconsiderate and not taking your feelings into consideration at all. You're feelings are valid."

Robbi reached around Kris to get the bottle of scotch off the top of the fridge. "Yeah, well, they're also thirsty."

Kris reached up and put her hand on Robbi's arm, stopping her progress.

"Kris…"

Kris held Robbi's gaze. "No, enough. You're not going to find the answer there."

Robbi sighed. "Yeah. It could never be that easy. What am I going to do, Kris? I love her."

Kris' look softened and she drew Robbi to her and put her arms around Robbi's neck and held her close. "Oh honey, I know. I know."

Robbi said into Kris' shoulder, "Missing her hurts. It really does." She tightened her arms around Kris.

Kris responded by returning the pressure, and then began to gently rock back and forth. It was almost as if they were slow dancing in the middle of the kitchen but they barely moved their feet.

As Robbi's tears began to soak through Kris' shirt and she began to shake with quiet sobs, Kris started stroking Robbi's hair and talking softly to her as if she were comforting a child after a nightmare. "It's okay. I got you. Shh. It's okay. I know. I know."

❧ ❧ ❧ ❧

Robbi sat on her couch, a drink in hand. She was alone this time. "Sarah, you promised." She took a sip and licked the fine, smoky whiskey off her lips. She was trying to stay calm. "But Sarah, I told you, this was important. It just seems like you don't take my needs as serious as you take…" She stopped talking while Sarah interrupted her. "No, I wasn't calling you selfish, but now that you mention it…no, no, I didn't say you were selfish, just that you could be…this is what I'm talking about, you never let me finish." Robbi was getting more visibly angry the more she listened, until finally, "Will you shut the fuck up for a minute and let me talk!…Oh, okay, fine, what the fuck ever. Just… bye!" Robbi angrily pushed the end call button and threw the phone on the other end of the couch. Then she ran her hands through her short-cropped dark hair and exhaled. "Fucking bitch!" She screamed out to the empty room.

She stood up from the couch, looking for something less expensive to throw, something that would make a nice crashing sound when it broke and her eyes fell on the glass decoration in the middle of the coffee table. It stood about a foot and a half tall, was made of a continuous tube of heavy rainbow colored glass on a square base in the shape of a treble clef. She had given it to Sarah on their third anniversary, before she had gotten the tenure track job teaching music at a liberal arts college in Seattle. As Sarah had been packing to leave she had said she was going to leave it because she didn't want to take the chance that it would get broken on the move. Robbi had accepted that excuse and even allowed herself to ignore the fact that Sarah had left most of the other gifts she had given her behind as well. She took the new car Robbi had cosigned for though, there was no question of that.

Robbi ran her hand over the top of the clef, feeling its smoothness and admired its perfect shape. It really was a thing of beauty and the colors were so vivid. Maybe she had liked it more than Sarah had after all. She ran her fingers down the neck of it and curled her fingers around it until she had a good grip, picked it up from the coffee table and heaved it into the corner, where it made a satisfying smashing sound before it fell to the floor in a rainbow-hued cascade mixture of chunks and shards. "Well, it sure as shit is broken now, isn't it?" Robbi stood next to the coffee table, adrenaline pumping through her and making her look around for something else to throw so that she could keep this feeling going. She spotted all the little tchotchkes that Sarah had insisted on placing on her bookshelves in the open spaces in front of the books. Robbi always liked keeping that space empty so everyone could look at and admire the books, as she often liked to do herself. Plus, Robbi hated clutter and didn't own tchotchkes of her own for this reason. They just took up space and Robbi liked wide-open spaces whenever possible.

She went to the useless things and looked at them. They were a hodgepodge of cutesy, breakable things, from little teddy bears, to dolls, to angels, to bells, to votive candles. Sarah liked to collect little mementos from adventures she had had with her friends and kept every small token a friend ever gave her. She had unopened boxes full of such things and that was the argument she used to convince Robbi to let her put some things out on Robbi's bookshelves. "I'm only bringing out some of my collection. You should be happy I'm not trying to bring it all out." In the spirit of compromise, Robbi had given in, thinking that it was part of being a couple and sharing your space. After all, she had wanted Sarah to feel at home. Now, she picked them up, one by one and threw them into the same corner as the rainbow-hued treble clef and the pile of broken things on the floor grew. She just continued to throw, one by one, until all the shelves were clear of them and contained only her books. She looked at the shelves and sighed a contented sigh and smiled. "As it should be."

Robbi put her hands on her hips and turned around and surveyed the damage and her smile grew bigger. "Just like our relationship, broken beyond repair." Robbi shook her head, then went to the fridge and grabbed the bottle of scotch off the top and took it back to the couch and sat down. She poured more into her glass until it was three quarters full, then sat back and propped her feet up on the coffee table and lifted her tumbler to the rubble on the floor. "Salud and happy anniversary, bitch."

❧❧❧❧

The next morning Kris found Robbi passed out on the couch, the bottle of scotch empty and tipped over on the coffee table, and a small black jewelry box sitting beside it. Kris took it all in and whispered, "Shit," then she went over to Robbi on the couch and touched her shoulder and lightly shook her. "Robbi, sweetie, come on. Get up." Robbi just groaned and rolled over onto her arms. Kris tried again, this time shaking her harder. "Robbi, you need to get up, come on."

Robbi managed to mumble a somewhat coherent, "No."

Kris stood back up and raised her voice, "Roberta Jean Baker, get your ass off this couch now, or I'll get the ice water."

Robbi groaned again but did sit up, albeit slowly. "Yelling AND full name?"

Kris stood over her with her arms crossed, trying to suppress the smirk that was coming. "Yes, you deserved it." She looked around the room. "What happened here?"

"I straightened up a bit. Cleaned off my shelves."

"If this is what you consider clean, I hate to see what you consider messy." Kris dropped her hands back to her sides and sat down next to Robbi and put her hand on Robbi's knee. "Talk to me." Robbi moaned again and started to lean over on the arm of the couch again, but Kris grabbed the sleeve of her shirt and pulled her back up. "No you don't. You will tell me what happened here last night or I will do what I can to annoy you. You know I'm capable." Kris wiggled her eyebrows at Robbi who snorted.

Robbi rubbed her temples. "Don't make me laugh."

"Talk to me then."

"What can I tell you? She canceled. Again. The only time it mattered."

"Why?"

"Why? Why does Sarah do anything? Because Sarah only cares about Sarah and doesn't give a damn about me. That's what I realized last night. You were wrong, you know?" Robbi looked at Kris and almost smiled.

"Wrong about what?"

"There are answers at the bottom of that bottle."

"Oh? So what answers did you find?"

"Mainly that Sarah's a selfish, coldhearted bitch. And maybe always was. But she sure is pretty. She was always pretty."

"Is that all?"

"Mostly." Finally, Robbi grasped Kris' hand on her knee and turned to face her. "I can't do it anymore, Kris. I can't. I'm tired of waiting for the phone to ring. Tired of waiting for her to remember that it's my birthday or our anniversary. I'm tired of waiting and being patient and making excuses. I'm just so tired." She put her head on Kris' shoulder and Kris leaned hers against Robbi's.

"I know, Sweetie. So, what are you going to do about it, other than break more stuff?" They shared a chuckle.

"Already did it."

"What?"

"Called her early this morning and left a voice mail. I broke up with her. I'm surprised she hasn't called and screamed at me yet. I guess she's going to miss our breakup as well."

"You know I'm going to help you heal through this, right?"

"Yeah."

"And you know what has to happen first, right?"

"Yeah." Pause. "Don't worry, I've already emptied all the alcohol in the house, I'm way ahead of you." Then she snickered.

Kris smacked her arm. "You're allowed this one but if I see it continuing after this, I will drag your ass to rehab. I mean it, Robbi."

"I know you do. I'm glad I have you to kick my ass when I need it."

"What are friends for?"

Robbi sighed. "I never should have broken up with you, especially not for her. God, did I fuck things up?"

Kris gave her a small smile. "Yes you did."

"I'm just glad you're still here. I don't deserve you."

"No, you don't."

They shared a chuckle again. "Why are you still my friend, anyway? I've been such a jerk."

"Yeah, you have. But I think you should know why."

They held each other's gaze for a bit, until Robbi smiled. "Yeah, I do." Robbi sighed, and then put her head back on Kris' shoulder. "Though I don't know why, I've been such an asshole."

Kris kissed Robbi on the top of the head and said with a sigh. "Yeah, it's one of the things I love most about you."

They shared a laugh and Robbi sat up and looked at Kris, then reached over and caressed Kris' cheek. "I've been so busy missing someone who was never really here in the first place that I couldn't see the one who'd been here all along. I'm sorry. I'm so sorry." Robbi leaned in for a kiss but Kris backed away. "What's wrong?"

Kris scooted further back into the corner of the couch so that she was no longer touching Robbi and held up her hand. "Robbi...what are you doing?"

"What? I thought we...that you and I..." Robbi sighed, and then ran her hands through her hair. "Dammit."

Kris's voice softened. "Robbi, I'm your friend and I love you, I always will. And I'm glad to help you through this and any other problem you have, but I'm not a life preserver and I'm not a fall back option."

Robbi looked at Kris. "I don't think of you as a fallback option. I just thought that..."

"You thought that something was happening between us because I was showing you affection." Kris gave Robbi a small smile. "Robbi, just because you're cute doesn't mean you always get the girl."

Robbi chuckled, somewhat derisively. "I'd like to, at least once."

"Baby, you had the girl once, and you let her go. You can have all the regrets you want but that doesn't change the fact that we will never be anything more than friends."

"I thought you said a minute ago that you were still in love with me."

"I did and a part of me still is."

Robbi moved closer on the couch and reached for Kris' hand but Kris pulled it back. "I don't understand this."

"Loving you is something I can't help. Sometimes I wish I could. But that doesn't mean we should be together. We weren't good as a couple. We can't gloss over that with false hindsight. You were kind of a shitty girlfriend and I told myself that I wouldn't let myself be treated that way again." Kris' voice never wavered and her posture was still rigid.

"I was a shitty girlfriend? You never told me that."

Exasperated, Kris smacked the back of the couch. "Oh my god, Robbi, I did! You just never listened! I was constantly telling you that you were always in your office, writing, and I hardly ever saw you. I tried to be understanding about it, knowing the life of a writer is one of solitude, but really, I couldn't, not after a while. Robbi, you shut me out all the time. You cancelled plans. You stopped in the middle of conversations to make notes and shhhed me when I tried to talk to you." She paused, then, with sadness said, "Do you know what's worse than missing someone who's far away and never comes home?" Robbi, looking on the verge of tears, shook her head. "What's worse is missing someone who's right next to you but still far away. As much as I love you and will always be here for you, I can't go through that again. And don't bother promising you'll be better. I don't want that. I just want you to know…I want you to know who you are."

"Oh god Kris, no joking this time, I was a complete asshole. And I was the worst kind of asshole because I didn't know I was asshole. You deserve so much better." Robbi didn't try to touch her again but she shook her head and closed her eyes for a moment.

"So do you." With humor in her voice, Kris declared, "Okay, it is resolved on this day that when we're each ready for a relationship again we will look for someone who's emotionally and physically available, someone who wants to make us their top priority, someone who will always have time for us. We deserve nothing less." Kris folded her arms over her chest and inclined her head. She was grinning.

Robbi laughed. "Can you twitch your nose and make it so?"

Kris tried and burst out laughing and uncrossed her arms. "Okay, so I don't have superpowers, but that doesn't mean we can't make that happen."

"Right." Robbi sighed again, and then rubbed her hands on her lap. "I don't know about you, but I feel like I just woke up from a bender. I think I need a shower. You want to stay for breakfast?"

Kris narrowed her eyes at Robbi and tried to fight back the smile and failed. "Yes, I will stay and make you breakfast."

Robbi tried to look innocent. "Let the record show that I never asked you to make me breakfast."

They stood up from the couch together and Kris crossed her arms again. "Let the record also show that every time you ask me to stay for breakfast that means you want me to cook it too."

Robbi mimicked Kris' gesture. "Not true. Sometimes it was my sly way of asking for sex."

"Oh yeah, so sly. Like no one's ever used that line before."

"It always worked."

"Only when I wanted it too. Now go take your shower. You smell like my alcoholic uncle Bill."

Robbi chuckled and backed away. "Okay, point taken." Robbi turned and started to walk out of the room, then stopped and said, "Thank you."

They shared a smile, then Kris said, "Anytime," then Robbi walked in the direction of her bedroom and Kris moved to walk into the kitchen. Just as she stepped around the couch she heard a cellphone ring and looked around for it, thinking it hers, when she saw Robbi's phone stuck between the cushions and pulled it out. She looked at the caller ID and sighed. "I don't think so," then she hit ignore before throwing the phone back on the couch, where it landed on a cushion with a dull thud.

Ms. Hayes currently has a novel published through Bold Strokes Books, entitled, A Class Act, and has a second novel coming out through them in August entitled, Sweet Boy and Wild One. She lives in Springfield, IL with four cats and a roommate.

Desperate Times

By Beth Burnett

I watched her from the other side of security as she went through the line. The last time I was in a long distance relationship, back in my twenties, you could walk all the way to the gate with whomever you were seeing off. Not so, these days. She said goodbye to me at the entrance to security, kissing me hard before getting into line. I smiled and said hello every time she passed until finally she told me to just go.

"You're making it too hard," she said. "Just go so I don't have to keep saying goodbye."

Stung, I lifted my hand once more and turned away. I walked away quickly, almost at a run. I didn't want to cry in the airport. When I finally made it to the parking lot, I dove into my car and started the engine, cranking the heat to the highest setting. Blowing into my hands, I shook until the car started warming up. By then, I had passed the urge to cry.

It had stopped snowing while I was in the airport, but it was cold and the roads were covered. I debated driving around to the cell phone lot to watch her plane take off. Her flight didn't leave for another two hours and it's not like she'd even know I was there. I'd know, but lately, I'd come to wonder if that was enough. It wasn't snowy enough to delay the flight, so I decided to just head home.

I pulled up to the attendant and paid my parking fee. He recognized me, and smiled when he greeted me. I'd been to this exit sixteen times, twice a month for eight months. And I'll be here again in two weeks when I picked Carol up for her next long weekend. That's all we get these days, long weekends. We'd been partners for twelve years, and it didn't occur to either of us to break up when her mother got sick and Carol decided she needed to go home to care for her. We had some long, intense fights about it. I didn't understand why her siblings couldn't step up. When that didn't pan out, I fought to have her mother come here. Her mother wouldn't consider it. She wasn't going to live in a den of iniquity, as she called it. That wasn't fair. Carol and I have a small house in the suburbs where we live with our two dogs and a giant orange cat. We watch Netflix and play cards and read, and sometimes we fight, or do laundry. If we have a gay agenda, it's trying to find a pet sitter so we can go to the National Women's Music Festival once a year, but that is hardly a hotbed of wildness. I had offered to move us to the second bedroom so Carol's mother could have the master bedroom with the attached bath, but that wasn't enough. Carol's mother was dead set against me, against lesbians, and she was not coming to our house. She would have had it good here. I'm a professional chef and I did some of my training in special diets. I've had Carol and I on an oil-free vegan diet for years. We both look better than we have in our lives even though I'm in my fifties and she is coming up on sixty.

I even offered to go there. I love our little house in Madison, and I never want to leave, but if I had to, I would pack up our stuff, and the pets, and drive a

U-Haul across the country to rent some dumpy piece of crap house in Phoenix so Carol could take care of her mother. Ultimately, that seemed the best idea, but Carol thought that was a ridiculous idea. We'd lived in Madison for thirty years, we had an entire life here, and Carol didn't want to give it up for what we had originally thought would be a couple of months.

Eight months had dragged by and Carol was starting to feel like a stranger. This last visit, she barely greeted me when I came home from work. We didn't even make love. When we crawled into bed at night after a late night spent on our respective computers, playing Facebook games, and checking email, we barely brushed lips before turning in our separate directions.

I pulled into our driveway and looked at our little home. The bushes were all covered and the flowerbeds were bare. It looked empty even though I knew the pets were waiting for me inside. As I came through the door, they ran to greet me, the dogs circling and wagging, and Toby the cat circled my legs in greeting.

I flopped onto the couch, surrounded by the furry kids. Did Carol still love me? I wasn't sure that I still loved her. I tried to remember the way my heart used to swell when she would laugh, the way my whole body used to strain toward her when she touched me. When we were first separated, the together times were precious. We would crash into each other at the airport barely able to contain our tears and laughter. She'd reach over and slip her hand under my shirt as I drove us home, resting her hand on my belly, letting our skin remember what it felt like to be connected.

One day, early in our separation, she grinned at me and slid her jeans off. Sitting on the passenger seat naked from the waist down, she said, "Do you want to touch me?" I stroked her until she came, one hand on the wheel, going five miles under the speed limit so as not to pass any semi-trucks while she was exposed.

I laughed thinking about that day. At first, the separation had been good for us. It isn't that we were bored with each other. But we had settled into a pattern, as long-term couples tend to do. Our sex life, while still loving and warm, had become routine. We knew each other's bodies as well as our own and that meant we knew what worked when it came to sex. We didn't explore anymore. We didn't look at each other with wonder.

Maybe the separation was a test for our failing relationship. We had started to take each other for granted and the separation was a way to temporarily shake us out of our complacency. It was the make it or break it moment of our life together and right now it felt as if we were falling firmly on the side of breaking it.

I tried to put it out of my mind as I went through my workday. A chef could not risk distraction. As I lovingly prepared each dish I remember how Carol and I used to make most of our meals together, brushing against each other in the kitchen, laughing when something spilled. Once I got regular work in the restaurant I just brought meals home most of the time and Carol ate while on the computer.

As I left work I checked my phone. Carol had texted to let me know she landed safely. I sent her an automatic reply.

"I'm glad. I love you."

Greeting the dogs and Toby, I went into the kitchen to put my take-home meal into the fridge. I was grateful to have free food as part of my Chef compensation. With the constant traveling our savings was dwindling fast. Even with all the airline miles Carol had accumulated from her last job, the cost of these plane tickets was prohibitive. If her mother didn't die in the next few months we'd be out of savings. We had tickets booked ahead for the next two months. After that, if her mother was still in need of care, we would take our visits down to once a month or every six weeks.

Back in the living room, I flopped onto the couch. I knew I should call Carol to say goodnight, but I was suddenly so tired. All I wanted to do was sleep. As I shifted to pull my phone out of my pocket the phone rang.

"Hi Gwen." Carol sounded as tired as I felt.

"Hey, how was your flight?"

"Uneventful. How was work?"

"Fine," I replied. "How is your mother?"

"Same as always," Carol said. "Sick, miserable, and spouting homophobic bullshit."

I sighed. "I still don't understand why you feel so obligated to take care of her. We could hire a full-time nurse for what we pay in plane tickets."

"She's my mother," Carol said. "And we've had this conversation a million times."

"It's because I've never understood," I snapped.

Carol took a deep breath. She always did that when she was trying to regain her temper. I could tell from her silence that she was mad. I knew her so well, I sometimes wondered if I could read her mind. She exhaled sharply before speaking. "Gwen, I'm seeing a side of you that I didn't think existed."

Stung, I sat up, gripping the phone in my hand. Toby immediately jumped into the warm spot left on my pillow. "What does that mean? I'm not allowed to be upset that she's disrupting our lives when she hates us?"

"My mother is dying. Whatever feelings I have for her and the way she raised me she is still my mother. If my siblings won't step up to help take care of her, I have to do it. She's confused enough as it is. I'm not going to have her spending her last days with a stranger."

"We don't even know if they are the last days," I said. "She could live another year. Or two. We thought this was going to be a couple of months."

Carol was dead silent for a few moments. "I can't believe that you're saying you wish my mother would die so we can have our lives back. Do you realize how horrific that sounds?"

"I don't mean it like that. I just feel like whenever we talk about options we have a fight about it. I need to have a say in this."

"You don't get a say in this," Carol yelled.

Defeated, I flopped back onto the couch. "I'm sorry I'm not being supportive enough. I'm sorry you think dealing with me is just adding to your stress."

"I just don't think you understand," Carol said. "I'm exhausted. I'm dealing with my mother's healthcare, phone calls from no-good siblings, the doctors, the in-home visits. And on top of that I have to spend two full days every two weeks in airports and planes. I'm tired, Gwen. I'm tired of doing this."

"Then let's talk about our options," I said, softly. "Let's talk about ways to be together again."

"One of our option discussions should be about ending our visits completely," Carol said.

I sucked in air. "You mean, end us?"

"I think it's time to think about it," Carol said.

"Carol," I pleaded. "It can't end like this. I can't believe you're even thinking like that."

It didn't help that I had been thinking the same thing earlier today. Part of me wondered if she was right. But the bigger part of me just wanted those days of cooking together and making love unexpectedly and laughing at stupid jokes to come back.

"We can talk about it next time I'm there," Carol said. "In the meantime, let's just not talk for a couple of days. I have enough to deal with from my mother. I don't want to lose so much energy fighting with you every day too."

Blinking back tears, I opened my mouth, but closed it again. I was afraid I would cry if I spoke. Finally, I managed to say okay without choking on the word.

"Okay. Bye Gwen."

"Bye."

I didn't bother getting up to go to bed. It didn't matter anyway. Carol was slipping away from me and I couldn't even talk to her or hold her or fight for her. I wasn't as supportive as I should have been. Her mother was a vile person. I hated that Carol had to go take care of someone who spent her life making Carol feel like shit for being herself.

The next couple of days passed in a blur. On Wednesday, I dragged myself off the couch yet again and rummaged in the fridge for last night's take-home. I was eating cold fettuccine alfredo straight out of the take-out container when I heard the front door slam. Stunned, I stepped into the living room with fettuccine in my mouth and the container still in my hand. Carol was squatting in the doorway petting the dogs and Toby. She looked up at me when I wandered in.

"You look terrible," she said, smiling.

"It's been a rough couple of days," I said.

Carol stood. "Do you remember that time you had a cold and I made you homemade chicken noodle soup with old carrots and you got diarrhea for days?"

"Are you saying I look that bad?"

She shook her head. "Just remembering how adorable you looked in your pajamas."

"I remember resting my head in your lap and you stroking my hair for hours."

She smiled. "I remember the morning you shook me awake shouting about how you finally felt good and we needed to make love right then."

"Oh yeah. I had lost ten pounds in four days, I stank, and my hair was a greasy mess."

"You were still beautiful to me," she replied.

"Carol, what went wrong?"

She stepped over the animals and walked into the room. "We stopped appreciating the fact that we are better together than we are apart."

"I did. I know I did. I started taking you for granted. I think it happened little by little until it was too big to fix," I said.

"It can't be too big to fix," Carol whispered. "I thought it was. I lost faith. I was so wrapped up in the trauma of seeing my mother through her sickness that I forgot about us."

I could feel the tears streaming down my face. "I'm sorry, Carol. I'm so sorry I wasn't supportive enough."

"How could you be in that situation? She's a mean person. She hates us, she hates all gays, and she abused me my whole life. How could someone who loves me the way you do be okay with me giving so much of my time and devotion to her?"

"I could have been more supportive," I said, wiping my hand across my eyes. "I could have been a better partner."

"You've always been the best partner. I let you go while dealing with my own hell instead of remembering that we have always faced hell together."

She put her arms around me and I pulled her close. "Wait, did your mother die?"

She shook her head. "No. My sister is going to stay with her for the next six months. Her kids are grown, she's retired and it's about time her husband learned how to cook his own meals."

I rested my face against her head, marveling at the way she felt against my body. "How on earth did you get her to agree to that?"

Carol giggled liked a teenager which made me laugh with her. "Remember when Lindsay and I went to Cancun in 2008?"

"Yes."

"She had a one-night stand with the concierge from our hotel."

I pulled back to look at her. "Are you kidding me? Uptight Lindsay had vacation sex and you never told me?"

"I was sworn to secrecy," Carol said. "I swore I would never tell."

I laughed, squeezing her even tighter. "And now?"

"I threatened to tell her husband if she didn't get off her ass and help with mom."

"I can't believe it. I really can't believe it."

"What?" Carol kissed me on the cheek letting her lips linger just long enough to send shivers through my body. "That she had an affair or that I'm blackmailing her about it?"

"Both," I said.

"Desperate times call for desperate measures."

"I've felt rather desperate for some time. But what happens when the six months are over?" I said.

Carol looked up at me and grinned. I couldn't remember when she looked so beautiful. I kissed her on the mouth savoring the sweet taste of her lips. She opened her mouth to me and I sighed when her tongue touched mine.

"When the six months are over I'm sure my brother will be happy to step in."

"Tom? Yeah, right." I laughed. Taking Carol's hand, I led her to the bedroom. I pulled her shirt off over her head and when her face reappeared she was wearing a deliciously devilish grin.

"Darling," she said. "I've got so much on Tommy that I could get him to take care of mom for a decade."

She pushed me onto the bed and crawled on top of me. "Gwen," she whispered.

"Yes, my love?"

"Remind me of why I never want to leave home again."

Beth Burnett is the Director of Education and the head of the writing academy at the Golden Crown Literary Society. Beth teaches women's empowerment classes, runs a Lansing women's networking group, and gives seminars on open communication. Beth has published four books with Sapphire Books Publishing and is expecting her fifth. In her spare time, Beth reads, walks with her geriatric dog, and works on perfecting her three-quarter shimmy.

Man-Trapped Madeline

By Eva Lefoy

April 16th
Butte, Montana

I'll miss you." I stood in the kitchen with my arms around Chloe, holding her as I always did, until the very last minute before she had to go catch her plane back to the big city. Never one for goodbyes, our relationship ironically seemed built around them. Like a butterfly, Chloe was always leaving and coming, arriving and departing. She and I had just shared two long weeks of bliss here in my rustic-but-modernly appointed home, and I was reticent to let her go, more so this time than ever before. Yet I refused to spoil our parting by starting another, move to the small town, argument.

She pulled back from my embrace. "I'll miss you, too. But you know I have to get back to work. Got bills to pay."

Knowing she did didn't make parting any easier. In my opinion, it made it worse. The same questions always floated to the top of my mind. Why couldn't she stay here with me permanently in Butte, Montana? Why did it always seem easier for her to leave?

Worry niggled at me. Did she have another lover

stowed in Cincinnati? Had she lied to me and was really married? Sighing, I gazed down into her mink brown eyes searching for answers.

Chloe stiffened in my arms.

"What? What is it?"

She shook her head and stepped out of my arms entirely, spinning around so I couldn't see her face.

I took two steps toward her trying to keep the alarm out of my voice. "What's going on? Are you okay?"

She whirled and flashed me a smile, but her eyes radiated worry. "There's something I'm going to do when I get home that I haven't told you about…yet."

I scratched my short-trimmed dark hair and prayed for patience, but unease quickly settled into the middle of my chest. It wasn't like her to keep secrets from me, at least not that I knew of. I sure didn't have any secrets from her. What she saw was what she got—a stocky mid-thirties rural veterinarian butch living in a comfortable, modernized cabin, who was ragingly in lust with her.

"All right. Is it about your job?"

She shook her head, swishing the cascade of blonde curls around her shoulders. The hair always made her appear young and innocent, but I wasn't quite buying it.

The worst-case scenario popped into my mind. "Are you…leaving me?"

She came forward and took my hand. "No, silly. But I have made a decision you might not like."

Oh boy. I was too afraid to ask, so I remained silent, waiting.

She must have gathered her courage from somewhere deep within and found enough of it because her head lifted and her chin came up. "I want a baby."

"What?" I screeched the word like a pair of squealing breaks on a two-ton pickup truck. If she'd of said she was moving to Mars, I would have been less shocked, but a baby? That was a whopper.

Chloe let go of my hand and backed away toward the door, the last place I wanted her to go.

Grasping for a straw, I stated the obvious. "But… we haven't discussed a family."

"I know."

Was that bitterness I detected in her tone? My mouth dropped open as I found myself suddenly on the defensive. Too stunned to move, I watched her move closer and closer to her suitcase.

"But I'm not getting any younger, Maddy." Her fingers made a brush over the top of her belly as if imagining a fetus nestled there. Then she bit her lip like she always does when she's determined.

"I need to get this done, so I've made an appointment with the doctors for in vitro. I'm getting my first round done as soon as I get home."

"Shit." I cursed not because of anger but more out of disbelief.

The whole two weeks she'd been here she hadn't said one word about her plan. Now on her way out the door she casually told me she's been sneaking around behind my back with this whole make a baby thing. I mean what the hell? I didn't even know where to start with how wrong this all seems. I rubbed my head some more and paced in the kitchen. I didn't know where I was trying to go, and the room hardly seemed big enough to hold all my troubles. I just needed air, or common sense, or both. Finally I stopped and stared at her wide-eyed.

"I'm not sure I'm ready for this."

Chloe crossed her arms under her breasts and stomped her foot, eyes blazing. "That doesn't matter. I am."

With that, she turned and yanked open my solid pine front door, throwing it aside as if it weighed no more than a saltine cracker. Her other hand snagged her luggage, and she started out onto the porch.

My feet were already moving. I might have been slow on the uptake, but I was no fool. My love for Chloe was real. I just didn't understand where this sudden change in her behavior had come from. There was no way I could have expected it, but I sorely wanted to fix it.

"Chloe, wait."

It wasn't fair. Being taller, my legs were longer than hers. I reached the porch and snagged her arm before she had a chance to get to the car door open. Carefully so I didn't hurt her, I spun her back toward me. She dropped the suitcase and it hit the gravel pathway with a thud. My heart joined it when I saw the tears in her eyes.

"Oh honey." I wrapped my arms around her and guided her head onto my shoulder. Her choked sobs instilled a new fear in me I'd never experienced—the fear that I'd hurt her without even knowing it. I held her close and rubbed her back in soothing circles. "Chloe, it's okay. I promise. We'll talk this out. Don't worry sweetie."

She sniffled a few more times then raised her head. "Really? It's okay? You're not going to be mad at me if I do this?"

I wanted to tell her I'd be pissed as hell, but the way her chin trembled made me reposition my answer.

"No." I traced her pretty pastel pink lips with my finger. "I wish I was going to be there with you when you had it done, though. I don't like the thought of you going through that alone."

Chloe brightened a little. "I'll call you and let you know, okay?"

What could I say? I nodded and watched her pull out of my driveway as I always did, but nothing was ever going to be perfectly okay again in my world.

April 18th
Butte, Montana

Two days later, I sat at the counter at the Roost and Rail bar where Chloe and I had first met. The bartender, Jeanie, was on her way back with my stout. I must have looked troubled because after Jeanie set my beer down, she paused and lingered.

"Everything okay?"

"Chloe just left."

"Aw, that's always hard on you, honey." She patted my hand sympathetically. Jeanie wasn't gay, but she was gay-friendly. She was someone I could tell my troubles to. "I wish that girl would get another job."

I picked up my beer. "Yeah, me too."

"The way she's always crisscrossing around the country, you'd think she was some little bird not a pharmaceutical salesperson."

I nodded, taking a sip. The beer went down cold and spicy, just the way I liked it. But I couldn't say the same for Chloe's job. I too, wished she'd settle down, move in with me in Butte and give our relationship a chance to grow into a full-time thing. God knows I'd brought up the concept to her many times over the last two years, more than once. But every time she rolled her eyes and got that uppity city slicker look in her eyes. Yeah, it was true Butte would never be as big or as busy as Cincinnati. It would never hold the same appeal for her, I supposed. But every time we argued about it, it made me feel like somehow I wasn't good enough for her either. Not just this town, but me. I gulped down some more beer, and was surprised to find Jeanie still leaning on the bar in front of me.

"What?" Her eyes bored into mine. "It's more than that this time though, isn't it?" She backed up and placed her hands on the counter, continuing to give me the once over. "You two get in a fight?"

I slumped in my seat. "Sort of." A glance at Jeanie informed me she wasn't going to let this issue go until I spilled the whole pile of beans. Fine. "To tell you the truth, I'm not really sure."

Jeanie put her hands on her hips. "Well, what did she say?"

Gawd this was embarrassing. I lowered my voice and mumbled. "She said something about wanting a baby."

To my utter shock, Jeanie threw her head back and laughed. Not a little, a lot. Bewildered, I frowned at her without the foggiest notion of how my situation was funny.

"A baby?" She slapped the counter and wiped a tear of mirth from her eye. "Well, don't that beat all."

I shifted uncomfortably on the bar stool, half afraid I'd have to call the ambulance to have Jeanie mentally evaluated. This was so not funny. Not amusing to me one iota.

Jeanie called down the bar. "Hey Frank, Chloe's gonna have a baby!"

A whole row of heads turned my way, some of them friendly, others just to get the gossip. Frank boomed out a congratulations and everyone else applauded politely. I took another sip of my beer, surreptitiously counting how many ambulances it would take to haul the bar's patrons away. To my dismay, Frank came up to me and shook my hand.

"Great news, great news! Couldn't have happened to a nicer couple." He beamed at me before wandering off to finish his drink. A few people raised their glass to me in approval and then went back to their drinking.

Jeanie reached across the bar and slapped me on the shoulder. "Well, sailor. How does it feel to be a daddy?"

All tangled up is what I wanted to say. I shook my head. "It's all a damn mess. She got the in vitro appointment without me knowing about it."

Jeanie's eyes widened. Maybe she was finally coming around to my point of view. "How old is Chloe?"

"Thirty-five."

"And how long have you two been together?"

"Nearly two years." I answered the question, but as I did a little warning bell went off in my head. I didn't know what it meant. Was it wrong to be with a woman for two years? No, not as far as I knew. I had been looking forward to many more, to be honest. Sure, I hated the fact we always had to part, but I accepted it as being normal for me, and Chloe.

Jeanie sighed and leaned on the counter again. "You ever talk about marriage?"

"No." Well, not in so many words. Our on-again, off-again arguments about living together were sort of in that category. Living together was one step closer to marriage after all.

"Well, you'd better go shop for a ring."

At Jeanie's announcement the alarm bells in my head got louder. Way louder. I looked at her helplessly, like a deer caught in the headlights.

Jeanie rolled her eyes at me. "Geez, even though you're a guy you're still a girl. Or a girl-guy." She waived away the train of thought that had been going nowhere. "Let me explain it to you, okay?"

I held my breath, not sure I even wanted to hear her explanation of anything right at that moment.

"I'd been dating Derek for let's see—" She tapped her fingers on her chin. "About two and half years. Yeah. That's right. And things were going well but," she shrugged her shoulders, "there was no ring."

My stomach started to knot. I suddenly knew where this story was headed.

"So…" Jeanie traced little wet circles on the wooden surface between us. "I got pregnant. And presto!" She snapped her fingers. "We got married the very next month."

The knot in my stomach grew so tight I could hardly breathe. In desperation, I grabbed my beer and took another deep gulp.

"I think they call it a man trap, or something. Only you, you're a girl-guy, but hey. Isn't it funny that the good old tricks still work, even on girls?"

I muttered something about how ironic it all was and dragged myself out of the bar. At thirty-six and very much a butch, it had never occurred to me I'd one day be subjected to the same shenanigans that men with dicks suffered. The term shotgun wedding echoed in my head as I rolled my Hummer toward home, still in a state of shock. I really should have seen this coming but I hadn't. I'd taken our inability to agree on our living quarters as a sign we'd continue on exactly as we were indefinitely.

Good luck, my brain told me. *That's all water under the bridge now.*

⁂

I thought about calling her but realized my grip on the phone was so strong that I'd probably crush it before I got to hello, so I tossed it in the desk drawer for safe keeping. I was in no mood to talk. I needed to think. Lying on the bed with my hand over my eyes, I sifted through the facts looking for answers.

Chloe wants to get pregnant so I will marry her, even though she doesn't want to live with me.

I haven't asked her to marry me, since she doesn't want to live with me, but maybe I should have.

Chloe's going to have a baby but it will live here and then there, and will it be hers or ours? Or both?

How did that even make sense?

Hell and damn. Perhaps I've been ignoring the obvious.

Groaning, I rubbed my head harder, as if I could pop the right answer out if I caused my head a little more pain. For God sakes she'd sprung this on me two days ago and we hadn't talked since except for a few texts to verify she got home okay. I wanted her safe and sound, even if I didn't know what kind of game she was playing. This just wasn't like her. She was always so organized, practical and honest. Where had this strange desire of hers come from?

I sighed. "Must be hormones," I told the ceiling. "Her clock is ticking." Mine wasn't but then mine never had functioned right. The thought of pushing a baby out of my body made my insides shudder in horror. I hadn't realized Chloe didn't feel the same way. I'd been an idiot.

The phone rang and I sat upright on the bed, my head jerking toward the sound. It wasn't a vet related call it was Chloe's ringtone. I raced to the desk and pulled the phone out before it went to voice mail and practically yelled into the microphone. "Hello? Chloe?"

"Hi, Maddy."

Her voice sounded so small and so far away. Vulnerable. I wanted to wrap my arms around her but I couldn't. Instead I went back into the bedroom where I felt closest to her and laid back down on the blue Woolrich blanket where we'd made love so recently I could still smell a faint trace of her shampoo lingering on it. Inhaling deeply, I closed my eyes.

"How are you?"

She sniffed. "Okay."

Even from a distance I could tell that she wasn't okay. I pictured her lying there next to me smiling, her shiny golden hair spread around her head like a halo. I'd given anything to make her feel that happy again. "I'm glad you called. How was your day?"

"I cancelled my appointment."

I sucked in a breath. "Chloe, I'm sorry. Really, I am."

She sniveled and the sound gutted me. The last thing I wanted to do was make her cry. I wanted her to be okay with her decision. "Look, you don't have to explain..."

"I don't know, I just. I have all these feelings and it just keeps getting later and later and I want to have a family, you know?"

I murmured an approval, not wanting to

discourage her dialog.

"And I don't even know if you want that. I mean want that with me. Do you think it will ever be possible? Do you think we'll ever..." Her voice fell to a small whisper. "Get married?"

"Yes," I found myself saying. "Yes. I do." What was strange is that I meant it. It didn't seem wrong to say it out loud. I mentally kicked myself for not saying it sooner. Leaving a hormonal woman on the hook wasn't really my style. "Listen, we are going to work this out, okay? We're going to get this all figured out the next time we're together. I promise." I made a mental note to shop for a ring.

"Really?" She sounded as though her mood was lightening and I breathed a sigh of relief.

"Yes."

I heard her sigh and then what sounded like her settling down between the covers. "Are you in bed?"

"Uh huh."

"Good." To distract her, I fell back on our usual call pattern, one that had worked for us during those long times apart. "Tell me what you're wearing."

Chloe giggled, a good sign she was in the mood to play along. "My pink lace trimmed nightie."

I stifled a groan as I pictured her in it. "I love that one."

"Yeah, I know. It makes me feel closer to you when I wear it."

I smiled for what seemed the first time in ages. "What kind of panties?"

"Teddy bears."

"Teddy bears?" We both burst out laughing. The thought of a grown woman wearing teddy bear panties hit me as absurdly funny.

"I can't help it. I haven't had time to do laundry and these were all that was left in the drawer."

"My God honey, do some laundry before someone sees you in those!"

She snickered. "Don't worry. I already have a load in the dryer."

"Good girl." I wasn't sure if she wanted to continue with our usual play but I thought I'd give it a try. "Want to be an even better girl?"

"Uh huh."

"Take them off."

I heard the covers rustle and pictured her sliding the panties off her slender legs. Then I heard more rustling and wasn't sure what she was doing so I just held the line. Finally she came back on.

"Okay, I'm ready."

❧❧❧❧

Desire slammed through me. It always did when I saw Chloe naked, or even imagined her naked. Reaching down, I unbuttoned my jeans and then rolled onto my side. I transferred the phone to my left hand and slid my right down into panties, where I was already sopping wet. "God, I want you."

Chloe giggled. "You can't even see me."

"I can. I can see you lying there with your legs spread, and your pert little breasts poking through the negligee. I bet your nipples are hard. Are they?"

She gasped. "Yes."

"Touch them for me. Pretend it's my tongue licking them."

I heard a light rustle of fabric and then she let out a soft moan. "Oooh, Maddy. Feels so good."

God, didn't I know it. My own fingers were

covered in my juices and my clit was already thrumming. I hadn't realized how much I'd needed her in the short time we'd been apart but my body was primed to explode. From my side I rolled more onto my front, trapping my arm beneath my weight. "Pretend I'm on top of you rubbing my leg between your thighs."

"Yes. Oh yes."

I assumed she was touching herself, as I was. "Are you wet there?"

"Mm hmm."

I groaned into the bed, her scent all around me. It wouldn't take much more imagination for me to come. My fingers were drenched. It sounded like hers were too. I wished I was there lapping her up. "I want you to rub all the way down your lips and back. That's right. Down and back. Make sure your fingers are nice and wet."

Pretending it was my tongue licking her in place of her fingers had me struggling not to fall over the edge into release. My body shook with the need of her but I refused to come first.

"Maddy," she breathed. "I'm so ready for you."

"I know baby, I know." No point in lying about that. "Now bring your fingers up to your clit and circle around it like my tongue does. Very slowly."

Her breath hitched.

"Slowly…"

It hitched again. Her tiny gasps of pleasure becoming higher pitched.

"Okay. Maddy…"

"Now I'm sucking you as hard as I can, pushing my mouth against you, pushing your legs open wider. Raise your hips for me. Fuck my mouth. That's right honey."

"Maddy!"

Her scream of pure ecstasy stole my breath. I lay there and listened to her, unable to speak. Under my fingers, my clit pulsed like a rapid heartbeat. I hadn't moved my hand in forever but a white-hot orgasm pounded out of me just the same. Hearing her come had taken me right along with her. I wasn't surprised. It almost always did. "Chloe." I groaned her name into the wool blanket, ending up breathing in some of the scratching fluff.

Her pants were short and cute, and enough to give me aftershocks. "Maddy. Oh, Maddy. God that was good. Thank you."

"No, thank you." I was still amazed at the way she ruled my body, even from a distance. We were about as connected, as two people could get who didn't live together. A fact I'd try to remedy as soon as a possible. Letting Chloe slip through my fingers seemed a very bad outcome, one I'd do my damnedest to avoid.

"I'm glad you're not mad."

"Of course I'm not mad. I was just shocked, that's all." I withdrew my hand from my jeans and rolled onto my back.

"I know, I'm sorry. I shouldn't have sprung it on you."

"That's okay. It's given me a good reason to think about things." I stared at the ceiling once again, trying to pull the wool hairs from my mouth.

"Well, I guess I'll go to sleep now."

I checked the clock. It was late her time. "All right. Get a good night's sleep and I'll see you soon."

"If you call two months soon." The pout in her voice was adorable.

"No, I'll be there sooner than that." I sat up, ready to execute a newly hatched plan. Apparently that orgasm had really cleared my head. "I'm rearranging my work schedule. Going to shuffle some patients to other vets in town. I'll see you in two weeks."

"You're what?"

"We need to talk about this Chloe. We need to figure out how this is going to work." I stared at the empty pillow on her side of the bed. "And Chloe if you do want to go ahead with the in vitro we can schedule it while I'm there but I want to be there when it happens, okay?"

"O—okay. You mean it? You really want me to…?"

"I want you to be happy, Chloe," with me, preferably. "I love you, now get some shut-eye. We can talk again tomorrow."

"Okay. Love you too. Night-night."

"'Night." I hung up the phone and shook my head. For a woman who'd been man-trapped I was pretty okay with it. Making Chloe my own permanently was a move I should have made long ago. I silently thanked Jeanie for her not-so-gentle nudge and suddenly realized everyone in the bar thought I was already a daddy. Standing, I zipped up my pants and corralled my courage. *Well then. I'd better get this show on the road.*

Eva Lefoy writes what thrills her and her tastes are pretty far from boring. She's forever sneaking FF action into the most unlikely stories in the hopes of showing that all lovers can prevail, given the opportunity. She lives in Washington State but hopes to someday travel the galaxy.

Two Months

By Kande Monroe

Music Round Chat A739421YU:

SmokyJazz401: Why is it that the world simply makes more sense when you are inside a Dylan lyric or lost in Benny Goodman?

dub56poet: I don't have a definitive answer to that. Suffice it to say, I agree wholeheartedly.

SmokyJazz401: You do? I have never made sense so readily to anyone before. Oh, how I am going to miss you. Usually, I am looked at with a quirk of the head and a smile that I know has been placed there to buy time until they can figure out what to say to me.

dub56poet: I have been the recipient of that look before! Sometimes, I even get to hear a little humming as they decipher what I just said and then they walk away, not even bothering to reply.

SmokyJazz401: Ah yes, the humming!

dub56poet: I will miss you too, especially how you make me laugh without being entertainment fodder. I grin with pride.

SmokyJazz401: Am I really about to do this?

dub56poet: Yes, you are! I will confess that I've been hopeful you'll come my way.

SmokyJazz401: No! Don't tell me where you are.

It would be too tempting to stay away. I don't think I could handle knowing where you are while I am roaming about. I need these decisions to be mine and not be persuaded in any way.

dub56poet: You can't blame me for trying!

SmokyJazz401: I never will! Oh dear, I am blushing.

dub56poet: I love that I have that effect on you.

SmokyJazz401: The words you type...

dub56poet: If you use that sexy imagination-inducing ellipse one more time, I might have to take care of something. I have been warning you about this for a month.

SmokyJazz401: I am flush now. Blushing and flushed!

dub56poet: You are so tangible. This is insane. We had better try and focus. So, Smoky, what are your plans?

SmokyJazz401: Focusing, focusing, focusing...

dub56poet: Delightful.

SmokyJazz401: First, I am travelling to—

dub56poet: Stop! No specifics. I also can't handle knowing where you are. I would jump on a plane and go. Wander around whatever part of the world you were in to try and find you. Knowing and not finding you would be torture. I think, best to stay mysterious, for both of our sanities.

SmokyJazz401: Fair enough. Tomorrow I am to visit my aunt. After that I am off to visit two different friends, one a city and one a person.

dub56poet: I love that you have befriended a place. I have done that with the ocean.

SmokyJazz401: Beautiful. After that, I want to live somewhere new, experience a different climate and region. I simply cannot decide or narrow it down. I cannot even narrow down the narrowing down.

dub56poet: Listen, you've already taken the gamble. You are throwing yourself into a life you didn't expect, to have a more fulfilling one—one without regret, without longing, or what-ifs. Why not take it further and gamble again?

SmokyJazz401: I don't follow.

dub56poet: Oh, you follow my lead just fine.

SmokyJazz401: You! I just stopped blushing!

dub56poet: I like keeping you in a perpetual state...

SmokyJazz401: I bet you do.

dub56poet: Get a map, close your eyes, point. It is the oldest trick in the world for wanderers and dreamers like you.

SmokyJazz401: And you, I dare say.

dub56poet: Perhaps. The beauty is that once you get there, you can change your mind. Keep the map handy and you will always know how to make a decision.

SmokyJazz401: Is this how you make your decisions?

dub56poet: Some of them, where people aren't concerned.

SmokyJazz401: You don't think people can be like maps?

dub56poet: I do, but more akin to atlases, that are too full of tricky mountain regions and county roads that dead end unexpectedly.

SmokyJazz401: Also, people are just as hard to fold up! Maybe people are more the topographical sort of map...they have to be read with Braille rather than words.

dub56poet: If that were the case, I would very much like to chart a course on you.

SmokyJazz401: For you, I'd be a willing map.

dub56poet: Smoky, how can we…

SmokyJazz401: I know, I know, this is so hard. I will not ever be able to thank you for this past month.

dub56poet: Shhh, hush now, you have given me so much, shown me love is real.

SmokyJazz401: Dub, I never knew it was possible to connect so purely with anyone, and I do not even know your name.

dub56poet: Just promise me, if you ever truly do need me, log back in and I will be here.

SmokyJazz401: No, we have to live and be open to fate. We swore it was the right thing to do!

dub56poet: I know and I want the world for you, but I also want to help and be there for you.

SmokyJazz401: Oh dub, we will never be able to function if we go down this path. Let's not end this month this way.

dub56poet: You're right, of course you are. I'm sorry. I will be strong and honor our pact.

SmokyJazz401: Listen to me. You saved my life by renewing my spirit and kissing my heart.

dub56poet: Right back at ya! Truly. Now stop stalling…you promised you would tell me tonight.

SmokyJazz401: Are you sure?

dub56poet: More than ever. Get yourself something to drink and hurry back!

The computer glowed in front of her as she sat down at her desk with a glass of wine. Glass, as a description, was a stretch. She had given away all of her actual glasses earlier in the day, which left her with only a Dixie cup. Luckily, it was the largest size they make or she would have felt silly doing what would be the equivalent of spritzer shots. The cursor blinked inside the little square. It winked at her, inviting her to answer a quest that started on a whim exactly one month earlier. It was a silly component to something that had meant more to her than she could have ever imagined, and it was the last piece of this magical unexpected expression of love. Answering it signaled the end. But they had made a pact, two strangers resigned never to meet. Could she answer it? Dare she?

SmokyJazz401: Okay, yes. I have a beverage. A wine spritzer of sorts, made out of the last of my Sprite from lunch and a forgotten solo bottle of wine. They were the only options besides water. And it is in a Dixie cup. I am very classy.

dub56poet: You slay me! I have a beer. Are you ready?

SmokyJazz401: Yes.

dub56poet: Do you have the bowl?

SmokyJazz401: Yes.

dub56poet: What do you call the bowl?

SmokyJazz401: The Wish Away Bowl!

dub56poet: Adorable.

SmokyJazz401: Hey, you promised not to make fun of me...

dub56poet: Oh, that ellipse of yours! I am not making fun of you. I truly do find it to be an adorable name. I find you to be adorable as well, though you probably figured that out by now.

SmokyJazz401: Don't make me blush. I'm already nervous.

dub56poet: And stalling.

SmokyJazz401: I am not!

dub56poet: Tell me how you did this again. You

just wrote down your wishes and put them in the bowl?

SmokyJazz401: Yes. Only I wrote them each on a separate slip of paper.

dub56poet: So they would each have equal importance?

SmokyJazz401: Yes, and room to grow. How did you know that?

dub56poet: I pay attention.

SmokyJazz401: You certainly do.

dub56poet: Are you ready?

SmokyJazz401: Yes.

dub56poet: Then here we go. Cheers to you, Smoky, and for the path that is coming up to meet you!

SmokyJazz401: Thank you, dub, and cheers to you too! Are you sure you want to experience every slip with me?

dub56poet: Yes. Every. One.

One Year Later

"Hey, you!" Cyn called and waved for Krista to come join them. Krista walked deliberately and maybe a little slower than her normal gait toward the table. Before she looked intently to the side, hoping to appear nonchalant, she felt Slide look at her. Slide had turned around when Cyn spotted Krista and had not reassumed her previous position. Their eyes locked briefly, which caused Krista to look slightly away. It was her only defense mechanism, and she regretted it. Especially if that was a smile she saw spread across Slide's face, a smile so subtle and dear that Krista blushed and then felt ashamed for believing it to be true. Those lips that had encouraged and held that smile...she had thought about those lips almost constantly for the past month, and she blushed again.

"You made it!" Drea said.

Slide stood and moved behind a chair and gestured toward Krista as she pulled it out. "Do sit down." Krista still had not gotten used to the chivalrous acts Slide subtly tossed in her direction, always for her benefit.

"Thank you," she managed, and was grateful when Cyn picked up the conversation, which helped to neutralize the attention being placed on Krista. The discussion mainly surrounded Drea's and Cyn's recent two-day honeymoon that immediately followed their beautiful wedding.

"Krista, how can we thank you enough? You pulled off a miracle. We could never have foreseen having to completely plan and have our wedding in less than a month! You are a wonder." The table erupted in applause, inasmuch as three people can applaud to create an explosion. Krista could not stop the reddening of her cheeks from the flattery. "By the way, my mom is doing well and has a chance at a recovery if her tests keep going well," Drea added, wiping a few tears from the corners of her eyes.

"Oh, I'm so glad. She is a lovely woman. I am so honored I got to meet her," Krista stated. Drea's mother, Maureen, had taken ill suddenly and her life expectancy was cut dramatically short. It was this revelation that expedited their wedding, as they didn't want Maureen to miss it. They had already hired Krista to plan the wedding. They'd simply had a much longer planning process scheduled in their original vision.

"What a month, huh?" Cyn asked. Krista thought it sounded rhetorical. "And we managed to stay so focused, even so far as postponing getting to know you better, Krista."

"And it's been killing us!" Drea said, and laughed. Krista stole a glance at Slide, Drea's best friend and the photographer they hired not only for the wedding, but also to document all of the planning that led up to it. "Tell us, our lovely new friend, what you do when you're not planning weddings?"

"She's a singer," Slide announced. It was the first thing Slide had said since Krista sat down, and the whole table was silenced by sound coming from her corner. Krista allowed herself another look toward Slide. It was really the only thing she wanted to do, but she was afraid it was too obvious.

"Well, we knew that. That's how we met her, after all. She sang at David and Erin's wedding. We must have mentioned that." Drea seemed flustered, as if she felt the need to justify her opinion to Slide.

"Did you?" Slide asked.

Krista wanted to ask Slide what was going on, though not in front of Drea and Cyn. Luckily, the waiter came to the table to deliver drinks and broached a completely different topic about the art on the walls.

"All of the proceeds from the auction go to Music First, a nonprofit that ensures music programs thrive in schools." The waiter delivered the required information with about as much excitement as sharing the specials.

"Good sir, we are aware of the auction. We have among us the artist who donated the work to be auctioned. It is precisely why we are here." Drea puffed out her chest and tilted her head back to Slide in a naked display of how proud she was of her.

Krista looked around the restaurant, at the lush urban landscapes interspersed with macro portraits.

They were all black and white, and they were stunning. Having been too preoccupied with her nerves, she hadn't noticed them before. They had a calming effect, which was welcomed as Krista was anxious to learn how Slide knew more about her than she would have ever thought possible.

"This is your work?" Krista asked directly.

Slide met her gaze with fierce eye contact of her own. It was intense, but not threatening or challenging, and it made Krista's insides clench low in her body. "Yes," Slide answered in a deep, sincere tone, which implied an answer to more than what the simple question posed.

"You can see why we begged her to photograph our wedding and process. She has such a great eye!" Cyn said. "Drea wanted Slide to videotape us, but I was against that idea from the start."

"But think of the podcasts we'll miss out on!"

"Honey, please. It's not like we met online or anything. No offense, Slide."

"None taken. Though you shouldn't knock something you've never tried." Slide's speech was tempered, measured and unapologetic. Krista liked that. *The words you type...*flashed through her mind and she wondered if Slide had an online romance of her own. "If the two participants are open and honest, it can be a beautiful and valid way to communicate." When Slide spoke, Krista heard jazz compositions—smooth, even, melodic tones with just a hint of agitation to keep it interesting.

"Come on, no one is real online. It is all pretending." Cyn continued to plead her point of view, and Krista shook her head and placed her hands on the table as she leaned toward Cyn.

"I'm going to have to disagree with you, Cyn. Granted, I don't have a lot of experience with social media interaction, but what I have experienced was most definitely real. I think it depends on how you approach it and what you are willing to bring to it. If you're open to cutting through all of those preconceived notions and the safety nets the internet inherently provides, then it can be very rewarding." Krista had experienced only one online dialog. It was one of the most meaningful months of her life, and she would defend the platform that gave her that gift.

"Sounds pure when you put it that way, but how do you know who's full of crap? You've got to have a good way of identifying and weeding out the cowards who are hiding behind the interface, and that's hard to do. Right?" Drea posed the question to the group, but it was clear that it was pointedly addressed to Slide.

"I've never said different," Slide answered calmly.

"Well, I'm glad we cleared that up," Cyn said, and she and Drea laughed tentatively until Slide joined in, followed by Krista. Slide's laugh was deep and low and sounded to Krista like sincerity personified. She hoped she would get to hear that laugh again and often.

As their laughter faded, their food arrived. Drea's and Cyn's meals, made it to the table boxed up and in a bag, while Krista's and Slide's were hot and on plates in front of them.

"Wasn't this great? We've got to get home. We took advantage of our dog sitter this past month, so we had to give her the night off. You two enjoy." Drea jumped up and swooped down to pick up the bag containing their dinner.

"Best of luck with the auction, Slide. Let's schedule lunch next week, Krista. Have a lovely weekend." Cyn laced her arm through Drea's, and they were off. Krista settled into her chair and let out a sigh. Slide took a moment before she turned in toward Krista.

"I believe we have been set up. Apparently, we're on a date."

"Do you mind?" Krista searched Slide's eyes for an answer before Slide could form a reply.

"Only that I didn't ask you myself. Are you nervous?"

"Not after hearing you say that." Krista could not believe how suddenly it felt easy to sit next to Slide. It was an excitement that calmed and enticed her. In a strange way, it made her brave. "How do you know that I sing?"

"Chapman's Corner."

"How do you know about that?" Krista couldn't believe Slide knew about that record.

"I was on vacation with my first girlfriend at her college on the East Coast. It must have been a few months after the album was released. Her college radio station played the Chapman's Corner's version of 'Cry Me a River' every day I was there. I made a mental note of the band and your name so that when we went into town, I could get the recording. Only, we never made it into town because we broke up before that excursion, and I came home. It wasn't until recently that I was able to get my hands on a copy of that song."

"That is crazy." Krista had only made one album with her parents, at their request. They were musicians, and Krista had been singing since she was born. "Chapman's Corner only pressed three albums total. There were two instrumental jazz albums and one with my vocals. My father engineered and produced them himself, and my mother took charge of promoting them. I thought my aunt and I were the only people on the planet who had that album. I can't believe we aren't alone."

"No, you are not alone." Slide's words were welcomed and Krista allowed a smile to linger on her lips.

"I haven't thought about that album for a while now, though I think of my parents every day," Krista shared. "A car crash took them from me shortly after we made that record."

"I am so sorry Krista." Slide put her hand over Krista's. Immediately and inexplicably, Krista felt that she really wasn't alone, not if she didn't want to be.

Krista gave Slide's hand a squeeze. "You know, they had to beg me to sing on that album. All I wanted to do that summer was travel through Europe with a friend. The last thing on my mind was spending a summer with my parents in their home studio in the suburbs." Krista paused to take in Slide's steady, open gaze upon her. Being this near Slide was similar to the sensation of being on stage singing a great song in perfect timing with your band killing it along with you. Everyone in the place completely tuned in to that moment, with you, in the music, and everything is right in the world. "Looking back, I am so grateful to have had that time with them. Once we got started it was a blast. I got to be with them as an adult, to see them differently but exactly as who they were…the three of us, in the music. Does that make sense?"

"Yes, perfect sense. All of that comes through in the album. Mind you, I have only heard the one track, but it is very powerful," Slide answered, her eyes never leaving their lock on Krista's.

I have never made sense so readily to anyone

before. "How did you know it was me? Krista may not be the most common name, but surely there are more Krista Chapman's out there."

"Not ones whose speaking voice is a song." Slide applied more pressure to Krista's hand.

Krista felt the blush rise on her cheeks. She pulled her hand away and picked up her fork. "We should eat before it gets cold." Slide's hazel eyes had a hint of grey that Krista wanted to drown in. Receiving that compliment forced her to concentrate harder on her meal. Otherwise she would not be able to resist smoothing her hands over Slide's broad shoulders. "And, maybe, talk about something else."

"Anything." Slide's eyes held just a hint of veiled desire, but behind that Krista thought she caught a glimpse of something that resembled more of a promise...of possibility. And possibilities, she thought, were totally worth a gamble—*Get a map, close your eyes, point.*

"Do you mean it? Anything?" Krista asked, completely aware of how seductive it came across.

"Yes. Anything," Slide answered immediately, as if she didn't need to think.

"Well then, when did you get that shot of my legs?"

"You saw that one, huh?"

"I recognized my shoes. I don't think my legs ever looked that good. You must have done some magic," Krista admitted.

"Not one fairy dust sprinkling. It's all you, all natural. I don't Photoshop anything. It's sort of a personal challenge of mine. I took that shot in Cyn's office before you knew I was there. I couldn't stop looking at you."

Slide's gaze continued to pierce her, and Krista wondered if there was more to the challenge than she was aware. Either way, she was enjoying her attention immensely. "It's a great shot. Thank you," she said as she pushed her plate away. Honestly, the only thing she wanted to eat was not on the menu. "What is your favorite shot?"

"Besides you?" Slide answered, and it felt like a seduction.

"Stop it!" Krista laughed to calm herself down. "Seriously."

"I am serious, but I will humor you with another answer." Slide smiled at Krista. "The coast of Ireland from a few years ago."

"Oh, I bet it is beautiful. Is that when you set up shop?" Krista asked.

"In photography? No. Can you see me telling people to say cheese?" Slide let out a free laugh. "I own a business in IT. That's my paycheck." Slide moved closer to Krista and smoothed her hand down Krista's arm. "Photography is my passion."

Krista licked her lips as Slide leaned in closer. She thought she could track the telemetry of Slide's face to hers in fine fashion, to prepare for the impact, but was completely shocked when impossibly soft lips met hers. It wasn't a chaste kiss, but one deep and wanting. Slide's hand went to Krista's knee and began to trail up to her thigh. Krista felt a brush of cool air as her skirt lifted slowly. It was enough to jolt her away from the embrace.

"Come home with me," Krista demanded breathlessly.

Slide didn't remember who paid the bill—or even if either did—but at once they were getting into a car and driving across town. By the time she regained her senses, they were safely inside Krista's apartment and had resumed kissing, Slide firmly guiding Krista onto the table.

"I love that you wear stockings," Slide whispered in Krista's ear as she moved her hand farther up. "But these have to go." Slide didn't have the patience to completely remove the panties before moving her fingers down them and through Krista's wetness. She cupped Krista's sex to say hello before concentrating her fingers between her lips.

"Slide..." Krista gasped at the touch, widened her legs a little more. Her hands were in Slide's hair, her breath choppy with increased desire. Its sound and heat drove Slide crazy. She stroked down again and entered her, overtaken by the sensation of being inside Krista. She slipped in another finger.

Krista's breathing transformed into hums and little moans. As Slide filled her up, Krista surrendered completely to her touch. Slide loved the way Krista felt wrapped around her and on her. She deepened her penetration, her pressure, and her speed. Feeling Krista on the verge was about to make her explode. Slide rested her head on Krista's shoulder to concentrate on her needs more than her own. Krista held Slide's shoulders, her heels locked tight under Slide's ass.

"Slide!" Krista screamed from the very back of her throat. She began to buck against Slide.

The feeling of Krista's sex clamping down and how it tried to push her out as she came made Slide orgasm, too. She did her best to hold on tight and stay inside Krista. She circled her arm tighter around Krista's waist to hold on for herself.

Krista gave Slide a half-lidded glance before Slide removed her hand, lifting her fingers to her lips to taste them, pointedly.

"Your wish is my desire," Slide said. Krista smiled deliriously.

"Why don't you put on some music while I catch my breath? The stereo has options."

Slide had been so entranced by watching Krista she hadn't noticed the cherrywood RCA stereo cabinet. It was in mint condition—a beauty, just like its owner. "Wow."

"I knew you would appreciate it," Krista said and kissed Slide's neck.

The top of the cabinet contained a turntable and a radio. The speakers were exposed on the front ends with a sliding door in the middle. Inside the cupboard Slide found a slew of albums, and a bowl with what looked like written upon slips of paper inside. Slide kneeled to get a closer look. She knew she shouldn't pry, but curiosity got the better of her. Most of the slips had been folded once. Slide picked out one of the unfolded slips and read, "learn to sew."

Slide was overwhelmed with a sense of déjà vu. This bowl couldn't be what she thought it was. The universe could not be that much of a trickster. She read another slip, one that had been folded in half, "sing again." This had officially become surreal. Reading one more slip could solve this riddle, and she was prepared for confirmation but not the next goal, "meet dub56poet in real life."

Slide grabbed the bowl and spun around. "What's this?"

"Oh. That's something I put together before I left Maine," Krista said. When Slide remained silent, she continued. "I set out to write down my wishes, and I put them in that bowl. I keep it with me because there are a few wishes that haven't come true yet." Krista's explanation was sweet and matter-of-fact.

"What do you call it?" Slide asked.

"It's silly. I call it the Wish Away Bowl," Krista answered. Slide's breathing became shallow and her eyes went wide. "What is it, Slide?" Krista asked, genuinely concerned.

"Oh...my...this is..." Slide found it hard to form words but she had to. This was too intense. "Are you SmokyJazz401?"

Krista's expression changed from concern to shock. "How do you know about SmokyJazz401?"

"I'm dub56poet."

Krista stared at Slide. "That...this isn't possible. I've only ever chatted..." Krista trailed off. "...Had one long distance relationship in my life... It was only a month but it meant so much to me." The air felt charged and alive. "And, it was with you?"

"Oh, whoa, it was you who gave me that recording? I was talking to you the whole time. Why didn't you tell me it was your song?" Slide hugged the bowl to her chest.

"We said nothing personally revealing. We shared no searchable details," Krista stammered. "I couldn't very well have said, 'Oh I am glad you like my song,' and not broken our pact."

"I love this bowl. I love your wishes. I have them all practically memorized," Slide said without shame.

"I can't believe that was you." Krista shared a giddy grin. "It makes sense, but it is unbelievable that we met on Music Round, the only website that can claim me as a member."

Slide set the bowl on the table and sat next to Krista. Being close again steadied her breathing. "I'm not a member of Music Round," she confessed. "I created it. It's my IT business. When my band, 56 Beat Poets, stopped touring, I had to keep the music alive."

Krista let out a sigh. "Of course you did." She placed her hand on Slide's cheek and gave her a reassuring laugh.

"Why are some of the wishes folded?" Slide asked.

"I fold them when the wish comes true," Krista answered sweetly.

Slide reached over for the bowl. She found the piece of paper that had wished to meet her and handed it to Krista. Krista read it and smiled. She held the paper to her heart before folding it over with her lips. Slide could feel their hearts pound in unison. She held out the bowl to catch the wish come true, for SmokyJazz401 had indeed met dub56poet.

"Are you sure you don't mind?" Krista asked.

"Mind? How could I mind? Two of my most favorite women are staring right back at me." Slide lifted Krista's chin and gave her a kiss as dub kissing Smoky for the first time. "Oh Krista, I have been falling for you from so many distances, long before I had any inkling of who you were. First, back in college when I heard your recording, then on Music Round in chat, and now all over again tonight."

Krista curled in closer to Slide, "What a night."

"What a month." Slide kissed Krista's forehead to seal the promise that was in her heart. "I love you, Krista." Slide said it out loud for the first time, though her heart had been saying it long before they had ever met.

"And I love you, Slide." Krista's kiss made Slide feel as if she had come home. She hoped with all of her heart that Krista could now sing the song her parents had arranged for her, the one she and Slide would compose as they went along together.

Kande Monroe has been writing stories in her head for decades. Sometimes she types them out and finds ways to share them. Her story, What Remains, is available in audio on networklisten.com. During the day she telecommutes from her home in Colorado. At night she dreams until she falls asleep. https://www.facebook.com/KandeMonroe/

The Big Gulp

By Sallyanne Monti

June 10, 1998 – Dallas, Texas

Amy Garel - Set Designer
Neiman Marcus Offices, Downtown Dallas

It's been an exhausting day of meetings at Neiman Marcus Headquarters in the Renaissance Tower on Elm St. in downtown Dallas. This latest high-profile client hired me to design Runway Sets for their Fashion Expo, and the project fell smack in the middle of my already full plate.

My head hurts from bobbing and weaving my way through the non-stop bickering within a sea of opposing opinions, from the large team of well-dressed, self-serving, high-fashion personalities whose snappy responses matched the spikes of their designer heels.

I look at my fitness watch as I squeeze the bridge of my nose above my black rectangular framed glasses to relieve the tension. The watch flashes 1:20 p.m. My anxiety level raises a notch as I realize the likelihood of making my three o'clock flight to Burbank out of Dallas is now slim to none.

I excuse myself from the meeting to call Southwest Airlines in an attempt to reschedule my flight. Luck is on my side as I enter the details of my new six o'clock departure into my cellphone calendar. I take a deep breath and walk back into the meeting to conclude what is amounting to one of the crappiest weeks in Dallas yet. I've redesigned the runway configurations six times and still the group can't come to a consensus agreement. I remind myself that I'm being more than fairly compensated for my one week a month in Dallas. This was a typical production meeting, with the agenda off the skids and everyone's patience running thin.

I thought about my beautiful Santa Monica beach house and the fully equipped gym I'm missing. Working out always makes me feel better. The adrenaline clears my head while the workout releases stress. The Fitness Center in the hotel is the size of my closet with mismatched free weights, stained wall of mirrors, Fitness Guru Tony Little's Gazelle Glider and a pitcher of tepid water next to a stack of bathroom sized Dixie cups. My intense urge to lift something really heavy is second only to my ongoing obsession with daily exercise. I shake my head as I reluctantly admit how gym-addicted I really am. I giggle to myself as I walk back into the meeting thinking, *If you're going to be obsessed Amy, it should at least involve an adorable woman who wants to ravage your body.* Maybe next trip I can replace my daily gym workouts with happy hours at Sue Ellen's, the renowned lesbian bar in Dallas. I open the door returning to the crowded conference room in the hopes of concluding this week's business on a happy note.

Shelly Johns - Director of Marketing
Mellon Bank Offices, Downtown Dallas

If I hear him zip and unzip one more time, I'm going to pull my hair out. What is he doing in there? How many zippers can one man's laptop bag have? You'd think by now Dave's leaving the office rituals would be nothing more than background noise. I've worked for Dave Reese for ten years. He hired me as a marketing intern and personal assistant straight out of College. Then, I convinced myself that the personal assistant part would include bringing him his morning coffee, picking up his dry cleaning, and ordering his wife flowers, all while taking memos and organizing departmental birthday celebrations. Instead, Dave took me under his wing, entrusting me with complex projects for high-profile clients and eventually promoting me three times to my current position as director of marketing for Mellon Bank in Dallas. Our division creates elaborate presentations, brochures, and forecast documents for VIP clients. I work closely with our Los Angeles team spending one week a month at Mellon's downtown L.A. Offices on South Hope Street.

I like my job well enough. It isn't necessarily challenging but it is devoid of repetitious tasks, which I detest as much as I detest Diet Coke. Ick. Most people start their day with a steaming cup of coffee. I start mine with a frosty cold Diet Pepsi, straight from the can.

Well I suppose I should start zipping and unzipping myself out of this place or I'll miss my six o'clock flight to Burbank.

I love landing at Burbank, a small airport in the middle of the Los Angeles chaos. I'll be off the plane and in my cab in ten minutes for the scenic drive through Laurel Canyon past Mulholland Drive until it dumps into Sunset Blvd. near Crescent Heights. Soon I'll be at my favorite hotel on Santa Monica Blvd., a short walk from The Palms, West Hollywood's epic lesbian bar. A one-night stand is a definite possibility.

❧❧❧❧

Fate
June 10, 1998 – Dallas, Texas

Southwest Airlines Flight
From Dallas, Texas to Burbank, California

Relieved to have made it to the gate in time, I examine my boarding pass, which reads "Garel, Amy Group C." My anxiety rises while watching the mobs of fellow passengers in Groups A and B advance ahead of me. As they slowly make their ways to the podium and down the jet bridge, they will no doubt settle into every available window and aisle seat while consuming every remaining inch of overhead bin space, leaving my carry-on suitcase homeless. As I began to sweat and swear under my breath a crackled voice screeches over the loud speaker "Group C and all other passengers please board the aircraft at this time."

I make my way down the crowded corridor to the plane's entrance, greet the flight attendant with a nod, and survey the sea of passenger heads in occupied seats as far as my eyes can see. As the line in front of me comes to a complete stop I think to myself, *Great Amy, only middle seats left. Shit!*

As I impatiently look around, my plan shifts to finding a seat next to someone who's already asleep. I quickly conclude that a seat closest to the front of the plane will mitigate the inevitable deplaning bottleneck upon landing in Burbank. Sweeping my glance from the available empty middle seats to the meager overhead bin space is stressing me out. I'm relieved to spot an open middle seat in front of me, and a small bin space opening that will accommodate my carry-on. As I began to lift my suitcase to slip it into the open bin, a passenger behind me slams his backpack into my shoulder pushing me forward into the seatback in front of me. As I grab the seat with my free hand to steady myself, the passenger lifts his backpack over my head and stuffs it into the last available bin space over my head, before I could lift my own suitcase into the same spot. I feel the angry heat rise up to my face, as I begin to swivel around to tell the rude passenger behind me to remove their bag from what was clearly my bin space—I am stopped by a woman in the aisle seat who gently touches my arm.

As I look down, I see an expression of sympathy in her warm brown eyes as she looks up at me and says, "I can move my laptop bag under my seat if you'd like?"

Shocked by her unexpected kindness, I'm dumbfounded and say nothing. Taking this as a yes, she stands up and hands me her giant 7-Eleven Big Gulp cup, saying "take good care of this, it's liquid gold."

I back up, holding her Big Gulp cup in my left hand and my suitcase in my right hand allowing her room to move into the aisle in front of me. At about 5'7", she easily removes her laptop bag from the overhead bin.

She nods to me as she bends over and slips her laptop bag under the aisle seat in front of her, stands up, grabs her Big Gulp cup from my hand and says, "Hurry up, get it in there before someone stuffs something else up there."

I can't help but smile as I stand on my 5'2" tippy toes, shove my carry-on into the small space and say, "Thank you, that's so nice of you."

"Well don't get too comfy, I like to man-spread on airplanes and this middle seat of yours is likely to shrink by the time the flight attendant replenishes my Diet Pepsi."

As I wiggle past her and lower myself to the middle seat, I look at her saying, "Diet Pepsi? You can't be serious. Ick."

As she lowers herself back into her aisle seat, she says, "Seriously addicted."

"That's a shame because I was really beginning to like you," I reply sarcastically.

She rolls her eyes and says, "Don't even tell me you drink Diet Coke."

I say, "Okay, I won't tell you, but if you'd like one, I'm buying."

"I'd rather spend the flight stuffed into the overhead bin space with your carry-on than drink Diet Coke. Yuck." She replies.

As I buckle my seatbelt, I watch her buckle herself in, noticing how smooth the tops of her hands are and the manicured shine of her neatly clipped fingernails. I can't help but glance at the lean shape of her fit body. She has long legs spread out in front of her, crossed at her ankles. Her muscular thighs are showing through the linen fabric of her grey trousers. Her shirttail is tucked into her slacks and lying flat against her firm abs, which only accents her full round breasts. A white silk button-down dress shirt is opened to reveal the indentation of her collarbone and a hint of cleavage.

She has perfectly round-shaped lips and a slightly upturned small nose. As my eyes work their way up her body to her face, I'm startled to find her staring at me. With a sly grin on her face, she holds my gaze as she slowly uncrosses her legs at her ankles and spreads them as wide as she can, stopping only when her right leg from ankle to thigh is pressed tightly against my left leg.

I raise my eyebrows and smile back at her saying "I might have to bill you for the cost of half my seat."

Her wavy dark brown hair is cut short to just below her ears. It bobs around her adorable rounded face with a hint of childhood freckles speckled across the bridge of her nose and under both eyes.

What started out as the worst day of the crappiest week in Dallas, has vastly improved. Less than an hour ago, as I ran to the airport gate, I wanted this flight over so I could get home to my beautiful beach house in Santa Monica and relax with a glass of wine in front of a cozy fire. As I continue to study the features of her animated face, I suddenly wish this flight would never end. *Had I really just thought that, I don't even know this woman?* Yet I immediately know this is no ordinary encounter. She has me under a spell and I don't even know her name. I feel profoundly affected and spiritually moved. Suddenly I want to know everything about her.

I somehow find what's left of my voice, stick my hand out and say, "I'm Amy Garel and I think I am going to marry you one day."

She slips her soft warm hand in mine and squeezes as she responds, "I'm Shelly Johns and maybe I'll let you cook me dinner first."

The flight whizzed by as we share the details of

our careers—me as a self-employed set designer and her marketing career at Mellon Bank. I learn she has two older siblings, a brother who is a Baptist Minister and a sister who is an Artist. She learns I have two younger brothers, a self-employed Engineer and a well-known Musician.

She tells me she grew up in the outskirts of Beaumont Texas with a large extended family whose Louisiana Cajun roots led to weekend crawdad boils while the men went off hunting for anything with horns. She stares in disbelief as I explain the six degrees of mafia separation in my Italian Catholic New Jersey family and the seventeen-course Sunday dinners that began and ended with pasta.

We giggle as we both proclaim how liberating it is to get away from our claustrophobic homegrown narrow-minded traditions. She loves her downtown Dallas condo as much as I love my Santa Monica beach house, each of us in awe of the other's courageous escape to points far removed from our birth families. She is as shocked to learn I spend one week a month in Dallas, as I am to learn she works one week a month in Los Angeles.

Could what started as an irreconcilable diet soda debate, of Pepsi versus Coke, be a fated encounter? I'm shocked to admit I've spent the last several hours sharing the intimate details of my life with a stranger, and yet it feels so natural like we've known each other forever. As I look down at our legs still pressed together from ankle to thigh for the duration of this flight I admit to myself I am wildly attracted to her. As we begin our descent into the Burbank area I know I want to make a bold move to keep the attention of this witty, feisty and sexy woman but time is running out.

It's now or never.

With a deep breath I lean towards her as I wrap my right hand around the damp and now tepid Big Gulp cup she holds. While encircling the cup and the long fingers of her left hand I whisper in her ear, "I'm only going to sip that battery acid you call Diet Pepsi because I'm incredibly attracted to you Shelly Johns and your persistent man-spreading has left the entire left side of my body on fire. And, well, because I want to impress you with my open-mindedness."

I push back my auburn shoulder length hair while looking over the rim of my glasses. My light blue eyes never leave her brown eyes that are alive with mischief. As I tighten my grip around her clenched fingers I pull her hand and the damp Big Gulp cup towards me. I challenge her to look away by raising my eyebrows and holding her gaze. As she tightens her grasp around the cup, I continue to pull it towards me as I draw her lipstick-covered straw to my lips. I slowly suck the tepid liquid into my mouth. My expression goes from a forced dramatization of sweet liquid ecstasy to a sour-faced scrunch.

Her expression goes from shock at my boldness to annoyance as I hold her gaze and brazenly say, "You may like Diet Pepsi and I may like Diet Coke but I've never had a Big Gulp I couldn't handle."

She lets out a sound somewhere between exasperation and a small grunt as she quickly recovers, stares deeply into my eyes traled utters, "Well Ms. Amy Garel, this Big Gulp, my Big Gulp is about to change all that."

Still holding the stare, she roughly grabs the cup from my hand and plops it down on her tray.

I smile the slowest sexiest smile I can muster as I

pull my business card out of my cellphone cardholder. I place it face up on the tray table in front of her and push it ever so slowly towards the now dented Big Gulp cup that begins to shake in the unexpected turbulence, secured only by the confines of that silly round drink indentation on the upper right hand corner of her seat tray.

My heart is racing while I memorize the soft features and freckles of her adorable face. I take a deep breath in an attempt to push out the quivering in my voice as I boldly say, "We'll see, Ms. Diet Pepsi, we'll see."

Before she can reply, the captain's voice booms over the loudspeaker saying, "Ladies and Gentlemen, it's going to be a bumpy ride down. Flight Attendants prepare the cabin for landing, seatbacks in upright position, tray tables closed and secured."

Shelly begins to stow away the items on her tray table as I reach over purposely brushing her right arm with my left breast. I grab the Big Gulp cup off her tray.

"On second thought, I'll hold onto to this cup. You can pick it up tomorrow at my beach house where I will cook you dinner and fill it to the brim with Diet Coke."

In the rumblings of the airplane's lowering landing gear, I hear her say, "Well, since you tasted mine, I guess it's my turn to taste yours."

As the plane lands and parks at the gate, Shelly stands up and steps into the aisle. She turns and faces me while pushing the button on the overhead bin cover to expose our suitcases. As I rise from my middle seat and turn towards her she seems surprised to realize that at 5'2", while standing perfectly erect, my hair barely skims the top of our seat row's lighting console above my head.

I look at her and shrug saying "One of very few advantages of being vertically challenged."

I watch as she scans the length of my body from my grey slip on Sketchers shoes to my black Sedona Red Rock T-shirt, tucked neatly into my tailored Vera Wang jeans, and my wide white belt with the cutout star shapes I knew accented the narrowness of my waist in comparison to my curvaceous hips. I was proud of my fit and toned body. Eating well and working hard six days a week in the gym is no easy task. In this moment, the look in Shelly's eyes is my reward.

❧❧❧❧

Destiny
June 11, 1998 – Santa Monica, California

Amy Garel
Santa Monica Beach House

With dinner prep done and a few minutes to spare I take my glass of wine out onto the deck and lower myself into my favorite chair with the big fluffy blue cushions. I feel the stress from pent up anticipation begin to leave my body with each thunderous wave that crashes into the white sandy shores of Santa Monica Beach. It's time to think about Shelly and the last 24 hours, before she arrives for dinner. I'm fairly certain, regardless of the outcome that I will never complain about Group C boarding ever again.

I still can't believe I invited a stranger to my house for dinner after declaring in no uncertain terms that one day I was going to marry her. *Marry her?* I could barely sustain the one long-term relationship

I've had over the five difficult years we were together. My ex-girlfriend Liz wanted an open relationship while I wanted Liz badly enough to agree. It ended a year ago with Liz leaving me for the love of her life, which she went off and married.

At age 39, I'm single and determined to create a lifestyle of one-night stands and illicit sexual escapades. I never expected fate to drop Shelly into my lap, on an airplane of all places. I wonder if Shelly shares my mantra as I replay it in my head, *Love will conquer all.* I lean my forehead on the palm of my right hand. *What if she isn't ready for a serious relationship? What if she wants an open relationship?* The timer on the stove rings just in time to stop my runaway thoughts and pulls me back into the kitchen where I continue to contemplate if Shelly Johns is in fact my destiny.

I take a deep breath as I look at my watch. It's five o'clock and Shelly will be here any minute.

As I putter around the kitchen putting the finishing touches on tonight's dinner I can't help but feel giddy. Not knowing Shelly's dietary habits, I decide on arugula and endive salad with balsamic glaze, vegetarian quinoa and mushroom main dish and an organic strawberry and mango flourless tart for desert. On tap, Diet Coke and the chilled bottle of Pinot Grigio I'd already cracked open on the deck.

❧❧❧❧❧

Shelly Johns
Ramada Hotel, West Hollywood, California

As I stand at the window in the swanky room of my Weho hotel, I am looking for a sign, any sign at all, to tell me that fate had dropped Amy Garel into my life so that I could finally get it right. *After 35 years on this earth could I really love someone without doing what I always do, reeling her in, only to break her heart as I run for my life in a commitment phobic panic.* I think back to my ex Julie, who I loved so deeply and yet hurt so badly just a year ago. Since then, I thought my one night stands with random women expecting nothing but sex would liberate me from my guilt and the pain and suffering I'd inflicted on Julie. As I pick up my room key and leave the hotel, I know in my gut that Amy Garel is my chance to get it right and that she is my destiny.

⁂

Amy Garel
Santa Monica Beach House

On this night of our first intimate encounter, after a romantic dinner, several rounds of Diet Coke, hours of personally revealing conversation and an evening in front of the fire, we make love on the beach. It's two in the morning and the seashore is dark and deserted. Her body, soft and warm under mine, is in contrast to the hard cool nighttime sand I can feel through the thin fabric of the blanket we brought with us. With the moon at my back, I can see the deep brown pools of desire in her eyes. Tonight they are alive with anticipation of what will lie ahead in the hours to come.

The smell of the sea and sounds of crashing waves surround us. Our desire for each other barely contained, I press into her. She moans and arches her body in the echo of my own moans. The night chill all but disappears as the heat between us rises. There are so many things I want to say, but there would be time for that. I touch her face. She turns her head into the moonlight. I trace her profile with my finger. For a brief moment I try to remember what my life had been like before she opened up every part of my heart and soul only twenty-four hours earlier. It feels like we've known each other forever, yet we just met. *I hope this is more than a one-night stand—I hope…*

The arching of her body and the desire in her eyes interrupts my thoughts. I grind into her, our centers meeting and moving as one, our lurid moaning drowned out by the sounds of the crashing waves. I slide my hand under her shirt and push up her bra as I desperately feel for the softness of her breast and the firmness of her nipple. I lower my head taking the tautness into my mouth and circling her areola with my tongue. She moans and rises into me as I kiss down her firm stomach, feeling the lengths of our bodies connecting. I gently remove her jeans and lace panties, exposing her glistening arousal. I kiss the soft downy fur as my tongue traces to the center of her. I flick her stiff clitoris, as it grows bigger in my mouth. As she continues to move under me I slowly slide my tongue into the sweet deepness of her, my tongue following her shape inside, as I push in and out licking and sliding up to gently suck her clitoris.

She is moving wildly now, thrusting her center into my mouth, my chin pressed hard against the cheeks of her beautiful butt. She is getting close to coming as I increase the intensity and pace of my lovemaking. My own thrusts against her firm thigh, matches her tempo. As I grab onto her hips and pull her closer to me, with each deeper thrust of my tongue, she screams.

"Amy, oh Amy, how can I love you already."

As her body convulses in the fog of her words I

say, "Oh Shelly, you are my destiny."

As my excitement rises to match hers, our bodies are moving in perfect rhythm as we both climax in an explosive orgasm. We bask in the glow of the moonlight in what I thought was the beginning of the rest of our lives together. We find our way into the bedroom where she falls asleep in my arms.

⁂

The Morning After – June 12, 1998

Shelly Johns
Santa Monica Beach House of Amy Garel

The morning after our first romantic dinner and incredible night of lovemaking, I wake up in Amy's arms in full view of the beach and ocean through the floor to ceiling windows of her bedroom. My heart is full of love and promise until I see it as I lift my head off the pillow to check the time. There on the nightstand beside me, is a can of Diet Pepsi, in a melted bucket of ice, an offering of Amy's understanding for our differences, cradled lovingly in a bucket of her generosity. No one had ever said so much while saying nothing at all. This woman loves me that much already. *Amy Garel, you scare the hell out of me.* I get up slowly, quietly dressing and leave before she wakes.

⁂

Eighteen Months Later - December 15, 1999

Amy Garel
Santa Monica, California

It's been six months since I last saw Shelly—last felt the heat of her body in my car that day in the parking garage of Burbank Airport.

Looking back, our instant connection was the beginning of a fast and furious relationship that would consume the next year of our lives. We saw each other every chance our fifteen hundred-mile long distance relationship would allow.

Despite how desperately we loved each other, we hurt each other on a regular basis. I was obsessed with her and wanted to consume her mind, body and soul. She was deeply in love with me but needed the space I couldn't give her. The closer we got the more she panicked and ran. The more she ran, the more I pursued her. The ups and downs of our relationship was like a rollercoaster that leaves your heart racing while you are on the dangerous exhilarating ride—and your stomach instantly sick as your feet hit the ground and it is suddenly over.

Every three weeks or so, like clockwork, Shelly would panic and then withdraw, usually via a text message that simply stated our relationship didn't feel good to her anymore, I wasn't any good for her, and I was not to contact her ever again. For Shelly it was a relief valve. For me it was devastation. I'd feel destroyed and demoralized as I tried to reason her into staying and then begging her not to do this again. She'd leave anyhow and cut me off, blocking me from her phone until her longing for me returned and then she'd beg me back for more of the same.

During these times, I couldn't eat, sleep, or think and every aspect of my business and personal life suffered. I swore to myself that when she left again I wouldn't take her back but I always did. She got parts of me that others never understood. She laughed at things others thought were lame. She loved me harder than I'd ever been loved before and I was madly in love with her.

The last time I saw Shelly, was a year into our relationship, as I drove her to Burbank Airport for her unplanned flight back to Dallas. It was an almost perfect Sunday until she disappeared again before my very eyes. We spent the morning in bed making passionate love and the afternoon on Santa Monica Pier eating slices of pizza and enjoying the sights and sounds of the beach. As we prepared for our evening together she was sitting on my sofa with her long legs stretched out before her. With my head on her lap she ran her fingers through my hair in front of a crackling fire with the bright red and orange of the setting sun shining through the giant windows of my beach house.

As I looked up into her loving brown eyes, I said, "I love you so much Shelly. I can't breath when I'm away from you." My heart was exploding with love for her. I took a deep breath and closed my eyes as I inhaled her essence in an attempt to keep her inside me forever. Exhaling slowly I opened my eyes expecting to still see the mirror of our love in the eyes of this woman I so desperately needed. I felt an icy chill enter my soul as I looked into the stagnant dark brown pools of emptiness that were suddenly her eyes. Absent was the warmth of love and in its place was the cold hard stare of despondency.

Then I heard her say, "Amy please take me to the Airport I can't do this anymore. This doesn't feel good to me."

After a year of Shelly's continual abandonment

and with no fight left in me, we slid into my car for the silent trip to Burbank Airport with Amy behind the wheel. As we parked in our usual area of the underground garage I turned to look at her. Unable to read the expression on her face I began to sob as she crawled over the car's stick shift between us and reached down and lowered my seat as she laid the length of herself on top of me.

As she began to feverishly grind into me she slipped her tongue into my mouth in a ravaging and frenzied assault on my heart. She was wilder than I'd ever seen her, pushing and grinding and moaning. For a brief moment I thought there was hope for our happily ever after. Deep down I knew this was nothing more than her desperate way of saying goodbye to me. With tears streaming down my face, in the echo of her climax, I sobbed, as she whispered, "Amy, love doesn't always conquer all."

When she finished, she rolled off of me and slid back into the drivers seat. As I moved my seat back into a sitting position, I ran my fingers through my hair, grabbed a tissue and wiped the tears streaming down my face. From the corner of my eye on the floor in front of me I noticed the empty Diet Pepsi Big Gulp cup we'd shared on the way to my beach house just two days earlier, when our relationship had been alive and hope was in the air. As she opened the driver's door she turned to me. With a blank expression and a dull stare, she said, "Goodbye Amy."

As my voice cracked and a sob escaped, I handed her the battered Big Gulp cup and replied, "Goodbye Shelly, this belongs to you."

Three weeks later when her cycle of panic subsided she texts me "I miss you." The pain of knowing Shelly would never fully commit to me was excruciating. And so I deleted her text, blocked her number on my cellphone, and drove straight to the 7-Eleven. I approached the beverage station and pulled out a fresh new Big Gulp cup. I stood there for what seemed like forever, rolling the cup round and round between the palms of my hands contemplating my choices. Through the tears that streamed down my face, I stared at the blurry side-by-side Diet Pepsi and Diet Coke drink dispensers. As I considered the choice that would define my future, with shaking hands I pushed the Big Gulp cup under the Diet Coke dispenser and thought, *Shelly never will, so I have to choose me.* And so I did.

Sallyanne Monti is an author and editor. Her fiction and non-fiction short stories, articles, poems, and edited pieces have appeared in numerous anthologies, magazines, and newspapers. In her spare time she plays guitar and composes music. She lives in Palm Springs California with her wife, Mickey, and their doggies Sola and Zorra.
Website: www.sallyannemonti.com

Fledge Day

By Lea Daley

Just before sundown on Cinco de Mayo, the young mourning doves fledged. I hoped they'd be as victorious as the warriors commemorated by that quasi holiday, because legions of predators awaited them. I'd been anticipating their leap into freedom ever since their parents built a nest outside my kitchen window, if you can dignify a loose, hastily assembled pile of sticks with that term.

The speed of the squabs' development was astounding. Two weeks earlier, they'd been skeletal little creatures, with the thinnest fluff of down. I blinked and suddenly they were covered with an elaborate mantle of feathers, looking more like winged pinecones than birds. They teetered on that ledge, flexing and preening, daring one another to lift off. I was watching the fidgety duo—hanging on their every flutter, waiting for them to summon sufficient courage—when something caught my eye, a flash of motion in the alley.

A woman, probably returning from the dumpster. She unlatched the O'Connell's gate and walked toward their back door. As she stepped out of shadow, I saw she wasn't just any woman. I'd recognize that free and easy glide a mile away, even though I hadn't seen it for years. Desi O'Connell, older, yet undoubtedly still wickedly charismatic. Ragged breath caught in my throat, right as one tiny dove took to the air. Its nest mate looked startled, then dejected. I knew exactly how it felt. I, too, had failed to launch. In minutes, though, the solitary bird crept closer to the edge. As it flapped its wings, instinct kicked in, and it rose against a crimson sky.

I tracked the pair protectively, before noting the adults hovering nearby. Feeling absurdly bereft, I turned away from the empty nest, murmuring, "Well done, kids. You've got more guts than I do."

A light flickered on in the kitchen next door, the first I'd seen there in ages. Because Joe and Maura O'Connell were long gone, transitioned a decade earlier to a distant nursing home near Desi's place, where Big Joe died with unseemly haste. But Maura had stubbornly hung on till a month ago. Throughout her long decline, their house had sat dormant, though Joe Junior checked on it every few weeks.

Word of Maura's death first broke where news always did in Doe's Run, at Beryl's Beauty. I was getting an overdue trim when Liz Goble said, "I hear Desi O'Connell's coming home."

I laughed. Desi had left this godforsaken town in seventy-two, immediately following high school graduation, and had rarely returned. I'd know. I've lived alongside the O'Connells my entire life. And I sincerely doubted that Des thought of Doe's Run as home. She was more the big city, adventure vacation type, always on the go. Photos of Machu Picchu, Angkor Wat, and the Galapagos populated her Facebook page—not that I'd been bold enough to send a friend request. Most likely, she'd only stick around long enough to finalize her parents' affairs.

Still, sitting there while Liz brushed clippings from my nape, I hoped we'd get a chance to talk. I'd always liked Desi—more than liked her, truth be told. But I was three years younger, which was the difference between being an awkward fifteen to her suave eighteen on the day she left for Radcliffe. So we'd never been close. Except for that one sunlit summer, my seventeenth, when she was a senior camp counselor, while I made myself indispensable as her junior assistant. The summer I could never quite forget...

Across the way, the O'Connell's kitchen went dark. I imagined Desi moving silently through her childhood home, alone and grieving, making her way to a color coordinated bedroom. Sleeping under a handmade quilt. Conjuring the absent mother who'd stitched that patchwork so long ago. I opened my freezer and extracted a loaf of banana bread. First thing the next day, I'd present it to Desi, along with a sympathy card. I could count on the cry of the mourning doves to wake me, long before I was ready.

When I stepped off my porch at eight, bearing that banana bread, Desi was unpacking her car from an early shopping trip. A giant package of paper towels swung from one hand. A broom and mop were tucked beneath her other arm.

"Hi! I brought you breakfast—and condolences."

She had to set down her supplies to take my offering. "How kind, Sheila! I appreciate it."

She looked harried, a woman with too much on her mind to pause for chitchat. And, of course, her mother had recently died. But it seemed premature to end the conversation. "Spiffing up the place?"

"In a manner of speaking."

"If you need backup, I can help."

"I couldn't ask that of you—of anyone."

"You didn't, Des. I volunteered."

"You'd need safety gear. Rubber gloves, a hard hat, a gas mask."

"It can't be that bad. Your mom always kept on top of everything."

Desi brushed a tan hand through shorn silver hair and then made a dismissive gesture. "Never mind. I won't impose on you." Her face—still fine-boned and arresting at sixty-two—was tense, her dark eyes impenetrable. "Thanks again for breakfast," she said, stacking my bread on top of those paper towels, retrieving the cleaning gear, starting up the stoop.

I'd clearly made some misstep, inadvertently offended her. And I wasn't sure there was a way forward. Still, I tried. "Des? I loved your mom—and I owed her a lot. No judgment, I promise. I'd just feel I was repaying some of her generosity."

Desi seemed to waver, then relent. "Okay. Anytime you want to stop by, I'll be here shoveling shit. Just holler for me—the door will be unlocked."

"Let me guess, you're hoping for a thief in the night?"

"That would solve a multitude of problems. A fire would be even better."

I let a day elapse before risking another contact. Then I filled a scrub bucket with cleaning supplies and cut across the grass to the O'Connell's front porch. The door swung open, just as Des said it would. I stepped into a floor plan that was a duplicate of the home I'd inherited, living room to the left, dining room to the right, stairs dead center. A tidy, pleasant space, if a bit run down now—and shockingly dusty. Even worse, an unpleasant odor prickled my nose. Clearly, Junior's maintenance duties hadn't included housework. I was rooted in place, convinced I felt Maura's mortification radiating from the great beyond.

I'd spent untold hours of my youth here, hiding out from my incoherent, alcoholic, semiconscious mom. The door was always unlatched back then, too, and I'd been given carte blanche to enter. So I'd dart inside after school, do my homework at the O'Connell's dinner table and then dog Maura's footsteps while she potted herbs, whipped up casseroles, baked muffins. I'd never seen her disheveled, never seen her so much as frown, had certainly never seen her drunk. If there really were a god, I'd have lived one door over on Clover Lane. Lucky, lucky Desirée O'Connell, the girl who had it all! Sighing, I plucked a picture frame from the mantel, the charmed mother and daughter smiling into one another's eyes.

I shook off my reverie, replaced the photo, and started for the stairs. With every step upward, that peculiar stench grew stronger, more nauseating. And at the top, chaos reigned supreme. Stepping through the looking glass, I gaped at the inexplicable, towering piles of magazines, bundles of junk mail, brittle newspapers, random jumbles of yard sale merchandise, sacks of outmoded clothing.

A narrow path snaked through the refuse. It was just possible to skitter sideways along it. Which led me past a jam-packed bathroom. Then to a bedroom stacked to the ceiling fan with more garbage. Des couldn't have slept there these past two nights—no bed was visible under those mountains of trash.

I wanted to run, wanted to shield her from the

knowledge that I'd witnessed this nightmare. But she was expecting me, so I made myself call out.

"I'm in Junior's room. Down the hall."

I crept ten feet more to that doorway. At first I couldn't see Desi for the clutter. Then she peered around a barricade of plastic bins. "Welcome to the horror show."

Since I was speechless, she filled the silence. "I'd offer you a place to sit, but..." There wasn't one—not even room for a folding chair.

"I don't understand?"

"It's simple. Mom was a hoarder."

"How could I not have known?"

"Partly because she got worse as she aged. But partly because she had just enough self-control to confine her madness to the basement and this level."

Thunderstruck, I leaned against a column of VCR tapes. Which was held in place by a firmament of paperback books, which was backed up by a foundational wall of vinyl albums. "I guess I didn't come upstairs."

"No one did—no one was allowed." Desi's voice sounded bitter. "I never had a sleepover, never shared a moment of privacy with a friend here. By the time I fled, there was barely enough open floor space to slither to my bed."

"But...your mom was perfection!"

"My mom was sick—and not just with the COPD that finally took her down. She always believed she'd come home, though—even when her doctor said she couldn't. So she made me promise not to sell the old homestead or discard her stuff. Junior agreed to keep things in good repair until our parents were gone. But I'm responsible for clearing everything out."

"Well, let's get busy."

Desi looked exhausted, defeated. "Got a match?"

I stood on tiptoe to set my bucket atop those bins. Weeks might pass before we uncovered a surface to clean. "Listen, let me help. This is harder on you than it would be for anyone else—you're far more emotionally engaged. Besides, I'm hell on wheels when it comes to organizing."

For the first time since meeting again, Desi unleashed a real smile. "I remember that—the way you always had the arts and crafts activities ready for me at Camp Minnelaka. The precise way you packed up my gear after I made that your punishment for some minor infraction…I forget just what."

"I think I'd sneaked out of our cabin to sleep under the stars."

"I think I wished I'd joined you." Desi's voice throbbed with suggestion. She held my eyes captive, allowing the moment to deepen. She let me imagine how it would have felt to kiss her in the moonlight. Let me experience a nanosecond of transcendent joy. Let me think how different life might have been if she hadn't left me to love her from afar.

"Water under the bridge," I mumbled, hoping she'd argue. But when she said nothing, I clambered over the heaps on Junior's bed and contorted myself until I could reach the window latch. Looking over my shoulder, I thought I caught Des checking out my ass—my old lady ass. How delusional was I? "Do you mind if I open this?"

"Knock your socks off."

It took a few thumps and jiggles, but the window gave way. Fresh air rushed through the opening, bringing a burst of birdsong with it. "Hear that? Those are my mourning doves."

"Yours?"

I shrugged, feeling a bit defensive. "They nested outside my kitchen window. Believe me, they were the best entertainment in Doe's Run." Before Desi could respond, my analytical brain finally kicked into gear. Without some system to attack her problem, I realized, we'd just run in circles. "Let's go downstairs and talk for a few minutes."

"Anything to escape this hellhole, however briefly."

In the kitchen, Des pulled bottled water from a Styrofoam ice chest. "I haven't dared to peek in the fridge yet."

We sat at a table where I'd decorated a zillion sugar cookies, and I scanned the familiar space. After our interlude on the suffocating second floor, the sense of order was almost disorienting. I took a long swig of water. "I'll help in any way I can, assuming you'll let me."

"I'm afraid that could become a lifetime commitment. I can't imagine ever getting to the bottom of those heaps."

"It's doable," I assured her. "But the time involved is proportionate to your need for privacy—and your sense of reverence."

Desi traced patterns in the condensation on her bottle. "It's tricky. I loved my mother, but I spent my entire childhood protecting her precious reputation. And I'm furious that she stuck me with this mess—that she's made it my last memory of her. Still, the place has to be ready to market before September, so I can return to work. After I leave, Junior will oversee the sale."

"Neither of you wants the house?"

"Nope, much bad juju here. Besides, Junior already owns a home, and this town's not for me."

My latest fantasy evaporated. Desi and I wouldn't grow old together—older together—rocking on adjacent porches. Suppressing a sigh, I said, "Well, you can do this the hard way, carefully considering the fate of each item. Or you can do it the easy way."

"Which is?"

I winced. "A dumpster in your back yard. A chute from the second floor..."

"God! Everyone on the block would see it—Mom would be so embarrassed!" Desi closed her eyes, apparently weighing the options. "All right. Let's do it."

"Here's another thought. After we empty a room, we'll have a place to stash things that deserve more careful assessment."

"That's positively brilliant. Because sooner or later we'll stumble on family papers and memorabilia."

"Once we have a little space to maneuver, we could strip another room and store yard sale items there."

"No yard sale. We don't need the money, and I couldn't bear that—everyone gossiping about Mom as they poked through the rubble."

"Then donate whatever's salvageable to some charity that'll pick it up and haul it off. Maybe the guestroom could serve as the staging ground for that?"

Cool, confident Desi O'Connell stared at me like I was a miracle worker. "You're really willing to be part of this? Days—maybe weeks—of gritty labor?"

Days or weeks in her intoxicating presence, after years of loving her long distance, and all I'd have to do was toss out trash? Paradise! "I'm retired, Des.

Besides, what are friends for? We could get started now, assessing which room to clear first, and so on. Once the dumpster arrives, we'll begin the real work."

"I always suspected you were an angel fallen to Earth," she said, turning an incandescent smile in my direction—and igniting a blaze in my foolish heart. "I'll spring for pizza later."

But Desi's mood seemed to darken as we headed back upstairs. *She's saying farewell to her parents,* I reminded myself, *however troubled their lives were.* Surely, I could afford to set aside my own shock and bewilderment until I was at home. Because *I* had only lost an imaginary mother when Maura died.

Our brief respite in the kitchen allowed me to view the second floor with fresh eyes. "The bathroom!" I crowed. "That's where the chute should go." By necessity, there was a clear path to the toilet and a sizable window at the end of that trail. "This'll make it much easier to operate."

I was energized by my vision, ready to roll, but Des slumped against the doorframe. "I've surfed Pipeline, Sheila. I've climbed Denali. This though...it's totally overwhelming."

I squeezed her shoulder. "Why don't you go make arrangements for a dumpster, then call for pizza? I'll stay up here to plan our attack."

We ate lunch on the O'Connell's patio that day. It was a low-key meal and Desi made only desultory conversation. When she said, "You're awfully young to be retired," I ran with the opening, stretched out the details, hoping she'd concentrate on her deep-dish special—because she was far too thin.

"I'm fifty-nine," I reminded her. "Two years ago, the school board presented us old-timers with a buyout package. They wanted to hire novice teachers to reduce costs. I accepted the deal when the superintendent sent a strong signal that later offers would be less generous." I let loose a sigh, before remembering that Desi was the one with the real reason for complaint. "I've struggled to adapt to retirement. Teachers never have a spare moment. Now, I've got nothing but. So, as sad as your project is, it's oddly welcome."

I woke the next morning to the crash and bang of an enormous dumpster being offloaded in the O'Connell's back yard. Over cereal on my sun porch, I watched workers connect bright yellow cylinders to form a long chute, then position it at the bathroom window. Estimating the dumpster's capacity, I said aloud, "Two loads...At least two loads..." Of course, I had yet to see the scope of work in that basement.

By nine, I was at Desi's front door. "You're the best, Sheila Taggert!" she said, waving me inside. She'd dressed for our task in a faded Rocky Horror T-shirt and cut off shorts. Already one of her cheeks was smeared with grime and there was a wisp of cobweb in her hair. "Come upstairs and see what I've accomplished. As soon as the chute was in place, I started pitching stuff—it's the most liberating sensation!"

She'd made real progress in the bathroom. The piles of paper under the pedestal sink had vanished. Stacks of magazines no longer lined every wall. Gone was a glut of freezer containers that had filled the tub to overflowing. The linen closet and the medicine cabinets were nearly empty.

"Hot damn!" I said. "Which of the bedrooms should I start in?"

"Mine, I suppose."

And so it began, the tedious work of undoing her

mother's tedious work. How many hours of Maura's life had gone into gathering those pathetic treasures, transporting them, arranging—then rearranging—the space so she'd have room for more? I blinked back tears as I ferried hundreds of pounds of yellowed newspapers from bedroom to bath. Where Desi hurled them down the chute with such energy that I had difficulty keeping her supplied.

By noon, I'd excavated a route to her canopy bed and had begun unpacking it. Maybe Desi wouldn't have to sleep on the couch that night. But when I finally uncovered a corner of her mattress, I knew she'd never lie there again. Mice had converted it to a combination hotel and playground. Filthy beyond belief or redemption, it was one source of that revolting smell. I should probably offer Desi my spare room for the duration.

I could see her on the bed there, slender limbs splayed across the sheets, sleek hair gleaming like platinum in candlelight...Better yet, in my own bed, in my arms, her warm back molded to my yearning front, as I breathed in the scent of her skin, her sex...

"Sheila? Are you still here?"

Snapping to, I yelled, "Coming!"

I quickly gathered a double armload of tabloid magazines, but couldn't meet Desi's eyes when I handed them off. I did manage to say, "Listen...your bed's pretty bad...if you'd feel more comfortable sleeping at my house, I have a guestroom."

Her face lit up. "You wouldn't mind?"

"Nope. And the ghost of my dysfunctional mother has long since been laid to rest."

"I'd love that. Mine still walks here. Obviously."

By sundown, we were staggering. We'd made a

serious dent in Desi's room, but the more debris we removed, the less livable it became, filth and decay were everywhere. And though we'd stripped the bathroom of Maura's junk, no one would consider showering there until the space was sterilized. "Des? Why not pack your bath gear, too?"

"You don't have to ask twice. And after I clean up, I'd like to take you somewhere nice for dinner."

"Not necessary. Besides, I made Alfredo sauce last night. If we eat in, we won't have to brave public inspection."

She looked relieved. "I'll agree, if you'll take a rain check."

"Wine and dine me at some later date? Absolutely. Just not when we're both spent."

"Speaking of wine, shall I go buy some?"

I laughed sardonically. "Hardly necessary—I still have plenty of Mom's secret stash in my basement. Let's close up shop and then you can pick out a bottle. None of it's special, but maybe something will strike your fancy."

At my house, I led Desi downstairs and pointed out a tall shelf packed with divided liquor cartons. She picked two whites seemingly at random, more intrigued by the vast, open space around us. "Not a stack of magazines, or a bag of old clothes, or a single sheet of moldy newsprint! Was it this pristine while your mom was alive?"

"Sure, because I lived here, too."

We were upstairs, sipping that wine, assembling a salad, when Desi asked, "Why have you stayed here all these years?"

Why, indeed? "Mom was never going to get help for her addiction. I had to choose between abandoning her to an ugly fate or providing some normalcy and oversight for her."

"You were a far better daughter than I. I could never have babysat my mother."

"Say what you will about me, Des, I'm loyal. To a fault..." *Haven't you noticed?*

"Do you ever regret your decision? It must have come at the expense of your own happiness."

That was a tough needle to thread. "Happiness takes many forms. I loved teaching, and I was damned good at it. I loved my students, loved knowing I made a difference every day."

Once again, Desi sought my eyes. "What about romantic love?"

I considered laying the usual BS on her. Elementary education was a vast wasteland with scarcely an eligible bachelor in sight, yada-yada. But I was heartily tired of that charade. "There were plenty of lesbians in the school district, but all of us—"*Us! I'd actually said it!* "—All of us knew we had to be incredibly cautious or lose our jobs. Besides, I would have had to build any serious relationship around Mom's issues, with every complexity that implies."

"So you never—?"

"Had a lover? Of course, I did! Just not the kind I wanted, not the kind of partnership that's possible today. Imagine! Weddings and kids and a totally open life! I hate that I missed out on that. Now I'm the proverbial dried-up old spinster. How about you?"

"Oddly, my story's not that different...I travel, I meet people, I move on. Maybe I never loved anybody enough to stay in one place."

Don't I know it! Pivoting away, I gathered bottles of salad dressing, a wedge of Parmesan. "The pasta should be done. Grab a plate."

The next morning, the seductive scent of coffee woke me. I followed the aroma downstairs, where I found Desi in my kitchen, arranging doughnuts on a plate. "If this is too decadent, I bought fruit and yogurt, too. They're in your fridge."

"Something's gonna kill me," I said, scooping up a lemon-filled concoction, licking powdered sugar from my fingers. "How long have you been up?"

"Just long enough to hit the grocery. Listen, Sheila, don't feel obligated to keep slogging through Mom's disaster zone—"

"You can't get rid of me that easily."

Her smile was dazzling. "Music to my ears. I'm heading over there now. Join me whenever the mood strikes."

We spent a week at the O'Connell house, hurling decades of trash down that chute. When the rooms were finally empty, I suggested hiring professionals to swab them out, but Des said, "I want to finish what I started." The pain in her eyes suggested something different. She was still protecting Maura's reputation.

She tried to exempt me from the sanitation process, but I can dig in my heels, too. So we spent another week together, scrubbing the upstairs from floor to ceiling. "A new coat of paint," I said, "and no one will ever guess."

Desi draped an arm over my shoulders. "No one but an exterminator—if I don't halt the rodent infestation pronto, all our scouring is for naught. You've been a godsend. Thanks for everything."

I swiveled in that semi-embrace, reluctant to break contact. Facing her directly, I said, "I haven't forgotten about the basement. You can't kiss me off just yet."

"Then maybe," Des said, "I can just plain kiss you."

I could only nod. She tilted my chin and brushed my lips gently before pausing for a response. In a daze, I cupped the back of her head, pulled her closer, intensifying the contact. I gasped as our tongues met. By the time we separated, my knees were wobbly. "That was unexpected…"

"Then I must be losing my touch. Because ever since my return, I've been signaling that I'm wild about you."

"All through our youth I believed you hated me."

"Well, I mostly did. Until that summer we worked together. Probably because Mom cared so much about you—I often thought she loved you more than me. You were the adoring downstairs daughter, while I was the sulky changeling upstairs."

"Oh, please! Maura talked about you all the time. She was so proud. I'd kill to have heard my own mother praise me like that just once."

Des gripped my hands so tightly they ached. "Really?"

"Really. Now show me the damned basement." Instead, she leaned in for another kiss, which I ducked, racing for the stairs.

If I'd thought the bedrooms were appalling, the basement was worse. Fortunately, it was a walkout model with a slider that opened onto hardscape, because we wouldn't have the benefit of a chute there—or gravity. But if we filled a wheelbarrow with as much weight as we could manage, we could use the patio for sorting. Thankfully, Desi agreed to take a day off before tackling phase two—just time enough for a tent company to erect a protective awning over that concrete slab. And time enough for us to regroup.

We spent those free hours lounging around my house, catching up with the world, griping about aches and pains and bruises. Desi entertained me with hilarious tales from her travels, and cogent observations about the human race. After dinner, though, she took a serious turn. Leaning across the table, she reached for my hands. "Don't think I haven't noticed that you're distancing yourself, Sheila. But I have a hunch you've always cared for me. God knows, I've fantasized about you forever. Shouldn't we at least try to figure out whether we could make something of this?"

Every molecule in my body went on alert. Every nerve ending craved her embrace. Still I balked. "I'm a bit old for new beginnings."

"I doubt it's ever too late for love. What's really holding you back?"

I looked down. "My body, for starters. It was never my strong suit, but it's definitely seen better days."

Desi dragged me upright, pulled me against her. "I won't let you be embarrassed, Sheila Taggert! And I'm no spring chicken, either. Besides, bodies are purely incidental—I'd actually be making love to your fine mind and bountiful heart."

I quit fighting and led her upstairs. Was this actually happening? I unbuttoned my shirt, unhooked my bra and dropped them. Des had enough insight to bare her own torso before touching me. We stood with our hands on one another's hips, spellbound, drinking in every detail. She, so long and lean. Me, all softness and curves. Both of us women of a certain age, far from the youthful camp counselors who'd once almost dared to confess our love. Yet she was exquisite.

I bent my head to one small breast, kissed ineffably soft skin. As I flicked a nipple with my tongue, I finally relaxed. The woman I'd adored forever wanted me, had offered herself to me. As she moaned under my assault, she found my waistband and tugged down my shorts.

I stepped back, stepped out of my clothing and divested Desi of her jeans. Then I drew her so close our bodies nearly merged.

"Wait!" she cried.

My heart stopped—had she changed her mind? Desi ran to retrieve her gym bag, and then rummaged through it. After surfacing, she tossed a slender cylinder on my pillow. "Lubricant," she said. "We're gonna need it, because I'm even older than you."

"Later," I rasped. "I want my mouth on you first."

"Not half as much as I do." She scooted to the far side of my bed. "Come here. Let me hold you."

We no longer possessed infinite energy or youthful flexibility, but we'd gained the gifts of laughter and accommodation. Slowly, with great tenderness, we explored delicious possibilities, admitting defeat occasionally and then modifying our moves as necessary. And within those constraints, an unending realm of delight unfolded.

Some long, uncharted period passed before I finally popped the top on that container of lubricant, pressed its dispenser. Cool gel pooled on my fingertips, then glided over Desi's intricate folds and tissues.

"Nice," she whispered. "Very nice...Keep going...Right there!"

My fingers slipped inside her warm core, curling, coaxing, and thrusting. I held her hard, refusing to free her until she found the ultimate release. And then it was my turn again.

Teasing my clit, Des said, "You're everything that's been missing from my life. I was mad to leave you."

I managed to gasp, "You couldn't have stayed here."

"True. So the next time I go away, you'll have to come, too."

"I'm coming! I'm coming!"

By dawn, the pair of mourning doves was back on my windowsill, refurbishing their nest for another cycle, preparing for the future. As Des and I watched, our arms wound around each other, I thought I felt my own wings lift and flex. It was long past time for me to fledge.

Lea Daley has written fiction while raising children, claiming a lesbian identity, earning a BFA, and directing a United Way childcare center. Her debut novel, Waiting for Harper Lee, was a Golden Crown Awards finalist. Her second book, FutureDyke, won a 2015 Goldie Award and was a Lambda Literary finalist. www.leadaley.com

The Speed of Sound

By JD Glass

Gillian: Four more hours, my love. Four more hours until I can see you, breathe in the same space with you.

Luna: Four more hours, my heart—I can literally feel you approaching, the nearing of you to me is an electric hum that fills me, is pouring out and over my skin. Four more hours—and I can breathe with you, here, besides me, breath the only distance between us.

Gillian: That, my love, that is what is pulling me, calling me, drawing me to you. I want that, too, to see you, to hear you, to hold you, with the only thing between us a shared breath.

Gillian: I'm back in the car now, love, and back on the road in moments. I'll stop to text you again in about two hours and then—and then it's you and me—it's us my love—and our shared breath.

My heart was pounding as I read her last text to me. Because this was so close to happening, she was so close to me, and I missed her, wanted her, needed her—her very presence—near me, next to me.

That we loved each other—there was no doubt, none whatsoever. And that we missed each other, with wrenching need, an ache of longing that at least for me, I knew nothing less than seeing her before me, holding her in my arms, would slake—I knew that, too.

But what we were to each other, besides precious, what we would become—these were the questions that had no answer, not yet, anyway, and four hours meant everything and anything was possible. Nothing was established nor set, save this: we missed each other, desperately.

We'd spoken on the phone last night—not too late, since she'd had to get an early start to drive, and I was still going to put in a full day of work before these days we'd decided on spending together—our first, really, ever.

What we had, what we already were—this wasn't something I could explain, not even to myself, never mind to any of the friends or even family that asked me the what and why of Gillian and I.

It was just…

We'd met because my company was a consultant to a division within hers. What had begun as me being on the work site in Boston for a month and running into her on occasions within the labyrinthine corporate structure evolved into a casual work friendship and the occasional, shared lunch.

She was dating someone, I was dating someone, we were friends, the job was done, and back I went to New York.

We kept in touch, albeit sporadically, and more by email than anything else, since work and home life kept us both busy. And then a year later, she was working for a company in San Francisco—who hired my team to reshape one of their divisions.

After the first official business lunch with her company's people and mine, all the rest of them after that we spent together—even managing to catch a dinner or two.

She was dating someone new, I was taking a break, and we laughed about all of the weirdness and sometimes stupidity that was dating, talked about the quilt work patches of San Francisco, and how different it was from New York, how different it was from Boston, what city she wanted to see next, what city I wanted to work in...

Then it was back to life, and my job, and the break I'd been taking extended. Still, Gillian and I, we emailed each other, and more often than usual, we talked—on the phone.

We'd even joked about how if we were ever single at the same time, well, neither of us would be single.

We both laughed—and continued to have an amazing friendship.

Until, I needed a break from that, too.

It was too much, all these feelings I wasn't used to having. She was involved, I was working, and it was all so damned intense. I was confused and needed time to think, to figure everything out. I'd even attempted a few dates, but every single one of them fell flat because not a single one of these twomen had a tenth of the humor and insight that Gillian had, and none of them could hold my attention.

I dropped it, dropped them, and dropped everything—except for work. And I spent the rest of my time alone, thinking.

Feeling.

And what I felt was the unbearable need to connect to her—to Gillian—in any way, whatever it was. I missed her—missed my friend—so much so that it ached, the insides of my arms stinging with the memory of the one time we'd hugged goodbye.

I was torturing myself.

I just couldn't take it anymore.

I got back in touch, and Gillian was graceful about it, forgiving my prolonged silence with my sincere apology for being such a taciturn jerk.

I'd hurt her, but I hadn't meant to, not like that—not at all.

She hadn't told me right away when the last thing she'd been involved with ended, I hadn't told her that I'd decided to continue my I'm-not-wasting-my-time streak. Thankfully, our reconciliation and reconnection was a quick thing, aided and hastened by honest conversation, real and true internal work done on both our parts.

The fact is, I had noticed something during all of this. Her name in my email inbox immediately made me feel good and light, brought a smile to my face.

And something had...changed. Our phone calls, which had once been sporadic things, had grown from occasional, to weekly, to daily. It wasn't just that I looked forward to them, I needed them, needed to connect with her and hear her voice, to the point that on the very rare occasions we didn't speak, I was—well, to say out of sorts on the occasion was probably kind.

Gillian and her lovely rich voice that could soar up into octaves of delighted surprise, cut with strength across the mid-range, roll and rumble in a throaty low that left me almost undone every time, her voice and her words, her whispers and declarations, her jokes and affirmations—I needed that, every day and every night I fell asleep with her voice in my ear and her in my head, every moment of every day.

And every day we told each other the truth: we loved each other.

We never said how, didn't give it a type or definition.

But the love was definitely there, and it was definitely real, and it was definitely driving us, me figuratively to finally arrange this get together with her, her literally, across state lines and miles and miles and miles, just to see me.

Now, with four hours to go before she arrived, and me with four hours to wait, and prep, wonder and worry, I busied myself with planning and making a meal. I wanted to make something real, something hot, something more than whatever she'd grabbed on the road to drive all this way, so I focused. I focused on my hands and slicing meat carefully, the right amount of spices, the angle I cut the vegetables at.

> Gillian: Two hours, my love. Two hours, until I can see you and hold you, tell you with my breath before you, to you, that I love you. My Luna. I love you.

> Luna: I can barely breathe, my Gillian, my heart. Come, my love. Come so I can hear you, so I can hold you, so I can show you, too, how much I love you, how precious to me you are.

My hands shook as I put the phone down on

the counter and I took a breath to steady myself. I'd planned this with her, our visit, the meal I'd make—but everything else was up to unknowns I had no control over.

My heart felt like it would burst through my chest, filled as I was with all the feeling I had for her, because of her.

I breathed through it, and once again, I picked up the knife. I was mindful not to cut myself. I let things sit the way they needed to, that temperatures were exact, that this would all be right, because this was the first meal I'd ever made for her. I was so achingly aware that this—this was the first time we were meeting, openly knowing—openly ready—to see what we had, what we could be.

I was full of hope because finally we would know—I would know—what it would feel like to hold her, exactly as I'd always wanted to, to tell her directly, my cheek against hers, that I loved her, feel her heart beat against mine, the solid length of her pressed closely to me.

Meat sizzled while a pot of rice simmered away and I stirred carefully.

I was full of fear, because what if she didn't feel the same? What if once we were together, in the same space and place, what if after that first initial hug, we felt nothing? What if we kissed? What if after satisfying this whatever that existed between us, we discovered that we were in fact just really good friends? What if we couldn't get away from each other fast enough, after? What if…only one of us still felt that pull, that draw, while the other felt nothing but friendly affection? That was the worst scenario I could think of—and I was afraid that it would be—

The ring of my phone made me jump.

I grabbed it one-handed off the counter, saw the caller ID was the one friend I'd confided some of this to, and answered.

"Hey! How's it going?" I said, as friendly and casual, as I could manage, with the phone set to speaker so I could continue to work the stove.

Brenda's laugh answered me. "Well, I guess she's not there yet if you're actually answering your phone!"

"Ha ha ha," I shot back sarcastically. "Because you have intentions of calling while she's here?"

She laughed at me again. "Me? Do a call-us interrupt-us? Of course not! Never, my friend!" she said, and I could hear the mock indignation in her voice. "Especially when I expect you to be fully immersed in each other, doing all sorts things that would make even me blush. And you know I'm not shy!"

"Uh huh," I said drily, not certain if I should be annoyed by the teasing, or grateful that it was taking my mind off my concerns. "Or so you've told me, repeatedly."

"I thought you might like to live vicariously through me," she said, and I could hear the laugh that still hovered in her throat. "But seriously," and her tone changed. "Are you okay? Are you ready for this?"

The meat had reached the right color. It was time to add the first of the vegetables.

"I'm kinda nervous, actually," I admitted. The carefully sliced peppers hit the pan with a satisfying hiss, and their aroma spiced the air as once again I stirred. "I mean, what if she's not into me like that, y'know? What if I'm not? What if this is all just a lot of wishful thinking and we've built this whole fantasy up in our heads because we've missed each other so much and—"

"Hey, hey, slow down, slow down—take a breath!" Brenda said over me, and I did, I took a breath. And another.

"What are you wearing?"

"What?" I asked, surprised. Everything in the pan looked right, time for the equally carefully sliced onions to join the rest.

"Oh Christ, Luna—it's an easy question! What are you wearing? Or," and her voice slid down a tone, became silky and sensual, "are you planning on greeting her in your birthday suit?"

This time, I chuckled. "Yeah…it's a suit, but it's because I'm still dressed from work," I admitted. "I look nice in it, though?" I hadn't meant for my voice to rise up at the end like that.

"Hot!" Brenda enthused. "She's sure to find you sexy as hell."

"Uh…I don't know, I mean, maybe?" I said, once again stirring the pan, careful not to break the plants that were finally becoming tender.

"You sound just like a teenager, nervous and excited all at the same time," Brenda told me with a chuckle. "You do know it's gonna be alright, yeah?"

"You think?"

"Oh my God—you're so nervous! I've never imagined you like this, and I've imagined a lot!" She laughed outright.

"Thanks, thanks a lot! It's always nice to know you're thinking of me," I said, a little amused, but somehow, not quite so nervous any more. "I don't think I want to ask just how you—oh shit!" I exclaimed, as my rice pan began to overflow.

"You alright?"

"Yeah…Yeah…I'm good," I said, as I adjusted the flame down. "I'm just making dinner, is all, and the pot—"

"You're cooking, as in actually cooking food? Why didn't you just order something so you know, you guys can just get right to it?"

I lifted the lid and sifted through the grains with a fork. I tasted and tasted thoughtfully. "She's driving hundreds of miles. That's a lot of effort. The least I could do is actually make her something decent to eat."

It was done and done well. I shut the burner off.

"Yeah, right, like food is what she wants to eat after driving all that way."

I decided to ignore the innuendo in the words, and the salty tone in her voice. "It's a lot of work to put into a day. It deserves something with at least a little effort put into it."

"After driving hundreds of miles, I'm pretty sure she's already got just one something in mind, and it's not Betty Crocker, unless she's into some strange kinda role play! You know there's no other reason to make a drive like that unless you know you're gonna get some, know what I mean?"

I hadn't thought about that, I mean not so definitively, not in that way. "Bren—do you really think so?"

"What?"

"That she's expecting to…I mean…that she and I—"

"What, get laid? Shit, yeah! Who wouldn't?" she asked, and I could not only imagine her rolling her eyes at me, it seemed like I could hear. "It's a lot of work to put into a day," she said, mimicking my earlier tone. "It deserves something with at least a little effort put into it."

I said nothing as I let that sink in. The meal was done. I turned off the flame beneath the final pan and found the appropriate cover. Would she expect that? Could that be what all of this was about? Just...Just a weird ruse of sorts, so that I would—

"Earth to Luna—are you there?"

"Oh yeah—still here," I said as I cleaned. I was still thinking about—everything.

"Okay, you've gone all moony—ha!" she laughed at her own joke. "I'll let you go, but before I say goodnight and good luck, lemme just tell you to go ahead and do everything I would do!"

Somehow the laugh in her voice snapped me out of my head. "I thought you'd say the usual thing, you know the classic don't do anything I wouldn't do thing."

"Too late for that, my friend," she said cheerily. "You already have!"

"Really? What's that?" I asked, braced for and expecting more jokes or sarcasm, or whatever witticism she'd prepared.

"You fell in love," she said quietly.

"Oh..." I swallowed. I stood stock still as I let her words the reflection of my inner reality echoed back at me, sink in.

"And she's lucky to have you," Bren continued in the same serious and low voice. "Don't forget that, huh? No matter what happens. Good luck."

I smiled. I couldn't help it. Bren's words made the wonders and worry in my head disappear as I let myself feel, simply feel. Because she was right, I was in love.

I let it wash over me, the weight and warmth of it.

My Gillian was coming...to me. And I couldn't

wait to see her.

"Well alright, you've got like an hour to go, so I'll talk to you in a few days—if you're awake!" Bren said brightly. "Ta!"

And with that, she hung up.

I gazed around at the kitchen, everything complete and ready to go, food prepared and counters clean.

Making certain I still had my phone with me, I walked out to the dining room, through the living room, checked myself in the bathroom, made sure my clothes seemed presentable. I ran a quick comb through my hair, reset the clip that held it away from my face, but loose over my shoulders.

Half an hour…

Thirty minutes.

That was one thousand eight hundred seconds… one thousand seven hundred and ninety-nine…one thousand seven hundred and ninety-eight…I walked to my room, everything organized and tidy, back through the hallway and into the living room…one thousand six hundred and eighty seconds… one thousand six hundred and seventy-nine seconds….

I turned lights on. I turned lights off…one thousand five hundred and sixty seconds…one thousand five hundred and fifty-nine seconds….

Finally, I pulled out a new magazine I'd bought earlier in the week, set the light the way I liked to when I wanted to relax and read, just the one to the side of the sofa and over my head so I could read, the only other light on the one over the stove in the kitchen.

I took a deep breath, and sat down.

I could do this. I could sit here, calm my rapidly beating heart and my nerves that were flaying me from within. I could read this article I'd found today about new discoveries in astro and quantum physics, because there was a neutron star that…

No.

I couldn't.

I leaned back against the sofa, and glanced over to my shelves. I decided to pick some random book—any book would do—since it would be something I'd read before, so even if I skimmed it, I'd still know what the story was.

So I did. Words and pages flew under my eyes and hands, some old story about some old familiar characters, discovering something new to them and old to some and eternally true to everyone about the human condition…

My phone buzzed.

Gillian: I'm here.

My heart lurched in my chest, a thump that was hard, painful, filled with the ache of want, pure want—no, it was need—to see her.

Luna: I'm opening the door.

I swallowed as I walked the few steps to open the door, was certain my fingers didn't tremble as I undid the lock and then set my hand to the latch.

She was already coming up the walk as I pulled the panel wide, bag over her shoulder, thumb in the strap, striding proudly, shoulders wide and strong.

She stopped when she saw me, and my heart, already pounding to urgency in my chest, became the thrum in my body.

Her shoulders relaxed, the bag eased off her

shoulder, and oh, the expression on her face, in her eyes, the soft curving of her lips.

She was at the door, and I was already reaching for her, barely inside and she was in my arms, and I was crying, she was crying, she and I together, in each other's arms, barely inside the door, holding each other and crying and happy, so happy to hold each other finally, for once…for real.

"I should come in," she said in our embrace and I agreed.

Still embraced, we moved in just a bit, and I don't know how I closed the door with us still wrapped up with each other.

I didn't stop or wipe away the tears as for the first time I rubbed my cheek against hers, and felt her skin…soft, silk…magic. She held me closer, or maybe I held her, I didn't know, I didn't care, because finally my arms had stopped aching and my heart hurting and I was full, so gorgeously, achingly full.

I had wanted this, needed this, dreamed of this for so long, her in my arms, me in hers, and here it was, real and now, and oh so damned perfect.

We stood like that for long minutes or maybe it was forever, it honestly didn't matter. My hair, long and fine, slipped out of the clip, tangled with the waves of hers. Her body, once so far away from mine, an unreachable unbridgeable distance, was long and strong, her curves a glorious fit to me.

"I love you," I said softly against her ear. My lips brushed through her hair to the tender skin beneath, no distance, no translated electrical signals through plastic and wires between us. I breathed her in, a combination of spice and soap and the heat of her skin.

"I love you," I said again, reveling in being able

to say it, here, now, safe and warm and loved in the circle of her arms.

And I did, I did, I loved her, completely and absolutely. I loved her breath on my shoulder, the beat of her heart against mine, the width of her shoulders beneath my hands, the jut of the muscle and bone beneath her coat, beneath her skin, a perfect fit within my palms. "God, Gillian...I love you...so much, baby. I love you so goddamn much."

She nuzzled against my neck, her cheek now a soft brush against me, even as she pulled me closer and closer and closer to breathe me in as I did her.

I pressed my face into her hair, breathed the heady scent of her in again, all of me alive and electric, felt and reveled in the strength in her arms, the strength in mine, even as I felt the slight shake of her. I knew she was crying as I did, even before I felt the wet of it against my skin.

We fit so close, so perfectly, and in the perfection of our embrace, suddenly I knew, I knew, with clarity, with certainty, we didn't fit as if we'd been made for each other. We actually had been made for each other.

"Luna, baby, I love you—I love you oh so fucking much." Her words were beautiful and warm below my ear, and it was just as she'd promised, the only distance between us was a shared breath.

JD Glass wrote ALA and Lambda Literary finalist Punk Like Me, Lambda Literary and Ben Franklin finalist Red Light, GCLS finalist American Goth, and X; selection editor of GCLS Award winner Outsiders. Newer works include Glass Lions, First Blood, a 10-year Anniversary edition of Punk Like Me, and Drawn Together.

Paulie

By Jenny Fresh

So, um, Paulie…Don't you think it might be time to exchange a picture?" Jill felt her pulse race as she typed the question. She and Paulie had met online and they had been communicating for almost two months. Jill chewed on her lower lip as she awaited her reply.

"We can do that, if you want."

Jill scowled. "Do you not want to?"

"No, it's fine. I guess it's probably time."

Jill's heart raced. She had already chosen a picture that was taken last year at the beach. Her long hair was tucked in a baseball cap and she was wearing her favorite red bikini. Her larger than average cleavage was on full display, which made her hesitate on this particular photo, but it was the best one she had of just herself. Holding her breath, she sent the picture to Paulie's email before she could think twice and chicken out. "Okay. You should have mail."

Almost simultaneously, Jill's own email pinged. Closing her eyes, she clicked the mailbox icon and waited for the attachment to load. She wasn't a vain person but she also prayed that Paulie's looks were as attractive as her personality. Exhaling loudly, she slowly opened her eyes.

Paulie was gorgeous! She had long blonde hair and light green eyes. The picture was taken in a forest and Paulie was wearing khaki shorts, a tank top and had a backpack leaning up against her long and tan legs. Her lithe frame was clearly toned, but she expected that based on their previous conversations and knowing that Paulie loved the outdoors as much as she did.

Jill couldn't stop the grin from forming as she typed, "You are beautiful! I can't believe you were worried about sending me this!"

There was a brief pause, but Jill could tell that Paulie was typing because of the floating bubble in their secure chat room. Finally, the words appeared, "Let's talk about gorgeous. Wow! It's funny but I didn't picture you as blonde. I guess that's something else we have in common."

Jill smiled. "I guess so. Where was that picture taken? That forest looks beautiful!"

"A hiking trail near Mt. St. Helens. There's a national forest and there are tons of trails to choose from. This is one of my favorites."

Nerves jumped in Jill's stomach before she replied. "If I ever make it out there I would love to see that in person!" She didn't want to seem pushy, but the more she learned about Paulie, the more drawn in she was by the woman. She couldn't help but fantasize about actually seeing her in person someday.

The bubbles at the bottom of the page started and stopped several times before the words showed on the screen. Paulie was obviously struggling with her reply, which only made Jill's nerves worse. She knew that Paulie was a reclusive writer and cherished her privacy, but what was the point of this online dating if it never progressed to more? Jill's thoughts were interrupted by the words on her screen: "I would like that."

Jill scowled. *Really?   That's it?* Paulie had obviously erased whatever else she had been typing. Maybe it was time to push a little.

"Paulie? Are you afraid to meet me someday?"

Once again, the bubbles started and stopped. Jill took a deep breath and forced herself to be patient.

"Yes, I'm afraid it will ruin everything."

Jill frowned. "Why would you think that?"

The reply was immediate. "Because you don't know everything about me."

The words were like a cannonball dropping in her stomach. Swallowing, she replied, "What's that mean, Paulie? You're kind of scaring me right now."

"No! No, I'm not like a serial killer or something. You know I have a hard time socializing, but when it comes to dating, it's always been a disaster for me."

"Why?"

"Jill, I'm different than most lesbians. Most women I've met, when things got to the physical part, they couldn't handle it. Some women—two to be exact—could handle it but the important things, the non-physical things, didn't work out."

Jill rubbed her mouth and shook her head, puzzled. "Paulie, I don't understand. What is it that you are referring to?"

"Well, you know I'm a writer. I actually write under two pseudonyms. One is the mainstream that you've heard about. The other is, um, erotica. Futa stories, to be exact."

Jill crinkled her brow. "Futa? As in Futanari? Women that have a penis?"

"Yes. Some have a penis and a vagina."

Jill read the sentence again and she felt tendrils of understanding begin to form. "Paulie? Why are you telling me this?"

The pause was brief, as though Paulie was resigned to just type the words. "Because that's what I am."

Jill exhaled. "You have a penis? Is that what you are telling me?"

"Yes, and a vagina. I was born that way."

Jill quickly scrolled back to the picture that Paulie had sent. Scrutinizing the woman in the photo, she couldn't discern anything to suggest she was packing something in her shorts. Her mind was reeling with this new information. "This is really confusing for me, sorry."

"I understand. It's a lot to take in. I can answer questions. I'm sure you have many."

Jill shook her head and mumbled to herself, "No shit." Much to her dismay, her mind immediately tried to visualize Paulie naked. She just couldn't picture it. Paulie was so feminine.

"You're picturing me naked right now, aren't you?"

Jill barked out an embarrassed laugh. Even now, Paulie's sense of humor surfaced. It's one of the things she liked most about the woman. Choosing to be honest, she replied, "Yeah. Sorry."

She was not expecting Paulie's reply. "Do you want to Skype?"

Jill exhaled loudly and leaned back from her monitor. *Did she want to Skype?* Replaying all of the conversations they had over the past couple of months, warmth enveloped Jill as she thought of Paulie. She was drawn to her, her wit, compassion, and intelligence.

She was the complete package. Jill snorted at the thought and again shook her head. Could she deal with a girlfriend that had a dick? She had been with men before and penetration was actually something she very much enjoyed. Of course, with women, toys were involved. Picturing a soft, smooth female form covering her body while a warm, hard, dick filled her made Jill fidget in her seat.

Her fingers started typing before her brain caught up. "Yes."

Paulie sent her the contact information for Skype and, before she knew it, the connection was going through on the computer before her. The dark screen was replaced with a close up of the woman who had monopolized her dreams for the past two months. She was smiling nervously. Her hair was down around her shoulders and she was wearing a faded T-shirt.

Paulie's voice shook when she finally spoke. "Hi."

Jill felt a blush rise in her cheeks. A smile formed immediately as she took in the shy and beautiful woman before her. "Hi, yourself."

Paulie's chuckle sounded exactly as Jill had imagined it would. "So. It's nice to meet you, Jill."

"It's nice to meet you, too, Paulie."

Paulie laughed. "This is kind of strange, huh?"

"Yeah, but it's nice to finally hear your voice and see you in person."

Paulie's smile was genuine. "It is. Your voice is very sexy, Jill. It matches your looks perfectly."

Jill blushed furiously. "Stop. You're embarrassing me."

Paulie's smile softened and her voice dropped. "I'm serious. You are very beautiful. Inside and out."

The words made Jill's body tingle from head to

toe and it was in that instant that she realized she didn't care about Paulie's little secret. She frowned slightly as she wondered how little her secret was.

Paulie, watching the expressions on Jill's face, chuckled. "Well, you haven't hung up yet, so I'm guessing you are trying to picture me naked again."

Jill's mouth dropped open. "I am not!"

"She doth protest too loudly." Paulie held up her hand before Jill could reply. "Do you want to see me? Naked? I mean, I would rather do this while we are thousands of miles apart than suffer the humiliation later."

Jill's heart sunk at Paulie's words. "Don't you ever feel humiliated with me." Maintaining eye contact, she continued, "I admit, I'm curious, but I never want you to feel uncomfortable."

Paulie searched her face. After a moment of silence, she quietly stood and stepped back from the computer, exposing her full body to the camera before her. Reaching down, she slowly lifted her shirt over her head and dropped it to the floor.

Jill's breath hitched. Paulie was not wearing a bra and her exposed breasts, with their dark and erect nipples, caused Jill's brain to short circuit. Her voice was barely above a whisper,

"You are beautiful."

Paulie smiled as she reached down to unbutton her jeans. Jill could see her hands shaking, but she remained focused on completing the task. Without looking up, Paulie dropped her pants and stepped forward slightly. She was completely naked. Jill's eyes were glued to the growing appendage between Paulie's legs. She was huge! She wasn't even fully erect and Jill had never seen a dick as large or as thick as the one before her. She felt her pulse accelerate and her clit tightened as she watched Paulie grow.

"Are you okay?"

The timid question forced Jill's eyes up to meet Paulie's. Nodding slightly, she realized her mouth had gone dry. She swallowed and cleared her throat.

"You are magnificent."

The shocked expression on Paulie's face was adorable.

"Really? I mean, you aren't disgusted, or…?"

Jill pierced Paulie with her stare. "No. I'm far from disgusted."

Paulie searched Jill's face for signs of deceit and then a grin started to form on her full lips. Reaching down, she gently grasped her member with one hand and slowly stroked its length, watching Jill for a reaction. Jill's voice broke when she said, "Have I mentioned that I have next week off?" Paulie laughed as Jill continued, "And I have over two hundred thousand air miles just sitting in my account."

Laughing, Paulie continued to fondle herself. "I wish you were here right now." Shaking her head she went on, "I've never been so open before, with anyone. But here I am with my dick in my hand and all I can do is smile." Her expression softened. "You are really special, Jill. You truly are."

Jill smiled. "What I am right now, Paulie, is horny."

Paulie raised an eyebrow playfully. "Oh? Maybe you should do something about that?"

Jill laughed. "Oh no you don't! You can just hold on." Jill dropped her eyes and continued. "Hold on, literally, until I can get my ass on a plane." Raising her eyes again, her voice sounded like a growl, "And then we can take care of each other."

Paulie's jaw felt like it hit the floor. Releasing her member, she moved forward and sat back down in her chair. "Then hang up and get a fucking ticket!"

Jill's laugh was the loudest thus far and it made Paulie smile. "Hang on, tiger. Let's quit this call so I can go find a flight."

"Done! Go! I will email you my details."

Jill waved, a smirk on her beautiful face. And then, with a wink, she was gone.

❧ ❧ ❧ ❧

Paulie followed the path once again across her driveway and tried to not look at her watch. It had been almost a week since their Skype session and Jill would arrive any moment. Trying to calm her nerves, Paulie took another deep breath just as she heard gravel crunching down the road. Her heart was beating so furiously she thought she might pass out when the Jeep Wrangler slowly came into view.

Jill slowed the Jeep to a stop in front of the woman standing in the road before her. The picture did not do her justice. She was stunning. A smile broke out as the woman slowly made her way to the driver's side door.

"Hi there."

"Hi yourself."

Paulie's smile was tentative. "You can pull up over there, in front of the garage."

Jill nodded and parked the car, Paulie following on foot behind her. When she went to open the door, Paulie beat her to it and reached a hand in to help her out of the Jeep. The strength and warmth of Paulie's hand immediately put Jill at ease and she pulled the taller woman in for a hug.

"It's so nice to meet you," she mumbled into Paulie's shoulder.

Paulie's arms wound tighter around Jill's frame, pulling their bodies flush. "I'm so glad to see you."

Jill nodded but didn't release Paulie from her embrace. When she leaned her head back, Paulie was looking intently into her eyes. Jill brought her hand up and cradled Paulie's cheek as the woman bent down to capture Jill's lips with her own.

When Paulie's soft lips met hers, Jill moaned and moved her hand to the back of Paulie's neck. Paulie opened her mouth and gently traced Jill's lower lip with her tongue. Jill responded by meeting Paulie's tongue with her own as they explored one another for the first time.

Jill didn't know how long they stood there, but she slowly became aware of something pushing against her mound, over her clothes. Something hard. Breaking their kiss, Jill gasped as she looked down and realized it was Paulie's dick that was prodding her body. Even with jeans on, the unmistakable bulge in Paulie's pants was huge. Without thinking, Jill reached down and gently grasped the straining member and squeezed gently.

Paulie moaned and a low growl escaped her throat as she bent down and took control of Jill's mouth. Her tongue, this time, was demanding as it probed her mouth. Jill increased the pressure on Paulie's dick and tried to rub herself along its firm length.

Paulie suddenly pulled back. Panting, her words were short.

"House. Now."

Not waiting for a reply, Jill's hand was grasped

firmly as she was pulled into the large cabin before her. Clothes immediately started to fly off as they made their way down the hall, stopping at a king sized bed.

Jill stood in front of Paulie, clad in only her bra and underwear. Her chest rose and fell in time with her rapid breathing. Without hesitating, she removed both garments as Paulie's hungry stare took her in.

"You are so damn sexy."

Jill smiled and reached forward to remove the only remaining piece of clothing on Paulie's body. Kneeling, she yanked the underwear down. Paulie's dick immediately sprang free the glistening head was only a breath away from Jill's mouth. Jill's instincts took over as she closed the distance and encased the swollen head with her mouth.

Paulie's body jerked when she felt Jill's tongue on her cock. Moving both hands into Jill's hair, she gently encouraged Jill to take more of her into her mouth. When Jill obliged, Paulie slowly started to fuck Jill's mouth, pushing in a little more of her length with each gentle thrust of her hips.

Jill tried not to gag as she enveloped Paulie's cock with her mouth. The girth alone was hard to fit, but the length was soon pushing the head into the back of Jill's throat. Forcing herself to relax, Jill eased the cock down her throat with each of Paulie's thrusts. At the same time, Jill moved her hands to the base of the dick and started to explore. Her eyes opened wide in shock as she discovered a moist cleft, with engorged lips and a clit. Jill traced the opening with her fingers and then gently brushed over the hard nub, causing Paulie to moan.

Paulie couldn't take any more. Pulling her dick away from Jill, she reached down and pulled the smaller woman to her feet. They shared a blistering kiss as Paulie nudged Jill onto the bed. Jill broke the kiss and moved farther back, her legs spread invitingly.

Paulie leaned forward and slowly lapped at Jill's center, savoring the taste and the sounds of pleasure coming from Jill's mouth. When she felt hands gently pulling her head up, Paulie complied. Jill's eyes were feverish.

"Take me, Paulie."

Groaning with need, Paulie made her way up so she was face to face with Jill. Positioning herself between the other woman's legs, she moaned when she felt Jill take hold of her cock and guide it to her opening. Knowing how big she was, Paulie started to slowly push her way into Jill's warmth.

Jill sighed as Paulie slowly filled her. It had been a long time since she was penetrated and she was glad that Paulie was giving her body time to adjust. She could feel the head as it forced its way toward her core, the warm and pulsing member felt so good inside her that Jill felt she could almost come.

When Paulie pushed the last few inches of her cock inside of Jill, both women sighed. Looking down, Paulie smiled.

"You took it all."

Jill bit her lower lip. "Yeah. Feels so good. Please don't stop."

Paulie slowly withdrew and then pushed forward again, each stroke longer than the one before it. Jill began to raise her hips to match the rhythm, making a small noise every time Paulie sheathed her lance fully inside Jill's warmth. As they begin to move faster, Paulie whispered, "I'm going to come."

Jill wrapped her feet around Paulie's thighs and

groaned when she felt Paulie unload inside her. The pulsating member pushed Jill over the edge and she cried out as her muscles gripped and milked Paulie's cock of every last drop.

Spent, both women remained where they were. Jill could feel Paulie begin to shrink inside her. The feeling of being so connected to Paulie brought tears to her eyes. She had never felt so full or satisfied in her entire life.

Hearing a sniffle, Paulie raised her head and looked worriedly at Jill.

"Are you okay? I didn't hurt you, did I?"

Jill smiled and gently pushed Paulie's blonde hair behind her ear. "No. You didn't hurt me." Looking intently at Paulie, she continued, "You are perfect."

The words caused Paulie's eyes to water and her throat clenched. "Nobody's ever told me that before."

Jill shook her head. "Well, get used to it."

Paulie raised an eyebrow. "Yeah?"

Jill nodded. "Yeah."

Jenny Fresh is a proud mom of three. She and her partner have been together over 17 years and both work in real estate to pay the bills. Jenny's love of reading began at a young age thanks to her Grandmother. The writing bug first hit in college, where she majored in History with a minor in English. She and her family live in the Pacific Northwest and enjoy the outdoors whenever the rain lets up.

Granite

By Shelley Thrasher

We were sitting in my parents' kitchen when the phone call came. My mom handed the receiver to my new girlfriend, Carla. "It's for you. Long distance from Seattle. A man."

Carla quirked a brow. A stony frown replaced her usual smile as she took the call. "Hello."

Mom walked back over to the stove and pulled a large ham from the oven. Its succulent aroma filled the air. Mmm. I was hungry and looking forward to a home-cooked meal. Living alone, I'd eaten too many sardines and peaches straight from the can.

While Carla talked to the mystery man, I grabbed four white Corelle plates from the kitchen cabinet and began to set the table. One of her sons was probably calling to wish her a happy birthday.

"Oh, no!"

I turned to Carla. Her tanned skin had faded to gray.

"I'll be there as soon as I can! Meet me at Sea-Tac." She dropped the receiver and leapt from her chair at the table.

I stared at her. Obviously, we were ending our visit sooner than we'd planned. "Carla. What's wrong?"

"Randy's been in a motorcycle accident." For my

parents' benefit, she said, "My younger son. He drove off a cliff into the ocean. It's a miracle he didn't freeze to death." She picked up the glass of water she'd been drinking and downed the rest of it in one gulp. Then she started to pace. "They're life-flighting him into Seattle right now. I have to leave."

We rushed down the hall to the guest room and tossed our newly unpacked clothes into our suitcases. Carla didn't provide any more details right then, though she thanked my parents for their hospitality as we hustled our gear into the trunk of my green Cougar. Mom shoved something in the driver's window as I started the car. My hand closed around a paper plate wrapped in aluminum foil. "Bread and ham," Mom said. "Be careful."

It was almost dark outside when we pulled out of the driveway. "What happened?" I asked as we headed for the airport in Houston, four hours away.

"My husband told Randy that we're getting a divorce." Carla's voice shook. "Randy ran out and jumped on his bike and tried to kill himself." She took a deep breath. "He's already lost a leg, and they're not sure he'll make it." Sounding choked up, she provided some other details she'd spared my parents.

"My God." I stared at her so long, she grabbed the wheel and steered us back into the correct lane of traffic. "It's all my fault. I never should have flirted with you this summer."

Now Carla sounded as hard as her face appeared, etched in the glow of approaching headlights. "Don't be silly. I chased you until you caught me."

The tired cliché settled into the dank atmosphere that was almost suffocating us. I caught a whiff of ham, suddenly ravenous, but didn't want to ask Carla about food right now. Maybe later.

"Do you regret what we did this summer?" I couldn't keep from asking, even though I knew her mind was elsewhere.

"No." She sounded steady again, almost normal. Maybe it was a relief to think of something other than her injured son. "I'd do it again." I heard the rustle of foil, caught the rich aroma of the ham. She nudged my arm, then silently handed me a sandwich.

As I drove one-handed, I recalled making love in a string of motel rooms through Missouri and Arkansas. That was our first trip together. We'd met at a workshop in Iowa and, afterward, doubled the length of time it should have taken to drive to Texas.

"I only regret that my little Fiat didn't have an air conditioner and your car did. I've never been that hot." She managed a gravelly chuckle.

I finished my sandwich and reached over to touch her, but she pulled away and offered me a paper towel. Her expression had changed, and I knew she was back in that dark place, thinking about Randy. I couldn't begin to comprehend how she must feel.

"He'll be okay, won't he?" Her voice teemed with gloom.

I wiped grease from my lips and gripped the steering wheel, staring into the blackness ahead of us. "He was really lucky someone saw him go over the side and pulled him out so fast."

I could see her shrug in the light from the dashboard. "Knowing Randy, he's still pissed as hell. He's always been determined to get his way. Just like his dad." She took my soiled paper towel and rammed it into a plastic bag on the floorboard meant for trash. "That's one reason I want a divorce."

My two marriages had ended for other reasons, but I could empathize. Yet I still couldn't wrap my head around what her son had done.

Carla sat rock-like during most of the long drive over back roads lined with towering pine trees and refused to eat a thing. I ended up with another sandwich.

When we reached the airport, she headed straight to the Southwest desk. It was closed that late at night, but she booked a flight over the phone. We grabbed a motel room for a few hours' sleep before she flew out the next morning, and she insisted on separate beds. I could hear her pacing until I finally quit fighting sleep.

Back at the airport early, waiting to leave, she looked so flinty I thought she belonged right up there beside Washington, Jefferson, Lincoln, and Roosevelt.

The next day, she called me from the hospital, sounding drained, totally unlike her usual energetic self. "Randy's going to make it thanks to that stranger." She sighed, as if a boulder had been pried from her shoulders.

"Thank God. Are you okay?" I'd just come home from teaching an American literature class and was standing in my bedroom half undressed.

"I will be, if I can get a little sleep." Her voice shook even more now than it had when she first told me about Randy. "I've decided to rent a cheap apartment near the hospital as long as Randy needs me nearby. Can you come see me some weekend?"

"Of course. Just let me know when it's convenient, and I'll be there." After I hung up, I changed from my colorful gauze skirt and peasant blouse into a pair of shorts and a halter-top. It was the middle of October but still in the 90s.

I flew to Seattle two weeks later. Randy had lost his leg but not his life. Carla didn't take me to see him and barely mentioned her husband except to say that her divorce was still in the works.

"Do you think I could teach some courses in the college where you work? I'd love to live somewhere warm for a change," she asked as we sat in her cramped Seattle apartment sharing a pizza.

"I'll see what I can do. If you want to be warm, you'll love Southeast Texas." I took her hand, and she let me hold it. "Are you positive about this?"

Carla and I had spent as much time together as we could manage since we met. After our leisurely trek from Iowa in late July, we'd left my car in Texas and driven to Seattle together, stopping to see the sights and exploring what was happening between us. Several days after we reached our destination, I rode the bus back to Texas.

With only a handful of aborted lesbian relationships in my past, I certainly wasn't an expert tour guide for Carla's flight from marriage toward lesbian bliss. But we were fumbling along together. We'd spent Labor Day weekend in San Diego. A couple of weeks later she flew to Texas to visit me. And two weeks after that, we'd rendezvoused in a Seattle hotel.

It was during her third trip to Texas that she received the news about Randy. Now, on this early November weekend, we were together in Seattle for the third time. Was it a charm? Maybe.

So far, Carla said she had done little except stay at the hospital beside Randy's bed and retreat to her small, temporary apartment. He'd stabilized, and she felt comfortable leaving him alone for a few hours. We didn't talk about her husband. I knew only that he had a very demanding job that took him out of town for extended periods of time. Carla's marriage, or what remained of it, was strictly her business. I preferred it that way, and she insisted on it.

Still holding Carla's hand, I asked, "What would you like to do while I'm here? Rest, talk, and sightsee? Though it seems a little chilly to do much of that." The high the next day was supposed to be 55, which was Houston's expected low. I could understand her desire to move south.

She ran her hand over mine, as if touching it for the first time. "I'd love to rest forever. But not in that bed." She pointed to the tiny bedroom, where she must have tried to sleep when she wasn't at Randy's side. "It's more uncomfortable than this kitchen floor."

Her gray eyes, which had dulled when she'd first heard the news about Randy, had regained a bit of the shine I'd noticed this summer after we met. Now they reminded me of a neglected granite countertop someone had just wiped clean. I hoped my arrival was at least part of the reason for the change.

The kitchen, evidently the largest room in the place, contained only a small, round table for two— where we sat—along with a gas stove, refrigerator, and sink. The rest of it stretched out into a sprawling empty space, just waiting to be filled.

Hoping to help her feel more comfortable, I said, "Let's make our own bed then." But I didn't move. Instead, I finished the piece of pizza I held in the hand she wasn't touching. I wasn't in any hurry to break off our tenuous contact, but I did want to give her what she wanted. She'd been through a lot, and though I tried, I couldn't keep from considering myself somewhat responsible for what had happened to her and her son.

Her granite eyes gained more luster. "How do you suggest we do that?"

I motioned toward the bedroom. "Whoever chose that mattress obviously had a pillow fetish. I've never seen so many piled on one bed." Then I pointed at the couch. "And that's one of the softest sofas I've ever sat on. With all those cushions, plus a sheet and a blanket, we'll be in business."

"You're so thoughtful." She smoothed her hand up my arm to my shoulder, her eyes shimmering now. "Tell me you don't blame yourself for what happened."

I shivered. Had she just read my mind? "If it hadn't been for me, you'd probably be home safe with your husband and two boys."

She shook her head and firmed her strong jaw. "They're not boys. They're men in their twenties—old enough to be on their own. But yes. I'd probably be there. Miserable. Wishing every minute that I was somewhere else."

My deep sigh ended with a shudder. I didn't want to think about her family. Though I didn't love her in the splendidly romantic way I'd dreamed of experiencing when I met the right woman, I did feel compassion for her. "How can I help?" I whispered.

With her hand still on my shoulder, she pulled me close, her lips soft, yielding as we kissed for the first time since Randy's accident. "What were you saying about all those pillows and cushions?" she murmured as she finally pulled back.

We covered the floor with them and a blue sheet, and then stretched out on our makeshift bed. "Hmm. Much better," she said, her eyes even more translucent now, though they still kept me at a safe distance. During all our trysts, she'd never given herself fully to me, whatever that entailed. It was as if she suspected I would try to trap her into something she wasn't ready for. Or, more likely, into the same type of situation she was struggling so hard to free herself from. I kept my distance too, trying not to appear too eager to commit to anything other than what we had together at the moment.

Carla was a painter, and she'd probably spent years perfecting her habit of carefully observing her surroundings and others. An introvert, I preferred to read and write about emotional entanglements rather than become involved in them, so we were an oddly matched pair.

That day, however, I could sense lava bubbling behind her deceptively calm façade. As I moved over her, I touched her in all the places she'd already taught me to please her, and she lay still, as if waiting for something. Yet I distanced myself from her, as if perusing one of her paintings. This was her moment, and I wanted her to experience it fully.

Gradually, she stretched out on that blue sheet like she was dancing with herself—slow, languid movements, full of grace and a type of natural beauty I'd rarely witnessed. She shifted from one side to the other as I caressed her with my fingers and my tongue, her body gradually loosening like that of a runner melting into her stride, at one with the air and the pressure building inside her. Suddenly, something inside her cracked broke through, threatened to erupt. She tensed and exploded in an orgasm that outclassed all the ones romance novelists could imagine. It seemed so honest, so real, so simple, so natural, and so easy. I assumed she had at last surrendered to feelings frozen inside her during the years of her failing marriage and was now finally releasing them.

However, as I watched her, I knew she and I were traveling very different paths. She had to find her own way, just as I'd been struggling to do for seven years, since my second divorce.

We did eventually live together in Texas, for several months, but that next fall she went to China to teach English. For a long time, I felt responsible for the decisions she had made. But, ultimately, I realized I had provided her a safe causeway across part of the stormy water she had to navigate in her journey from one way of life to another.

She had repaid me with the sight of a perfect orgasm.

I'd never seen one before, much less felt one, and I'll never forget that gift.

I still see her lying there, radiant, on that kitchen floor, spilling herself, granite transformed into cooling lava.

Shelley Thrasher published The Storm, First Tango in Paris, and Autumn Spring—a Lambda lesbian romance finalist—with Bold Strokes Books. Her first book of poetry, In and Out of Love, was recently released by Sapphire Books. A retired English professor, she edits novels from her home in East Texas.

It's All Academic

By Jules Worth

"I respectfully disagree, Dr. Kaplan. You are missing the point of the genesis of the European Union." The speaker stood up among the audience, a microphone in her hand.

Georgiana "George" Kaplan peered intently into the audience and stared at the speaker. She took a deep breath. She figured her department rival would be at her panel discussion to harass her, that infuriating sexy auburn haired vixen, Dr. Laura Holt. George caught herself. *Sexy, what the hell was wrong with her?*

"Dr. Holt, do expound on your comment please. I would definitely like to know what points I have missed." George spoke into her microphone, her blue eyes telegraphing Laura's glacial to cool green ones.

"Point one, Dr. Kaplan, the EU originated with economic impetus, the political aspects happened much later. It had its underpinnings in economics." Laura Holt explained comfortably as she turned to face the audience.

"Well done on the panel discussion George and you too, Laura for your comments and contribution. What a terrific way to introduce the department to a batch of new students, especially those who are not sure of their majors yet. I will see you both later at the cocktail hour." Dean Marks congratulated both as he walked out of the auditorium.

"Really Laura, you couldn't find a better way to insert your point, than 'I disagree, Dr. Kaplan?' I can't believe how you upstaged me." George looked sufficiently peeved.

"George, it was not as bad as you make it sound. I thought we had a good discussion going and by the end of it, the audience clapped loudly for you. So what was wrong with me pointing out a few facts for you?" Laura raised her signature eyebrow.

George pouted and ground her teeth. She refused to answer and packed up her papers, ready to stalk out of the auditorium. Laura looked at her in amusement and chuckled softly.

"Come on, Georgie, let me buy you a drink at the cocktail hour to smooth ruffled feathers." Laura said, leaning towards George with her palms on the table.

"Drinks are free, Laura, you don't have to pay for them." George answered, looking up from her papers, surprised that Laura was leaning so close, even more surprised when her eyes strayed towards Laura's cleavage, visible from her white silk blouse. George's breath caught and she felt her face flush.

"Manner of speaking. So what do you say, join me for a drink? No hard feelings?" She stuck out her hand to shake.

George slowly straightened her back and stood ramrod straight, towering over Laura. She was powerless against a set of charming dimples that appeared on Laura's cheeks as she smiled.

"Sure, why not." George gripped Laura's hand, the warmth and solidness of the grip, warming her all over.

I am in so much trouble, George thought as she felt her heart pound out an erratic rhythm and the familiar fluttering in her stomach whenever Laura was near. She could no longer lie to herself. She was attracted to the petite spitfire.

Laura Holt approached her lectures as she did with everything in life with gusto and passion. She was confident, calm and collected, everything that George was not. George was the quintessential nerd, preferring research and publication to lectures and public forums. George adjusted her black frames and picked up her briefcase.

Laura offered her arm to George and raised her eyebrow at her, "Shall we?"

"We shall." George took Laura's arm and they headed into the hall. As they entered the Hall Laura went to get a drink.

"Dean Marks, this is a very nice turnout for the first shindig of the semester." George said to her boss.

"Yes, when you offer free booze, everyone turns out. Plus we have a student band performing too. So free booze, free music and a dance floor, it'd be a hit for everyone."

"George, there you are." Laura put an arm around her waist and squeezed.

"Hello Laura, just chatting with our boss. How many have you had?" George asked, looking in surprise at Laura's comfortable familiarity with her.

"Actually, only one. But I have decided to follow through on my new resolution. When I see something I want, I go for it." Laura looked directly at George, her demeanor coy and yet direct.

"Huh, I'm not following." George was starting to perspire. *Did she mean what I thought she meant?*

Laura wanted her? George shook her head thinking it was hard to believe.

"Let's dance, George, you'll get my meaning soon enough." Laura pulled George with her towards the dance floor.

As she wrapped her arms around the object of her fantasy, George could not believe that Laura felt the same attraction as she had. But here they were, doing the slow dance, with their arms around one another and their bodies moving with the familiarity of lovers.

"Hmm, you smell good." George whispered as she dipped her head to Laura's ear.

"I taste good too. Want to try?" Laura's voice glided over George as she hugged her closer.

George stumbled in her step and almost tripped over Laura. She looked at her for a moment before answering.

"Maybe we should take this somewhere else. Come to my place?" George asked, her blue eyes turned a darker shade, hinting of arousal.

"I thought you'd never ask." Laura replied huskily as she took George's hand and led them towards the exit.

As George drove the car, she cast a shy glance at Laura, who looked steadily back at her.

"I am still somewhat in shock that you're here with me? Why?" George said looking bashfully.

"You're doing that sexy geek thing again, that bashful, shy, nerdy thing that you do so well, Dr. Georgiana Kaplan. I have tried to avoid this attraction, believe me, I didn't want an office romance, but lately, it's been really hard to ignore these feelings I have for you." Laura said, holding George's hand.

"I am so glad I wasn't the only one feeling it. I was

pretty much tongue-tied every time you were near. In fact, the only way I could hold a conversation with you was to be antagonistic and make every conversation a debate. Sorry. I was a bit of a jerk." George admitted ruefully.

"Baby, can you drive any faster? I am in a bit of a hurry." Laura said, stroking George's thigh, moving dangerously close to her crotch.

"I don't want to crash before we even have a chance to get to know one another. So you'd better stop that." George put her hand down to grab Laura's and hold it against her thigh, preventing further movement.

As soon as the car stopped, George released her seat belt and kissed Laura firmly on her lips. She opened her car door and rushed over to help Laura out of the car. They both ran hand in hand to George's apartment. George hurriedly searched for her key in her pocket.

"Found it!" George said.

She turned the key and found herself pressed up against the door as Laura launched herself on her, kissing her fiercely. George gripped Laura's buttocks and lifted her, leaning forward as Laura wrapped her legs around her waist. Laura slipped her hand down the waistband of George's trousers, feeling for her.

"Oh, you're so wet." Laura nipped her lips and sucked on her tongue.

"Laura, please. Oh, you're killing me. Touch me please." George moaned.

Laura rubbed her thumb on George's clitoris and slowly inched her finger inside.

"Baby!" George groaned, "Yes, more."

Wow what a dream I had, George thought, as she awoke groggily, staring at the rumpled bed sheets and suddenly realizing, she was naked. *Naked too? I definitely had too much to drink.* She shook her head and finger combed her brunette mop that felt sore as if it had been gripped too hard too many times in the night.

"What a dream!" George said aloud, as if affirming that she was awake.

"No, I don't think you could call it a dream." A sexy drawl drew George's eyes to the doorway.

George swallowed audibly. Leaning against the doorframe, wearing a white unbuttoned shirt was Laura, holding two cups of coffee, her long auburn hair all tousled with green eyes soft and amused looking back at her. Laura came over and sat on the edge of the bed and handed the mug over to George. Leaning closer, she kissed her on her lips.

"Good morning. You have really good coffee. Illy. My favorite brand." Laura said, leaning back to take a sip of the coffee.

"Good morning to you. You look like you slept well." George fingered an auburn curl around Laura's neck.

"Yes thanks to you. I finally had those months of frustration worked out last night." Laura said, laughing bashfully as she held the mug with two hands and looked at George.

"Hmm, I'm not sure if I was that thorough in my research? I think I need to investigate some more." George murmured, reaching out to take the mug from Laura's hand and moving the shirt off her shoulder as she slid towards her.

"I've always liked this hardworking side of you. Work on me some more." Laura leaned into George's kiss and deepened it.

❧❧❧❧

Laura walked smartly down the corridor to George's office and gave the door a quick rap with her knuckles

"Come in." Came that familiar voice.

"Hi" Laura said, leaning close the door.

"Hey you, what a surprise." George stood up to her five feet seven inch frame, towering over the smaller woman and giving her a warm hug.

Laura kissed George on the side of her neck and reached up to nip her chin. "Dean Marks surprised me today. He wants me to head over to California, Santa Clara University. One of the professors there fell ill and had emergency surgery. Will be out of commission for the whole semester. He wants me to fly up over the weekend and take over as substitute professor for the time being." Laura rushed the words out. She looked unsure and frazzled, quite unlike the cool calm demeanor she always wore.

"Oh, that is a surprise." George took a step back, and dropped her arms from around Laura. She adjusted her glasses and looked away. Her heart took a tumble at the news. Her relationship with Laura was still very new but George had already known she had fallen hard for her favorite professor.

"What should I do George? I know I should go and help. It's a great opportunity to teach at Santa Clara but I don't want to leave you." There, Laura made the opening. She was afraid to hear what George had to say. But the words were exactly what her heart had dictated.

"Baby, it is a great opportunity. You'd have Marks

in your pocket for stepping up. We can make this work, honey. It's California, not another country. It's just a few hours away…we can text, Face Time, and see each other on weekends. The usual long distant affair." George tried to rally as she pulled Laura close into a hug, resting her chin on top of her head, soothing her back with rubs.

"Is that what we have? A long distant affair?" Laura leaned back in her arms and raised an eyebrow at her.

"No, we are more than that, much more, Laura." George said and kissed her.

"So, I should say yes? If so, I have to do a lot of packing and talk to Marks about my classes here." Laura said wistfully.

"Sweetie, I'd go with you to help you settle in. Don't worry about your classes here. I'll talk to Marks. Maybe I could take on your sessions. After all we do very good research together." George waggled her eyebrows suggestively and Laura laughed, pinching her sides.

"Okay, we'll make this work. I am not ready to give up my research on you yet." Laura affirmed kissing George firmly and then breezed out of her office as quickly as she came in.

❧❧❧❧

"Hey, the academic housing here is so much better than what we have in Vermont." George said, looking at the lecturers' houses on the Santa Clara University campus.

"Yeah it's not too bad. But…" Laura trailed off.

"What?" George asked, lifting the luggage from

the car to the porch.

"You're not going to be here with me." Laura pouted. George laughed and tweaked her nose.

"Come on, don't do this. It will make it harder to say goodbye. It was already hard enough to get on the flight together, it'd be worse for me to fly out alone. Sweetheart, come on, smile for me." George coaxed, using her finger and thumb to pinch Laura's cheek. After a few hours of organizing the apartment, filling it with groceries and water, George was ready to take her night flight back to Vermont. Laura clung to her on the sofa as she sat astride George.

"I don't want you to go, darling." Laura's tears fell unchecked as she laid her head on George's chest.

"Baby, I am only a few hours away from you. I'm connected to you by phone, on text and on Face Time, even on this flight if you need me. You'll be okay and before long, you may not even want to come back to Vermont's weather, having experienced the mild California weather." George pushed aside the hair covering Laura's face and leaned her forehead on hers.

The sound of a car horn signaled the taxi for George.

"I will text you when I arrive. You get some rest hon. Tomorrow is a big day for you. First day of school." George kissed her lightly and walked towards the door.

Laura walked with her and stood at the door, holding on to George's coat as she leaned up on tiptoes to kiss her. "You'll walk in my dreams every night I am not with you, darling." Laura whispered.

"I love you." George said as she kissed her softly and walked out.

Laura stood by the door and stayed there even

after the cab pulled away from the curb.

≈≈≈≈

George looked at her watch. It was 12:30 in the morning, Monday morning. The plane ride had been smooth and she managed a quick nap from the time the flight took off till it landed.

Monday, 12:30 a.m.

"Hey, I've arrived. Grabbing a car home now. Love you," George texted.

Monday, 3:30 a.m.

George heard a ping on her cellphone and looked at the clock on the dresser next to the bed. It was 3:30 a.m. George was already in bed. "Laura," she said softly to herself...

"Glad to know you're home safely. Miss you," replied Laura.

Monday, 3:36 a.m.

"Why are you still up? School today," asked George

Monday, 3:43 a.m.

"Can't get to sleep in new place, you're not here. Pout," replied Laura.

Monday, 3:55 a.m.

"Go to sleep, hon. I need the shuteye. 9:00 a.m. lecture, and then I cover your class at 10:30a.m." George messaged.

Monday, 4:05 a.m.

"My class? Ok, darling. You get some rest. I know you'll be great. Kiss, kiss."

Monday, 4:08 a.m.

"Kiss, kiss. Love you," replied George.

Monday, 4:12 a.m.

"Love you back," texted Laura.

The first week was torture for both Laura and George. But by the fourth week, with multiple calls into the night, sometimes even sexting, the separation became more bearable. The workload George was handling was double what it used to be, as she assumed responsibility for Laura's classes. She also came upon an idea of a joint academic paper with Laura, conceived one early morning over text as they talked to each other.

Friday, 11:00 p.m.

"Baby, got an idea for you." George texted.

Friday, 11:30 p.m.

"Hmm, what idea Sweetheart?" Texted Laura

Friday, 11:35 p.m.

"Since taking over your class, I have an idea for a joint paper or book, that we could work on." Replied George.

Friday, 11:45 p.m.

"Sounds like fun. What do you have in mind?" Laura asked.

Friday, 11:55 p.m.

"Glad you're on board. Will send you proposal in email. Now I want to know what you're wearing?" George texted.

Friday, 11:58 p.m.

"My, my, you sound horny...again. Well, let's see. I just came out of the shower, with nothing but a towel." Replied Laura.

Saturday, 12;05 a.m.

"Towel huh? Nice. Imagine my hands running down your body, drying every drop of moisture from you." Replied George.

Saturday, 12:15 a.m.

"Every drop? Even in those hard to reach places?" Laura replied.

Saturday. 12:20 a.m.

"For those places, I'd use my tongue and mouth. Some moisture needs to be sucked, lapped and drunk up." George replied.

The cellphone rang and George smiled answering, "Yes?"

"Are you trying to kill me?" Laura rasped.

"No, Baby. Helping you sleep."

"Darling, putting me into a perpetual state of arousal is not helping me sleep. In fact my students are already calling me the grumpy professor." She groused.

George laughed warmly. "Seriously, are you doing alright Baby? The students, professors are nice to you?"

"Nice? You sound like my big bad professor girlfriend, ready to pick a fight for me if they are not nice to me." Laura said warmly, her smooth as honey voice gliding over George like a hand caressing her body.

"Of course I would. No one picks on my baby. I miss you. How many more days to go?"

"Seven months, 28 days more to go. But who is counting right?" Laura sighed.

"See Baby, that's why we have a project together, keep our intellectual curiosity sparring with each other while we explore our mutual admiration of bodies." George replied.

"I like the way you think, Dr. Kaplan. But seriously, love I miss you so much. I didn't think just three months of absence from you would be so difficult. I do love you, darling." Laura said with heartfelt emotion, her voice conveying all that she felt.

"I miss you too, Baby, very, very much. It hasn't gone unnoticed in the department that I eat my meals alone and spend more time alone in my office than I normally would have while you were here. Besides, I know I am not going anywhere. I will be waiting for you to come home." George caressed the phone with her hand as she whispered her longing.

"I'm going to say goodnight now, love. I have a panel discussion tomorrow where I am moderating. Think of me in your dreams." Laura said.

"You know I will. Goodnight, my love. Sleep tight." George made a kiss over the phone as she hung up.

It was not easy being alone again when she realized how good it was to be together as a couple. Dinner was lonely and breakfast was lonely. Hell, who was she kidding, she was now in a worse state than she was before getting intimate with Laura. She was going to have to surprise Laura with a visit to her campus during one of the upcoming weekends.

"Dr. Kaplan, a word with you." Dean Marks called out to George as she was leaving the lecture theater.

"Yes, Dean?" George asked as she waited for him to catch up to her.

"I think I may have loaned out one of the best lecturers in our department for too long. Santa Clara now wants to extend Dr. Holt's stay." He was frowning as he said it.

"What? You can't, Dean. I mean she has tenure here and her classes too." George was clearly upset by the announcement.

"Walk with me to my office and we'll talk." Dean Marks took her arm as if to escort her.

George sat stiffly facing Dean Mark's desk. He shut the door and sat behind his desk.

"George, I know what Dr. Holt means to you," he explained as he saw her widen her eyes.

"Laura told me about your relationship before she left. She would not entrust her class to any other lecturer but you. So I am aware of what the news means for you both if Santa Clara makes her the offer to stay. I cannot stop her. The Dean over there and I are good friends, which is why I agreed to send her over when I received the call. But now, I have to consider what that will mean for our own program. I cannot afford to lose a lecturer of her standing. Her students love her. Can you talk to her?" He asked George.

"Henry, you know I won't jeopardize her career or worse, use our relationship to pressure her. I will let her broach the subject with me first." George offered.

"That is good enough, George, I can't ask you for more than that since I created the problem myself by being a Good Samaritan." Dean Marks acknowledged.

George was troubled. She was worried that Laura would seriously consider the offer and actually stay. But how could she stop her if she loved her? Would telling Laura not to accept the offer come back to hurt their relationship? George was not sure she was ready to take a chance on that. As she walked back to her apartment, she felt a vibration in her cellphone. She checked it and it was a text from Laura. It said, "Call me."

"Hey Babe, everything okay?" George tried to keep the worry out of her tone.

"I'm not sure, Georgie. Dean Philipps spoke to me today. He asked me to stay for an extra semester and wants to offer me a full time contract at the university." Laura paused and took a deep breath, "I don't know what to do."

"Do you want to stay?" George asked, her breath hitching as she waited for Laura's reply.

"I don't know yet. There is so much to consider, you, my house, my students. What do you think I should do? I want to know what you think." Laura wanted George to ask her to come back to Vermont. She needed to know where she stood with George in their relationship.

"You have to consider what this opportunity means for your career. You could be the head of department sooner rather than later if you accepted the offer. I can't make that decision for you." George averred she would not push Laura on this.

"Georgie, you do realize there are two of us in this relationship right? This is a big decision that will impact us. Do you want there to be an us, or not? We have to decide together." Laura pushed her.

"Laura, I cannot tell you to accept or not accept. This is your career. You have to make the choice. Yes I want there to be an us. It will be difficult with us being bicoastal but doesn't mean it can't be done. Many couples do that and still survive." George said, trying to be rational.

"I am not surviving this separation George. I am barely sleeping and when I do, I am in a constant state of arousal that it has become a chronic condition for me. No, I am not going to do this long distant thing for such a long time. We might as well not be in a relationship if it came to that." Laura's anger was palpable on the phone.

"What are you saying, Laura, you want to break up with me?" George was aghast. How did the conversation take such a turn?

"No, no, you're not listening. I am asking you, what do you want George? I need to know how you feel." Laura tried to calm herself. She was clearly getting wound up at not getting a clear answer from George.

"I don't have the right to tell you what to do Laura, that is what I am saying. I will support you and stand by whatever decision you make." George responded, giving the answer her head suggested instead of what her heart wanted to say. *No, don't take the contract come back to me.*

"Is that all you have to say to me George? I'm saying goodbye now. You don't get it." Laura hung up.

"Wait, don't." George yelled into the phone but Laura had already ended the call.

Shit! She thought. *What did I just do? I cut her loose without even trying to fight for her, fight for us.* She panicked. She had to get to Laura and explain herself in person before the misunderstanding damaged their relationship completely. She looked at her watch. It was only 7:30 p.m. and 4:30 p.m. in California. *I need to go see her tonight*, George was certain of that.

"Hello Mrs. Marks? Is Henry there? It's George Kaplan."

"George, hello." Dean Marks came on the line.

"Henry, I need to head to Santa Clara tonight...I screwed up royally. Can you cover for my lecture tomorrow please? I only have one class...Um...I will be gone for two to three days if need be...Yes, I am going to get her back, hence the flight now...Thanks I will need the luck. Bye."

George hurriedly packed a small duffle bag and went to her dresser looking for that jewelry box. She needed to give Laura a reason to come home and George could not think of a better one than the engagement ring she purchased last weekend. The thought of losing Laura to a contract on the West Coast sent her heart plummeting. She felt so nauseous. *I don't want to lose my love because I was afraid to fight for her, fight for us. I'm not afraid anymore.* She closed up her apartment and walked quickly to her car to drive to the airport.

※ ※ ※ ※

Laura's eyes were red from crying as she sat on the sofa with tissues strewn about. The call with George had sent her world off kilter. She had thought George would actually demand for her to come home and be with her. Had she misread their relationship so badly like?

The doorbell rang.

Laura looked at her watch. It was almost 10:00 p.m. *Who could that be?* The bell rang again, followed by urgent knocking. Laura wondered if it was one of her students in trouble. She quickly washed her face at the basin and wiped it dry with a paper towel. The door had a latch to it and Laura carefully opened the door and asked, "Who is it?"

"It's me, Baby. Let me in please." George looked disheveled with her hair finger combed and her clothes rumpled.

Laura threw open the door in surprise. George marched right in and dropped her duffle bag, using her back foot to close the door. She locked it from behind her, never taking her eyes off Laura.

"I am so sorry Baby for being an ass. Please forgive me." She said, holding Laura tightly in her embrace.

Laura wound her arms tightly around George's neck, as fresh tears seeped out.

"You're here. You came." She said softly in wonder.

"Yes, I came for you. I will always come for you. Don't ever doubt that please. I think some things are better said in person. I was miserable without you. Every single day, every single night, you were on my mind. I missed you so much. I love you so, so much. Don't accept the contract, darling. I have a better proposition for you." George said earnestly, as she searched in her pocket.

Holding the ring in her hand as she got down on one knee, with her other hand holding Laura's, George looked up at her, with love blazing in her eyes, she said,

"Laura Holt, you are the love of my life. I want to spend my every waking moment with you for the rest of my life. Will you make me the happiest woman in the world and be mine forever? Marry me, Laura."

Laura was openly crying now, but she managed a tremulous, "Yes, a thousand times, yes" as George stood up and placed the ring on her finger. She wiped her tears away tenderly and kissed her with gentleness. Laura laughed shakily as she looked at the ring on her hand. "My goodness, Dr. Kaplan, I leave you alone for a little while and you make these grand gestures. What happens when we are together for the rest of our lives?" Laura teased.

"Well, my love, you'll have to find out when we start the rest of our lives together. It's all academic, if I promise you the moon and the stars right now without us being on that journey together. What do you say? Ready for an adventure of a lifetime?"

"Absolutely. Let's start that adventure with a trip

to my bedroom." Laura led George by the hand down the hall to her bedroom.

Jules Worth is a budding author. She is presently a student with the Golden Crown Literary Society Writing Academy, class of 2016-2017. Jules lives in New Jersey. She works in Corporate America by day and moonlights as a writer by night.

Ten Hours

By C.d. Cain

Middle windowpane, combined seal and spacer with six seal alignment tabs. Outer windowpane, passenger window frame, held in place by window retaining clips…ten altogether.

Cassie stared out of the thick plastic. She was mentally clicking off each layer of the airplane's passenger window. Her eyes drifted down to the bottom of the window where the tiny hole was found.

"Breather Hole. That's a nice term for it." To say she hated to fly would be an understatement in every sense of the word. "I wish there was a tiny hole in my head to equalize my pressure."

"Excuse me?"

Cassie realized she had said that last bit out loud and turned to explain herself to the flight attendant.

"Oh, no. I'm sorry."

She paused when she noticed the woman standing beside the vacant seat next to her was not the attendant at all but rather a tall woman with long red hair that fell somewhere between ginger to classic red in color. Cassie shook her head.

"Sorry. I was mumbling out loud," Cassie said.

"Aw."

The woman reached her long arms up to tuck

away her carry-on bag into the overhead compartment. Cassie flashed back, recalling her own attempt at the same task being quite a bit more difficult at her five foot two stature.

Cassie turned her focus back to the window when the woman sat down next to her. It wasn't that she didn't want to talk. After all she was a proper southern woman raised by the finest example of the term. No southerner can ever be true to her upbringing and not carry on a full conversation with a perfect stranger. But today…on this flight…she simply didn't have it in her.

"So…" the woman said. She stopped her task of getting her MacBook, books and magazines organized around her to look at Cassie.

"Flying out of London for adventure or returning home?" Her voice was raspy and reminded her of Kathleen Turner.

"Returning home."

The woman shook her head as if in understanding—understanding that Cassie wasn't really in the mood for small talk.

"Were you here for business?" she said.

Or maybe she hadn't. "No." Cassie again looked out the window.

"Good afternoon, Ladies. May I offer either of you a pre-departure beverage?"

"Do we have time for that?" Cassie said nervously to the flight attendant.

"Yes ma'am we do. I have a variety of beverages to choose from." The flight attendant, Holly or so her name badge read, had an unwavering smile.

The woman who had claimed the seat looked back and forth between Cassie and the flight attendant as she said, "A drink would be wonderful, Holly. Can you tell me what wines you're serving today?"

"Yes ma'am. We have two California wines to choose from—a Stuhlmuller Chardonnay and a Freemark Abbey Cabernet. Both are excellent choices."

"I'll have the Cabernet," she said as she looked over at Cassie who still hadn't answered or even acknowledged a question had been directed her way.

Cassie's mind had not yet left the fact that they obviously had enough time left before takeoff to drink a glass of wine. Which meant she had even more time to be stuck in the metal tube known as an airplane, which was soon to be suspended thousands of miles in the air for what seemed like an impossible amount of time. No. She did not like flying.

Apparently realizing Cassie was at a loss for words, the woman took it upon herself, and ordered two glasses of Cabernet.

"Hope you like red because I think you could use it," the woman said.

Cassie felt the blush color her cheeks. She didn't embarrass easily but this was certainly reason if any. She was a grown-ass woman acting like a child at the pediatrician's office. She knew her face had the look she had become accustomed to seeing on the faces of children, when she entered the exam room. She shifted in her seat to face the woman.

"Red is perfect and you're absolutely right...I could use one. Or well ten—one for each hour of the flight."

The woman laughed and held out her hand.

"I'm Kendall."

"Cassie," she said.

Kendall's hand was deceptively soft. Cassie had to admit she had already noticed the woman's hands.

It was the first thing she generally noticed on a person she was meeting. Something about the hands always seemed to give a hint to the person that used them. When she saw Kendall's she had envisioned they would be dry if not a little coarse. She was mistaken. This hand was soft, warm and nearly perfect within hers.

"I take it you don't like flying." Kendall dropped her hand in her lap but kept her eyes focused on Cassie.

"That obvious is it?" she asked.

"Oh, just a wee bit."

The lines at Kendall's mouth were highlighted when she smiled. Cassie thought perhaps they were the same age. She too had begun to develop the nasty little lines at the corners of her eyes and mouth, not to mention what was going on with her neck. Nonetheless this woman wore them well. She truly was very attractive. It wasn't like Cassie was dead...divorced, yes—dead, no. There was a distinctive difference.

Holly brought them their wine, which allowed a pause in the conversation. Kendall pulled out her briefcase that mimicked a large handbag, put on black-rimmed eyeglasses that matched her linen shirt and began to deliberate over her folders. Yes, folders. She had the old style Manila chart folders once found in doctor's offices everywhere. Cassie settled deeper into the black leather first class seat and turned her attention back out of the window. To be honest, she wasn't the type of woman to choose first class in anything. It wasn't just the expense she probably shouldn't incur, but also the fact that she didn't believe in wasting money frivolously, a job hazard she had incorporated years ago. When it came to flying, first class was the best guarantee she would see no part of the wing. If her mind obsessed over the layers of the windowpane,

Lord knows what it would do with the number of bolts to each metal sheet found on the wing. *When on earth are we taking off?* The half drank glass of wine was not easing her anxiety and she wished the hell they would just take off already.

"You're starting to fidget again," Kendall said. She didn't raise her head from her papers as she looked from the side of her glasses.

"I am?" Cassie said. "Wait." She turned fully in her seat. "What do you mean again?"

Kendall laughed. "Again…as in repeatedly… as in once more. You know? Again." She tucked her hair behind her ear and smiled assuring Cassie of her playful nature. "Each time you drift off into that window, you fidget."

"I'm really not fond of flying."

"Yet here you are on a ten-hour international flight," Kendall said.

"There is that."

"I'm not usually one to repeat myself," she said.

Kendall pushed her glasses back off of her face taking her long hair with them as she studied Cassie. The setting sun shined in the small window and highlighted the lighter strawberry-blonde strands in her hair. It also gave a flash of light to her green eyes, which made the brown flecks all the more visible. Her ears were double pierced with small gold hoops and what looked to be one-karat diamond earrings.

Cassie instinctively twirled the white gold stud she wore in the second hole of her right ear. She rarely changed her earrings. As of late she seemed to find comfort in the known, even such small things as the same four earrings in her ears, studs—diamond and white gold.

"Yet you are about to repeat yourself?" Cassie said.

"Apparently, as I'm wondering what possessed a woman so terrified of flying to get on an airplane from London to Atlanta. My assumption is work, which means it must be one hell of a job."

"And why is that your assumption?"

"I would think if it were for pleasure and you were this afraid to fly then you would have someone with you. Yet..." Kendall fanned her hand across her lap. "Here I sit."

Cassie couldn't stop the smile playing at her lips.

"Here you do," said Cassie.

Cassie looked out of the window briefly as she debated on furthering the conversation. Yes, she could turn into the reclusive bitch she found herself to be as of late. Broken. Resentful. Disgruntled at life and how it seemed to have worked out for her. Or...she could tell herself she had the opportunity to possibly enjoy conversation with a wildly attractive woman who seemed articulate, intelligent and genuine. Qualities she had not found in the women of the few dates she had gone on over the last several months. *Few? Do three qualify as a few?*

"Oh good, ladies. It seems you're nearly done with your glasses of wine."

Holly, still wearing her smile, had one arm draped over the seat in front of them and the other reached for their wine glasses.

"I'll be making my preflight announcements soon."

"Do you think that smile is real or part of the job description?" Cassie had grown tired of Holly's smile.

Kendall crooked her head to the side to look at

Cassie.

"Well now…that's the first thing of substance you've said to me yet."

"Ladies and gentlemen, my name is Holly and I'm your chief flight attendant. On behalf of Captain Jackson and the entire crew, welcome aboard Delta Flight 242, nonstop service from London Heathrow Airport to Atlanta International Airport."

The flight attendant shifted her weight from her left to her right. Cassie couldn't see Holly's feet from her seat as Holly stood in the aisle next to the row of seats in front of her. She imagined her heels must kill her feet by the end of the day. She looked down at her own tan Chuck Taylors and was very thankful she had chosen them for her trip.

"Our flight time will be nine hours and fifty minutes. We will be flying at an altitude of thirty-two thousand feet at a ground speed of five hundred twenty-five miles per hour. At this time, please make sure your seat backs and tray tables are in their upright positions."

"Are you okay there?" Kendall interrupted Holly's near perfect repeat of the announcement Cassie had heard a week earlier when she made the flight to London. "You look a little pale."

"Mmm Hmm. I'm fine," Cassie said.

Cassie swallowed hard when the doors were pulled closed and the plane began to push back from the terminal. She felt herself start to perspire at the small of her back. It was cold against the leather seat.

Holly returned to stand at the front of the aisle.

"Ladies and gentlemen, I would like to direct your attention to the television monitors. We will be showing our safety demonstration and would like the next few minutes of your complete attention."

The screens on the chair backs in front of them turned on. Cassie was glued to the video. She didn't notice that Kendall had leaned across the armrest to be inches from her ear.

"You know, I don't think you're going to have to pass a test before you'll be let off the plane," Kendall said.

"Oh, yeah. Right."

Cassie ran her finger across the top of her lip to wipe away the beads of sweat that had formed there. She wasn't sure if it was the anxiety of the takeoff, which had sent a trail of chills up her spine to her neck or if it had been the sensation of Kendall's breath against her ear.

The plane continued to taxi with a few turns until it slowed to a stop. Cassie leaned her elbows across each armrest, and let her hands fall to grip the corners as she watched the runway lights flash in the twilight sky.

"Are you alright?" Kendall's face had genuine concern on it.

"Yes. I'm sorry I don't like the takeoff." Cassie bit her bottom lip. "Or well, the landing. And to be totally honest, I'm not overly crazy about the part in the middle of each either."

"So, basically you don't like flying," Kendall said.

Cassie forced a smile. "Basically."

She pushed her back into the seat as the plane began to speed down the runway. Her stomach flipped over itself as the plane accelerated and lifted into the air. She swore she heard every single nut and bolt shake loose from its positioning as they became suspended above the ground. She sucked in an audible breath when she not only heard, but also, felt a loud clank against the bottom of the plane.

Kendall's hand was warm as she touched the skin of her arm.

She said, "It's the landing gear. That's what you heard. They brought up the landing gear."

Cassie took in a deep inhalation as she nodded. She rested the back of her head against the seat and closed her eyes. Mentally willing herself to keep them closed until the plane had reached its altitude. She cursed herself for not having her ear buds in. The redhead next to her had surely distracted her from her prefight routine.

By the time Cassie opened her eyes the sky had become nearly black. The airplane's cabin was also darkened but for the tiny overhead lights that had been flicked on. Cassie watched Kendall unnoticed. Shadows hid the full detail of her face as their overhead lights had been left off. However, it didn't take much light to notice the tension in Kendall's jaw as she stared at her left hand and twirled the gold band on her ring finger. She would slip it up over her knuckle, twirl it some more and then slide it back into place. Married. How had Cassie not noticed this? Perhaps it was the whole metal tube suspended thirty-two thousand feet in the air thing? Absentmindedly, Cassie rubbed her thumb across her bare left ring finger. Sometimes she still imagined she felt the band that had been worn for more than fifteen years.

Cassie reached up to turn her light on. "According to Holly we have nearly ten hours to kill. Do you want to talk about it?"

"I'm sorry?" Kendall turned her light on.

Cassie looked down at Kendall's hand. Her

fingers were still clasped around the ring. "Do you want to talk about that?"

"Aren't you a mysterious woman?" Kendall gave a half smile. "A woman who's barely answered my questions is now asking me one…a personal one at that."

"I'd like to think it's related to oxygen deprivation," Cassie said.

"I do believe the airline designs the plane so that the pressure is equalized to prevent such a malady." Kendall rubbed her hands along the top of her thighs, patted them and then said, "You know what? Let's don't and say we did. I'd much rather we have pleasant conversation. Tell me what brought you to London."

"I thought we were going for pleasant conversation?" Cassie said.

"Aw. Okay." Kendall nodded. "Got it. I'll tell you why I was in London. Business not pleasure. I attended the International Society of Stem Cell Research annual meeting. It was an excellent meeting. I've been kind of pumped to get home and get back to work ever since it concluded."

"Atlanta is home?"

"No. San Diego," Kendall said.

Cassie gave a quizzical look to which Kendall replied while gesturing with her hands. "I actually won't get back home for another couple of days. I'm meeting a colleague at Emory. My focus is on stem cell therapy as treatment for cardiovascular disease, particularly with critical limb ischemia. Currently patients have limited options when it comes to that and the healthcare expense is astronomical. They start with stenting procedures, which leads to open grafts if they are lucky enough to be candidates. Sadly, the outcome for most is amputation which starts a whole cascade of adverse outcomes to include physical disability, poor wound healing, ulcers." Kendall shook her head. "So much. But with stem cell treatments we are seeing new blood vessels form that can perfuse the limb and prevent the need for those sort of things." She smiled broadly. "Anyway, he's doing a study I'm really interested in."

Cassie returned her smile. "I can't tell you how refreshing it is to meet someone who is passionate about their work. I was beginning to think we as a society had started to lose that. I struggle myself sometimes not to let the, it is what it is, take over."

Cassie pinched her lip wondering how much more she wanted to share. Her career was both the best and worst of her.

"I'm the Director of Health Promotion for the Georgia Department of Public Health. Atlanta is my home. I started out as a pediatrician. Had a pretty good practice actually when you consider the competitive market in a place like Atlanta. If only I could've left it like that but no...I had a calling."

Cassie used her fingers to make quotation marks in the air.

"I couldn't keep my attention on common colds and flus. My attention was on the child and the family that brought the child in. I began volunteering with a non-profit organization that supported free, sustainable healthcare programs internationally. Before I knew it, my passion had absorbed me and I was no longer in private practice."

"I think that's remarkable," said Kendall.

"Yes, well not everyone feels the same as you. My divorce is a prime example," said Cassie.

Kendall put her hand on Cassie's arm that had not yet been removed from the armrest. "I'm so very sorry."

"It's fine."

"Is it?" Kendall asked.

"It is now." Cassie said.

"Ladies, the Captain has turned off the Fasten Seatbelt sign so I can now offer you another glass of wine or beverage." Holly and her smile had returned.

Cassie looked at Kendall who gave a resounding bob of approval.

"Yes, please Holly. We'll each take another glass of the Cabernet," said Kendall.

"It took me several years to say it was fine." Kendall continued after Holly stepped away to question the other passengers of first class.

"On a happier note, I'm assuming your practice is in academics…research? Tell me about that." Cassie said.

"Not sure how much of a happier note that subject is. Here's where I falter. I work for Stem GenEx. Not in academic research—which would be my passion. Stem cell treatment is a lucrative practice for Stem GenEx. It affords me a living."

Kendall looked down and began to twist the wedding band around her finger again.

"A nice living. When I initially accepted a contract with them, I was told I would be able to invest the majority of my time in research projects. I thought a company like that would be better for my goals. You know…money on hand instead of having to apply and lose grants. Lately with my contract coming up for renewal, I've been thinking it's time for me to move on."

Kendall slid the ring over her knuckle, spun it again before sliding it back in place. "The CEO and Chairman of the Board are not at all happy with my desire to seek an academic position."

"I can understand they wouldn't want to lose you but does it really matter to your future choices what the CEO of the company thinks?" Cassie said.

"It does when she's your wife." Kendall said.

"Wife?" Cassie knew she hadn't done well with hiding the surprise in her tone.

"Yes. Is that a problem?" Kendall tucked her hair behind her ear and let her fingers linger in the strands as she brought it down along her neck.

Cassie watched intently. Even though her inner self wanted to moan a response of "Quite possibly," she managed to say a more appropriate reply. "No. Not at all." Knowing Kendall was a lesbian made her all the more uncomfortable.

"Here we are. Round two." Holly placed the glasses of wine on their tray tables. "Dinner service will begin in about an hour. Please don't hesitate to let me know if you should need any type of snack or wine refill."

Kendall may not have liked the perpetual smile on Holly's face but she had begun to thoroughly enjoy her impeccable timing for interruption.

"So your wanting to change jobs has put some tension between the two of you?" Cassie said.

"Oh, it's a wee bit more than that. I filed for divorce before I left for London. Apparently, we were on the same page as I heard from my lawyer while I was there that she's not contesting it. All it is at this point is deciding what goes where," Kendall said.

This time it was Cassie who reached for contact.

She placed her hand on Kendall's knee. "I'm sorry. I know how hard a divorce is."

"Yes," she paused, "and no. Even before all of the contract stuff, I realized we had grown too far apart." Kendall pinched the bridge of her nose. "This will probably make no sense at all but I felt entirely too lonely. Yet I had the perfect marriage."

"It makes complete sense. I've been single now for three years. Of course, I've felt loneliness in that time. When I want to see a movie or show. Take a walk in the park." Cassie gave a half-hearted smile. "Or international travel, and no one readily available to share that with. Yes, I've felt loneliness. But it can't compare to the loneliness I felt lying in bed and feeling utterly alone as I laid next to the one that I was to share the rest of my life with. Sure we did things. Sure we looked like the happy couple but put us alone within the four walls of our home and there were nothing between us. No conversation that sparked either one of us. No affection or passion to kiss each other silly. Lying in a bed you share with your lifelong partner without a hint of expressed love finally became too unbearable for me."

Kendall took in a deep breath and whispered, "I get it. I so get it. But tell me how is it you're still alone? You're such a beautiful woman with a magnetic personality. Hell, I thought they were sitting me next to Charlize Theron."

Cassie's laugh got away from her before she could suppress it. She quickly covered her mouth with her hand and hoped the blush of her cheeks wasn't apparent under the overhead lights. "Thank you. But I hardly look anything like her. She's gorgeous."

"Are you kidding me? The hair. Blue eyes. Body.

You could be her twin. There must be something seriously wrong with the men in Georgia."

"Or women."

Kendall moved back away from her as she looked at Cassie with surprise.

"Is that a problem?" Cassie asked.

"Quite possibly," she moaned in a low, hoarse voice.

The women stared at one another in the acknowledgement that any attractions they were feeling could be reciprocated. For the first time, it was Kendall who appeared nervous. She reached across Cassie's chest to cover the small hole found at the base of the window with her index finger.

"I've always wondered what this was for," Kendall said in a pale attempt at changing the subject.

She looked surprised when Cassie grabbed her hand and interlocked their fingers as she pulled Kendall's hand away from the window and said, "No. Please don't do that."

"Okay," Kendall said but didn't let go of Cassie's hand. "Mind telling me why?"

"That hole equalizes the pressure between the windowpanes."

"And you think that covering that little hole in the window with my finger may somehow alter the pressure?" Kendall said.

"It's plausible. Not highly likely but plausible." Completely unlike anything she's ever recognized in herself, Cassie let her thumb trail down the side of Kendall's hand. "I'm sort of enjoying this flight a little too much to want it to go down in flames at the moment."

Kendall's smile stretched into a wide grin. "So

am I."

The two women shifted in their seats with their knees bent and bodies facing one another as they chatted. The meal service came and went. Glasses of wine were poured and drank. Overhead lights were turned off and on as the other passengers slept and awakened. Neither woman felt tired or desired sleep. They talked. They shared. They cried. They laughed. Lost in their unexpected connection the hours passed by as if they were mere seconds. For much of it their hands remained touching. Fingers intertwined in a near perfect fit, fingers sliding along the sides of the other, tracing the inside of the each other's wrists. The dance of their touch seemed benign yet both women knew it to be much more than that.

Kendall closed her eyes as her finger traced further up Cassie's arm. Her perfectly curved lips let out a slow exhale. "Cassie?"

"Mmmm Hmmm." Cassie rolled her arm over to allow Kendall's fingers passage to the break at her elbow.

"I can't tell you the last time I felt touched so intimately and all we've done is hold hands," Kendall whispered.

"We've done more than that." Cassie trailed her finger along the back of Kendall's arm as it lay across her own.

"Far more than that." She brought Kendall's finger up to her lips, slowly ran the tip of it across her bottom lip and kissed it lightly.

"You've touched my soul...awakened me to possibility—to hope." She left Kendall's finger against her lips as she talked. "Maybe I can feel again. Care for someone again. Let them in past these walls." With the words spoken, fear began to trickle in.

"Ditto." Kendall said while she ran her free hand through her hair, squeezing at the roots. "I'm in Atlanta for a few days. Would it be entirely crazy to ask you to go to lunch or maybe even dinner?"

Cassie looked out of the window.

"It wouldn't be crazy at all but would it be smart?" She gestured between them. "If this intensity is felt between us within the first..." she said as she looked down at her watch, "nine and a half hours of meeting, what are we setting ourselves up for if we meet again?"

"Happiness?" said Kendall.

"Ladies and gentlemen, as we start our descent, please make sure your seat backs and tray tables are in their full and upright position."

Holly. Cassie thought. *Damn her and her interruptions.*

The women finished the flight in silence. Cassie's thoughts were a rapid succession of firing arguments with herself. She had accepted being alone. She had accepted the fact that love had not been meant for her—not a real love. She'd been so distracted in her thoughts she hadn't noticed the plane had landed until the cabin was fully illuminated. Kendall's beauty in full light nearly took her breath. She watched her as she packed up each of the materials she had carefully laid out hours before. Materials Kendall never looked at during the flight.

Kendall looked at Cassie with a smile that did not reach her eyes.

"Well, I suppose this is it." She stood to open the overhead bin compartment and pull down her bag. She extended her hand to Cassie. "Saying it was a pleasure to meet you doesn't at all fit what I'm feeling right now."

Cassie took her hand and shook it lightly. "It was beyond anything that can be described in words."

"Yes. It was that." Kendall said.

Holly spoke to Kendall as she exited the plane and disappeared from Cassie's sight. She watched several passengers pass her before patting her blue jean-clad thighs. "It is what it is," Cassie mumbled to herself.

Holly grabbed Cassie's elbow as she walked past her. "It was a pleasure being a part of whatever happened between you two tonight. I've read of things I witnessed tonight but Lord knows I never thought I'd see it in real life."

"Oh yeah? And what was that?" Cassie said.

"Love at first sight. True love. Authors write stories about what happened tonight on Delta Flight 242."

Cassie smiled as she tried to choke down the lump that was forming in her throat. She walked with heavy footsteps down the jetway wondering what in the hell she had done turning down Kendall's offer for lunch. She cursed herself for her stupidity in keeping up her defenses—always afraid of being hurt again. She thought for a moment of running to catch Kendall.

"Cassie?"

Cassie turned to see Kendall. Kendall let go of the bag she held in her hand and took two quick steps toward Cassie until she was inches from her face. Without words she slid her hand along the side of Cassie's neck until her fingers were buried in her hair. She pulled her closer until their lips touched. Cassie dropped her bag and wrapped her hands around Kendall's waist to pull her in even closer. Their lips melted into one another's. Their mouths parted, deepening their kiss allowing the softness of their tongues to sweep Cassie into a world without walls...without defenses. She became both disoriented and found in Kendall's kiss. She couldn't pull Kendall in tight enough against her. Her hands roamed up and down her back, into her hair, along her neck and face. Anywhere she could touch she tried to touch.

Kendall broke the kiss but left her forehead against Cassie's.

"I'm a mature, responsible, well-educated woman who has always had a level head on her shoulders."

She caressed the side of Cassie's face with her hand and left her thumb to linger along her bottom lip that was still tingling from their kiss.

"It's crazy. Insane even. This can't be the end of us. Yeah so I live on the other side of the U.S. but this is the first time I've felt something this real. I need this to be a beginning—not an end."

No walls. No barriers. No defenses. Cassie smiled before answering Kendall with another kiss.

Love at first sight—a first love.

C.d. Cain writes to tap into her reader's emotions while bringing them the beauty, culture and characters of the south. When It Raynes was a finalist in the Rainbow Awards and the GCLS Ann Bannon Popular Choice Award. It Pours, won in last year's General Contemporary Fiction in the Rainbow Awards.

Fragile Attachment

By Rowan Avery

Ann stood by the window, phone pressed to her ear. Her mouth stretched into a warm, loving smile and she laughed softly.

"Oh Dell, I love you, so much," she whispered. "I can't wait to see you this weekend." Ann turned away from the window and pulled out a suitcase from under the bed.

"Yep, I've got it here," she said into the phone. "You don't think it's silly, do you? I mean it's Monday. We'll be seeing each other Friday." Ann unzipped the case and flipped up the cover.

"I'm holding it now," she said. Ann cradled the phone between her shoulder and left ear and held up a small purple vibrator. She was tempted to use it, had been tempted to since she'd bought it three days ago but wanted to wait until she was with Dell. This was something she bought for both of them to share and she didn't want to use it until they were together. Keeping it in the suitcase helped minimize the temptation but didn't remove it. It had been five weeks since they'd been together and Ann's body was aching. She craved Dell's touch, had since the moment they'd met.

"It's small, but not too small," Ann said, describing the vibrator. "The silicone covering has a lovely silky feel. Do you want me to turn it on?"

Ann cradled the phone again and pressed the silver button at the one end and the vibrator began to gently buzz in her hand.

"The clerk at the store said it has five settings. Different vibration frequencies." Ann pressed through the options.

"I don't, know, I think I like the one that starts slow then increases speed and drops off to start slow again. I think it would be a nice tease." Ann laughed and her cheeks flushed pink.

"I can't," Ann whispered. She looked out the window, watched a car move down the street then looked at the closed bedroom door. She was alone in this room but not in the house. "I'm at my brother's house and everyone is home right now."

She'd used this excuse before. When they were living together, Ann felt no need to touch herself when they were apart but since she took on this contract and was away more than she was home, things were different. Ann knew Dell was only suggesting it because she couldn't at this moment meet Ann's needs. But Ann didn't want to. Thinking of it felt strange. She'd masturbated thinking of Dell before, that wasn't the problem. It was having sex, masturbating while Dell listened on the phone that made Ann feel strange. What if she really liked it? What if this is what their relationship became?

Ann heard footsteps approaching and turned towards the bedroom door.

"I have to go," she said into the phone. She hated hearing the sadness in her own voice. She wanted to always be the one positive voice in Dell's life. She wanted to always be a comfort to her lover.

"I'll call you before I go to sleep," Ann whispered. Sometimes whispering hid the sadness but not this time. She wiped a tear from her cheek.

"Yes, even if you don't answer, I will leave you a voicemail."

"I know, Dell. I like waking up to voicemails from you as well,"

"I love you, my sweet."

There was a knock on the door just as Ann hung up. She looked briefly at the phone before dropping it on the bed and heading downstairs for dinner with her brother. She loved him and loved his family but liked it so much better when she had been able to visit with Dell. It had been over a year since she and Dell had come up to her brother's for a visit. This wasn't a visit and didn't feel like it. She felt like an outsider without Dell by her side.

She had six more months on this contract. Her brother gave her an open invitation to stay with him until the job was done. His oldest was off to university and only came home for holidays and Ann made sure to go home, to be with Dell for all holidays. It worked and she had to admit, having family around took away some of the loneliness. It did nothing to alleviate Dell's solitude. Dell had no one other than the few friends they'd made. They visited Dell occasionally but they had their own responsibilities and neither Dell nor Ann expected them to make visiting a regular part of their lives.

When they decided Ann would take the contract—they desperately needed the money—they both had agreed Ann would only come home once a month. And they'd stuck to it, building a schedule around the various holidays. Sometimes it was five weeks between visits but other times it was three. Each time Ann came home, she waited for Dell to ask her not to leave again. To beg her to stay, money be damned. She knew they couldn't do it, but she desperately wanted to hear that need in Dell.

Each time Ann came home she wanted to tell Dell she didn't want to leave again. She wanted to plead with her, to work out some other arrangement that wouldn't keep her so far from the woman she loved. But she knew she couldn't. Ann needed to work this contract. They needed it to survive.

Ann liked living with her brother. On the weekends she would help him finish the basement. In the evenings they would plan out where the rooms would be and research DIY toilet installation and plumbing and electrical. All things she wanted to do with Dell but hadn't had the chance. All things she hoped they would be able to do one day.

❧❧❧❧

Friday morning Ann loaded her suitcase in her car. She said goodbye to her nieces and nephew and promised to take them for ice cream when she came back on Sunday. Home, they said. She smiled to herself. For them, yes, but for her, home was always with Dell, no matter where they were. But she liked that they liked having her around. This was one positive to come out of her separation from Dell.

The drive was uneventful but work had taken longer than she anticipated and it was much later than Ann had planned when she was finally on the highway headed home. She tried calling Dell but received voicemail. Unusual. It worried Ann.

Ann stopped once on her drive, for gas and

something to eat. It would be too late when she got in to share a meal with Dell. Anxious to see Dell, she ate quickly and tried calling again. There was still no answer. This was worrying. She ran her hand over her face, cleaned up her meal, and tried to ignore the growing pain in her head. The last thing she wanted was a migraine.

At six minutes past eleven, Ann pulled up to the building and slipped into the first vacant parking spot. She grabbed her purse from the front seat and decided she would wait until morning to bring in her suitcase. She'd just be crawling into bed with Dell anyway.

The receptionist greeted her quietly as Ann entered the building. She waved her response and turned towards the elevators. It was too late and she was too tired to take the stairs. Minutes later she stood outside the door to Dell's room. It was dark but there was a little light on in the corner and Ann could see the slow rise and fall of Dell's chest as she breathed. The room smelled clean and there was a carpet on the floor that hadn't been there the last time Ann had been home. She made a note to ask Dell about it in the morning.

Teeth brushed and dressed in one of Dell's T-shirts, Ann quietly slipped into bed beside Dell. She kissed her on the forehead then curled against her side, arm across Dell's waist, and fell asleep.

"Good morning, Ann," a woman's voice woke her. Not Dell. She opened her eyes to find Dell gone from the bed. She looked around the room, trying to find her lover in the small space.

"She went down for treatment about half an hour ago," the woman, Nurse Maggie said, answering Ann's unasked question. A wave of sadness came over her. When had she become so comfortable sleeping on her own that she no longer missed the presence of Dell?

"She's doing alright," Maggie said. "It's been a rough week but she's going to come through it just fine." Maggie pushed the bed curtain aside and checked the readout from the monitor, tearing off the small paper graph and attaching it to the clipboard she carried in her left hand.

"Yesterday was the worst." Maggie wrote something in Dell's chart then smiled at Ann. "She didn't say anything but I could tell the pain was horrific. She's a strong woman."

Ann sat up and swung her legs out of bed. She needed to be with Dell, to hold her, comfort her. She felt a hand on her shoulder before she could stand.

"Dell wanted you to have an easy morning," Maggie instructed. "She'll be back in about fifteen minutes, relax in bed. The food cart will be by at 8:30 and Dell made sure they had French toast for you. She'll be back in time for you two to have breakfast in bed." She smiled at Ann then gave her shoulder a pat.

Ann didn't know what to do. She hated Dell going through treatment alone, hated not being there to comfort her lover, hated being away when she wanted nothing more than to be next to her partner. She rose from the bed and slipped on her jeans. This wasn't right. This wasn't how it was supposed to be. They were supposed to always be together.

Looking around the room she struggled to decide what to do next. A noise behind her startled her. Ann jumped and turned to find Dell rolling towards her, an orderly pushing the silent wheelchair. She burst into tears. The last time they had been together, just five weeks ago, Dell had been able to walk. Now she looked thin and pale and wasted. Ann could feel the exhaustion emanating off Dell. She placed a hand over her mouth and started sobbing.

"It's ok, my love, it's ok," Dell soothed. She felt a hand on her back and opened her eyes. Dell was now standing beside her. Ann hesitated only a moment then wrapped herself around Dell's frail body. She tried not to squeeze too hard but she needed desperately to hold Dell, to feel her body in her arms. She remembered how Dell's body had felt before she got sick, soft and warm against Ann's muscles and bones. She ached to feel that health again.

"I'm so sorry," Ann whispered into Dell's hair. Sorry you're sick, sorry I'm not there for you, sorry I'm not the one sick in your place, she thought.

"It's better," Dell said. Though her body was frail, Ann heard strength in Dell's voice. She pulled back and looked Dell in the eye.

"This was a bad one but it's better. I'm getting better," Dell said with a smile. Ann studied her face.

"Honestly," Dell said. She laughed lightly. "The doctor said it would get bad before it got better." She took Ann's hand and led her to the bed. They sat down, side by side, Dell rubbing Ann's back. Ann closed her eyes and leaned in to Dell. They were quiet for a moment and Ann could feel the stress of the drive and the worry and the uncertainty slowly ebbing.

Dell kissed Ann's hand. "That was the bad, my love. It just gets better from here."

Rowan Avery, a graduate of the GCLS writing academy, has had a love affair with words for most of her life. Though she spent most of her career in the technical world, Avery has recently left to pursue writing full-time. Avery lives in Canada, but she's dreaming of warmer climates.

A Caramel Macchiato with a Friend

By Lila Bruce

I'm sorry, but I'm having a caramel macchiato with a friend right now."

"What?"

"Did I speak too fast? It's simple…you look at her and say, I'm sorry, but I'm having a caramel macchiato with a friend right now.'"

I cocked an eyebrow at the LCD monitor in the center of my Toyota's dash, looking at the rectangular screen as if it was the face of my best friend Katy. I opened my mouth to speak, but quickly closed it into a frown as I caught a glimpse of a faded blue Ford Explorer abruptly crossing over into my lane. Swearing under my breath, I braked just in time to avoid slamming into its heavily rusted rear bumper.

It was a struggle to keep the irritation out of my voice. "I heard what you said the first time," I said, white-knuckling the steering wheel. "It just doesn't make any sense."

"How do you mean?"

"Katy, that just sounds…" I was honestly at a loss for words. "Ridiculous."

"What's ridiculous about it?" came the deeply Southern, slightly shrill reply over the sedan's Bluetooth system. "I told you…" Katy gave an aggravated sigh.

"You didn't hear a word I said, did you?"

Actually, I had only been half-listening to my best friend drone on as I drove, my thoughts focused on my destination. It wasn't until I had turned off the interstate and into congested traffic running parallel to a shopping center that what she was saying registered.

Katy heaved a sigh before continuing. "Seriously, Lauren, you kill me sometimes. I saw this whole thing on a television show the other day—*Mornings with Morgan*, I think it was—anyway, the security expert they had on said that when getting together with a stranger you've met online for the first time, in addition to meeting at a public place, you should also arrange to have a friend call. That way, if you're getting a bad vibe or the person isn't what they said they were—that kind of thing—you say that an emergency has come up at home and leave."

"Katy—"

"But, if things are going well," she continued, seemingly oblivious to the threatening tone of my voice, "then you say a code word or phrase that means you want to stay and get to know the person better. For meetings at coffee shops, they suggested saying 'I'm sorry, but I'm having a caramel macchiato with a friend right now'."

"I'm not meeting a stranger, Katy," I said, shaking my head. "I'm meeting Dana."

"Who is a stranger."

"Who is someone I've known for months," I countered quickly, maybe a little too quickly. This wasn't the first time we'd had this particular conversation and, now that the idea of meeting the woman I'd met online was becoming reality, I had to admit I was getting a little antsy. Not that I'd tell Katy that.

"Chatting with someone online is not really knowing them, Lauren. For all you know, Dana—" I could all but hear the air quotes as Katy said the name— "is actually some fifty-year-old perv who drives a white van and lives down by the river."

"I've done more than just chat with her online, thank you. I talk to her over Skype all the time. I assure you, she's not some creepy old guy." She's far from it, actually. I smiled as an image of Dana popped into my mind.

It'd been almost three months since we'd connected. After a series of dead end dates, I had decided to take the plunge into the online dating pool. Okay…maybe not so much plunge as dip my big toe. I more or less lurked for the first few weeks, reading profiles and scrolling through pictures of women who lived within a five hundred mile radius. Even though I've always been outgoing, I found myself feeling… well, awkward about the entire process. What should I say so as not to come off as being lame or just plain weird? And then there was that seed of self-doubt— what if I made the first move only to be met by silence?

That's not to say I didn't have any interaction with other members of the dating site. Almost immediately after joining, I'd gotten several waves. That's what the site called it when you were attracted to another member. Under each profile picture was a tiny hand that, when clicked, would send a wave to that person from you as a means of saying hello. Unfortunately, the bulk of the waves sent my way were from either straight couples looking for a third to party with or from women who were way more into kink than I ever thought about being.

Way more.

I mean, okay, who doesn't like the occasional bedroom toy to liven things up? I'm as up for that as much as the next gal. But some of things these girls were talking about.

Quick piece of advice—when a woman who's wearing a leather bustier and little else in her profile pic asks if you are into something that you've never heard of before, do not go and Google said thing. Definitely do not choose the see images option of said thing. All I'm saying is that I may never look at a fig newton in the same way again.

Beyond that, just sex was not what I was looking to find on the dating site. Hell, if I wanted that, then I'd have just stayed with my last girlfriend. No, I wanted a relationship with someone who was attractive, shared my common interests, and had a good personality. You know—the Rainbow Unicorn.

Now, I did receive some waves from a handful of—for lack of a better word—vanilla women who were looking for the same thing I was. After a few messages back and forth, though, it was clear that none of them were my unicorn.

Dana's profile had been one of the first to draw my attention and one that I found myself coming back to night after night. I think it was her username that initially drew my attention. I'd seen so many SexyGurl69 and ImaAnimalLover type usernames that hers—Amalthea—stood out. That and the way she smiled in her picture. It was the kind of smile that took over her whole face, from the curl of her lips to the glint of humor reflected in her green eyes. It was the kind of smile that you wanted to be on the receiving end of.

Not that her smile alone was enough to get me over the fear of doing anything other than lurk. No, it was actually my cat, Mister Pickles that made the first move. I'd been up late one night eating ice cream, listening to my Mary Lambert playlist on Spotify, and browsing through the dating site, when Mister Pickles decided my laptop's keyboard looked more comfortable than his side of the couch. It was about a second after I'd extricated him from the keyboard that I realized one of his paws had hit the mouse pad and waved at Dana. I panicked, started hitting buttons on the keyboard like I was a roadside chicken, and then went into a cold sweat as I realized there was no way to un-wave.

And then she waved back.

Then she messaged, to which I messaged back. Messages turned into email, emails into phone calls. Over the past month, we'd taken to talking over Skype. Last week we agreed that it was time to move to the next step, and picked out a spot that would be halfway for each of us. And so, there I was—at the end of a thirty-minute drive to a shopping center just outside of Birmingham.

"So, maybe she's got a partner," Katy said, dragging my thoughts back to the ridiculous discussion we were having. "Like on one of those shows on the Discovery Channel? You know...*Killer Couples* or *Unsolved Mysteries* or one of those."

"The only unsolved mystery here is why I'm still having this conversation," I muttered, spotting the large green and white sign that marked my destination. I clicked the switch for the blinker and turned in the parking lot, pulling into an empty parking space near the front of the coffee shop.

"Look, I've spent fifteen years training you—"

This little tête-à-tête was going to give me permanent frown lines. "Training me?"

"Yes, trainin' you," Katy continued, her southern drawl becoming more pronounced. "And I'm not in the mood to go lookin' for a new best friend to whip into shape because you just had to meet this chick you found on the internet." She humphed. "I still don't get why you couldn't have hooked up with someone the normal way, like I did,"

I switched off the Toyota's ignition, taking the Bluetooth with it. I retrieved my cell from the cup holder and brought it up to my ear. "You mean in frozen food section of Kroger?"

"Lauren..."

"Look, Katy, as hard as it may be to wrap your lovely little heterosexual mind around this, there's not a plethora of lesbians in our little corner of Alabama," I said, in what may have been the understatement of the year.

"A plethora? Is that what they call a group of lesbians? I thought it might be maybe something like a crew or a flannel," she said with an audible smirk. "Yeah...I can totally see that. A flannel of lesbians."

"I'm hanging up now"

"Okay, that was out of line," she said, having the good grace to sound apologetic. "But seriously, you're my best friend. I'm just lookin' out for you."

"I know you mean well." Groaning, I threw my head back onto the headrest. "All right, I'll go along with your nonsense..." Lord, the things I let her talk me into. "I don't drink caramel Frappuccino's. Don't you think it'll be odd if I say I'm drinking something that I'm not?"

"I said macchiato, not Frappuccino."

"I don't drink that either," I answered, squinting as I tried to make out the faces of the people sitting scattered around the dozen or so tables outside of the coffee shop. I didn't recognize any of them as belonging to Dana. A quick glance back at the LCD monitor in the center of the dash told me I was a few minutes early for our meeting.

"Well, what do you drink?"

"I don't know," I shrugged. "Just coffee."

"Oh, good lord." Katy's voice was taking on that shrill tone again. "You cannot seriously be meeting this girl for the first time—at a ten dollar coffee shop no less—and planning on ordering a plain ol' boring coffee."

"A minute ago you were calling her a serial killer, and now you're afraid that I'm going to embarrass myself in front of her?"

"A minute ago I thought you had good sense."

If I hadn't spent close to an hour on my hair that morning, I would have pulled it out. As it was, I settled for a deep eye roll. "Katy—"

"Don't Katy me," came the terse reply, cutting me off. "You are not going to roll in there like country come to town and order a plain coffee." There was a brief silence in which I could hear her making a tapping sound, and then she continued, "You'll order a latte."

"I don't drink—"

"I don't care what you like to drink, Lauren. You're going to act like a civilized person and order a latte. A French vanilla latte, at that."

I glanced down at the clock again. It was a few minutes after eleven and no sign of Dana. Trying to ignore the tension that was building up in my shoulders,

I ran through our last conversation in my head. Eleven o'clock sharp was the time we'd agreed on, and I knew that I'd come to right place. I scanned the front of the café again, and then the parking lot. Nothing.

"Fine, I'll order a French vanilla latte." Too late I realized that I had snapped the words out.

"Okay." There was the slightest hesitation in Katy's voice. "Well…I'll let you go."

Damn. Shaking my head, I blew out a long breath. Katy had been my best friend since middle school and while she could be a little overbearing at times, I knew she meant well. With every passing second the dread that Dana was going to be a no show grew more and more, but that wasn't Katy's fault.

"I really appreciate you watching out for me," I said, softening my tone.

Katy took the olive branch that I was dangling. "I know you think I'm crazy, but those things do happen, Lauren. I want you to meet this girl and have a good time, but just be careful."

"I know and I will. I'm here now, so I better be going."

"Okay, have fun and be listening for my call."

"Yes, ma'am." The call with Katy ended. I leaned back into the leather seat, closed my eyes, and took a deep breath to steel my nerves. Worst case scenario, this had all been some sort of elaborate catfish and Dana—or whatever her real name was—was a thousand miles away laughing with her friends right now. If that were the case, then I'd just treat myself to a coffee and then hit the mall across the street for some therapeutic shopping. Of course, I could never tell Katy the truth of what happened. I'd have to make up some story about—

The sound of my cell phone buzzing cut into my thoughts. I picked the phone back up from the cup holder where I'd dropped it after hanging up with Katy and looked at the screen to see that I had a text message.

Biting my lower lip in anticipation, I tapped the icon. It was from Dana.

"Hey sweets just pulled up."

I smiled and shook my head, berating myself for being so quick to assume the worst.

"Just got here myself," I texted back." Meet you out front."

I tossed my keys and the phone into the small canvas messenger bag that sat beside me on the passenger seat. After a quick check in the rearview mirror confirmed my hair was in place, I stepped out of the car. I threw my bag over one shoulder and brushed off the wrinkles from the front of my polo shirt.

I had taken two, maybe three steps toward the coffee shop when I heard my name. Recognizing the low, slightly husky sound of Dana's voice, I quickly looked around, eager to finally meet the woman who had come to consume my thoughts day and night.

"Lauren," the voice said again.

I turned in its direction and found myself face to face with a balding, slightly overweight man climbing out of a white van. I felt a presence behind me and then a hand seized my arm. The opening scene of every *Criminal Minds* episode I'd ever watched flashed through my head just before I gripped the strap of my messenger bag and slung it behind me as hard as I could. The bag hit with a thump, followed by a loud yelp. Spinning around, I reared back to deliver a second blow to my attacker only to see Dana crouching next to the bumper of my Toyota, her arms shielding her head in the universal please-don't-hit-me position. A movement caught the corner of my eye and I looked back over my shoulder to see that the man in the white van was now helping what looked to be his elderly grandmother out of the vehicle's side door and into a wheelchair. Both threw me a look like they thought I was a lunatic—probably because that's what I was right then.

"Oh my God, Dana," I exclaimed, falling to my knees beside her. "Are you okay? I am so sorry! I saw the guy in the van and then felt someone grab me and then, you know, killer couples and—" Realizing that I was babbling, I bit down hard on my lower lip to shut myself up.

Dana lowered her hands a fraction of an inch and peeked up at me like she wasn't quite sure if she stay put or run as far and as fast as she could.

"Let me try that again," I said in what I hoped was a more serene voice. "The man getting out of the van over there," I bobbed my head in his direction, "looked sketchy. Then when I felt you touch my arm, it startled me and I…uh, overreacted."

Dana tilted her head to look past me and then, after a long minute, said, "No, it's my fault. I shouldn't have come up behind you the way I did."

I rose to my feet and offered a hand out to her. "What do you say I help you up and we start this whole thing over?"

She nodded, her long fingers curling around mine. "Sounds like a plan."

"Wonderful," I said, pulling on Dana's hand to help her stand. Pushing against the Toyota's bumper for extra leverage, she rose from the ground.

And rose.

And rose. And kept rising.

The funny thing about internet dating is that you never actually see the person. I mean, sure, you can view their profile pictures and whatever photos they share on their social media pages. But you don't really see them. Even on Skype, you're really only talking to a head and upper torso, so it's hard to get a gauge for things like, for instance, whether or not the woman you're speaking to could in reality pass for the Jolly Green Giant.

Well that's not right.

As Dana reached her full height, towering nearly a foot above my relatively diminutive five-foot-three, I was suddenly struck by how goddamn gorgeous she looked in person. I tried not to gawk—or at least be obvious about it. Standing there in the parking lot, casually dusting off the knees of her otherwise crisp khaki pants, Dana could have passed for a supermodel. Like Elle Macpherson only…well, butchier. Her blonde hair was cut short, as usual, and fell in a curl just above the collar of her plaid button-down shirt. A breeze passed us and I caught the faint scent of sandalwood and roses.

I noticed then that she seemed to be taking an extra long time brushing the asphalt from her khakis. Catching the movement of her eyes, I realized that she was trying to subtly size me up. I wondered if—hoped really—she liked what she saw, and threaded a self-conscious hand through my hair.

"So," she said, running her hands over the front of her pants one last time, "what do you say we go inside and I buy you a coffee?"

"That sounds wonderful. But," I added, beginning

to walk toward the entrance of the coffee shop, "why don't you let me buy you a coffee? It's the least I could do for, uh…"

"Playing Whack-a-Mole with my head?" she said lightly, her lips curling up into a grin. Witnessing her face light up into a smile in person, with her eyes dancing as they looked down at me, almost took my breath away.

Well…it was either that, or the curb I chose that particular moment to trip over.

"Oh my God, Lauren, are you okay?" I heard a second after my face hit the warm concrete. Surprising strong hands wrapped around my shoulders and helped me back on my feet.

"No, no, I'm good," I rushed out in a croaking voice. I wasn't sure what was burning hotter right then—my cheeks or the now skinless area of my palms.

"Are you sure?" The bridge of her nose crinkled into a cute little worry line.

"Oh yeah." I hoped I sounded more convincing than I felt. "Just fine."

"Okay," she said, sounding colossally unconvinced, "if you say so."

Dana held the door to the coffee shop open for me as we stepped inside. Probably to make sure I didn't go crashing through it.

"So, how was your drive?" Dana said as we stood in line at the register, her eyes darting back and forth between the overhead sign displaying coffee prices and me.

"It was fine," I answered, feeling my nerves finally beginning to compose. "Yours?"

"Good," she nodded. "Traffic got a little heavy once I got into Birmingham, but otherwise it wasn't bad at all." Dana looked awkwardly at me, and then crossing her arms, turned her full attention to the register display.

Shifting from one foot to the other, I nodded back. Wonderful, I thought, trying to ignore the throbbing in my skinned-up hands. After months of emails, phone calls, and text messages, I'd finally met the woman of my dreams in person, only to have nothing outside of traffic patterns to talk about. What would be next—the weather?

"It's a beautiful day today, isn't it?"

I smiled the sort of smile that you force yourself to when all you really want to do is laugh at a situation. Or cry at it, or maybe both.

"Sure is," I chirped and gestured toward the front window of the shop. "We should sit outside at one of those tables."

She nodded as we finally made it to the front of the line. Dana ordered an iced coffee and, with Katy's voice running through my head, I asked for a French vanilla latte. After paying for our drinks, we stepped away from the register.

"I don't think I've ever had one of their vanilla lattes," Dana remarked as we crossed over to the, pick your drink up here area of the counter. "Are they good?"

Honestly, I'd never had a latte—vanilla or otherwise—in my life. "Mmhmm," I answered in what I hoped was a convincing voice. "The best."

"I'll have to try it sometime, then."

I gave a noncommittal nod and looked around the room, hoping to change the subject. It really wasn't anything more than a little white lie, but it was a lie nonetheless. That's not how I wanted to begin our first date. Although, at the rate that I was going, the odds of there being a second date were looking slim.

I noticed the barista sliding our drinks across the counter and stretched across it to retrieve them. "Oh look, there's our order. Here, let me gets yours."

"No, I can get it," she said, reaching for the drink I already had in hand. I saw what was going to happen, but it was too late to stop it. My elbow collided with her arm, the impact jarring loose the cup's thin plastic lid. A tsunami of iced coffee crashed across the blue and white design of her shirt.

"Oh my gosh, Dana!" The words spilled out of my mouth as what little that remained of the chilled drink splattered to the ground along with the plastic cup. I grabbed a handful of napkins from the counter and started dabbing furiously at her shirt.

"Lauren."

"I don't know how that happened." I wiped harder, but only succeeded in grinding little bits of shredded white napkin into the wet, ruined mess that was now Dana's shirt. "Oh damn, I'm so sorry," I said, continuing my futile efforts.

"Lauren," she repeated, her fingers closing around my wrist to pull my hand away. "It's okay." Trying not to burst into tears, I looked up at her. Somehow, she was smiling. "Really."

I swallowed and then croaked, "Okay."

Dana motioned toward the outdoor tables. "Why don't you find us a seat while I go in the restroom and cleanup?"

I was fairly sure that was code for, "Why don't you go that way while I go this way in search of a back door to escape through," but simply nodded and made my way outside. Just as I walked out of the building, I heard my cell phone begin to ring from inside my bag. Recognizing Katy's ringtone, I dug the phone out and slumped into a chair at one of the empty tables on the patio.

"Hey," I mumbled, propping an elbow on the table.

"How's it going?" Katy whispered from the other end of the line. "Are you alone? Can you talk? Do you need rescuing?"

"Yes, I'm alone. Yes, I can talk. And, no, I'm not the one that needs to be rescued." I glanced over into the parking lot and, somewhat surprisingly, saw no signs of Dana driving away. She must've still been looking for the back door.

"I don't understand," Katy said. "Is it going well, or not?" Katy made an exasperated sound. "Lauren, you're supposed to use the code phrase if you like her and want to stay to get to know her better, remember?"

I sighed and rested my forehead on the bruised, aching palm of my hand. "Is there a code phrase for unmitigated disaster, Katy? Because that's what this has been."

"What? What's happening?"

"I've screwed this up royally, that's was happening." Seeing Dana step outside onto the patio, I sat up in the chair. "I'll call you back on the drive home and tell you all about it." Not waiting for Katy's reply, I ended the call and dropped the phone back into my bag.

I started to stand as Dana approached the table, but she waved me down. "No, don't get up," she said, sliding into the chair next to mine. She sat a paper cup down in front of me. "You left your coffee inside."

I noticed that somewhere between the restroom

and the patio, she'd stopped to replace her own coffee.

I shook my head. "Dana, I am so sor—"

"No." She flashed a hand up between us. "You don't have to apologize again. It really is okay."

My eyes fell to the brown splotchy stain that covered most of her shirt. Grimacing, I shook my head again. "God, I can't believe I did that."

Dana shrugged and gave me a lopsided grin. "Well, I was hoping that our first in-person meeting would be memorable."

"Yeah, I think I've taken care of that little detail for you." I managed a smile, but deep down knew that she was just being nice.

Or, at least, I thought she was.

If we were on the computer or texting, then I would know immediately by how quickly she typed back or by what emoji she used, or if used one at all, what she was thinking. That's the Dana I knew. This Dana—the one that I'd assaulted, thrown a drink at, and otherwise humiliated myself in front of—I didn't know. I knew that I'd like to get to know more of this version of her, but I was afraid that, after today, I'd lost all incarnations of Dana altogether. I just wished there was some sign, some way to know how she really felt.

Dana stared at me as she took a long sip from her iced coffee. After a minute, she smiled—it was the same smile as in her dating profile picture, the one that had drawn me to her months ago. She opened her mouth, but whatever she was about to say was interrupted by the ringing of her cell phone. With a small frown, she unclipped the phone from her belt.

"Sorry," she said apologetically. "I hate to be one of those people who talks on the phone during a date, but that's my sister."

"Sure," I nodded. "Don't worry about it."

"Hello?" Dana chirped into the phone. "Hey there. Mmhmm. No." She twirled the straw of her drink, staring at the swirling coffee inside the clear plastic cup as she spoke. Dana tilted her head, her green eyes rising to meet mine. She smiled again. "I'm sorry, but I'll have to call you back. I'm having a caramel macchiato with a friend right now."

Lila Bruce makes her home in the mountains of North Georgia, where the air is sweet and the summers are hot. Lila loves to read and write contemporary lesbian romances, consume unhealthy amounts of coffee, and has always been a sucker for a happy ending.

A Wonder of the Goddamn World

By Allison T. Gruber

At thirty-eight, I arrive in Arizona for the second time in my life.

The first, I was thirteen, with my parents. We drove for three days from Chicago to see the Grand Canyon. I spent the trip feeling bored, unwilling to look out at what seemed to me nothing more than Biblically scorched earth and prehistoric holes.

At Grand Canyon National Park, I refused to leave the car, stubbornly turned pages in a tattered copy of *Watership Down,* until a series of escalating threats culminated with my father exhaling a frustrated burst of cigarette smoke through his nose, shouting, "For Christ's sake! This is a wonder of the goddamn world."

Even then, I knew wonder could not be commanded, but nevertheless emerged from the van long enough for my parents to snap a photograph of their eldest daughter in pink shorts looking petulant before *a wonder of the goddamn world.*

The second time I arrive in Arizona, by way of a turbulent six a.m. flight from Milwaukee, I am nervous and giddy. I listen to George Harrison, drink too much coffee, and take pictures on my phone of the pink earth below, uploading them to Facebook with the caption, "Breast Cancer Awareness Desert."

People comment on the photo, "Where are you headed?" But I do not reply.

❦ ❦ ❦ ❦

Four years prior, halfway through twelve courses of chemotherapy, I decided I wanted a quieter life, spared of all unnecessary shocks and pain—including those wrought by romantic relationships. Cancer made it clear to me that lack of a lover was not lack of love, that there were worse ways to die than eating alone and choking.

Loneliness, after all, was just a branch on the tree of boredom that could be easily snapped off and repurposed—buy a dog, watch Netflix, get a tattoo.

In the meantime, I got a therapist so I could talk through the experience of having cancer at thirty-four, so I could sort out my thoughts about death, but mostly I ended up discussing women I had loved. How they all, ultimately, made me feel bled out whether murdered or cleansed.

And then, because it too is a symptom of cancer, I started a blog.

On my blog, I wrote about doctors, fellow cancer patients, and the side effects of treatments. My readership was limited to friends and family. And when I no longer had cancer, I stopped blogging.

Years after deleting the cancer blog the Polar Vortex came to Wisconsin.

It was so cold my dog refused to piss outdoors, so cold I swore into my coat while waiting for the bus—*fuck, fuck, fuck*—and didn't care if I seemed crazy. It was so cold idiots scalded themselves trying to demonstrate flash freeze by tossing pots of boiling water into the wind, transforming their desire for YouTube hits into emergency room bills.

Crazed with cabin fever, I started The Polar Vortex Blog, which was political, polemical, and written under a pseudonym. The blog alleviated boredom, filled the hours when I wasn't teaching myself to cook elaborate meals I would ultimately throw out, or grading tedious essays where students chronically confused its and it's.

I usually posted a new entry once a week. After several Twitter and Facebook shares, I developed an unexpectedly large readership, on my best days, garnering over fifteen hundred views.

Unlike my cancer blog, the Polar Vortex blog outlasted the winter that had begotten it, and at the start of summer, a friend who knew my true identity, asked if she might introduce me to a woman named Sarah, who was an avid reader of my online work.

"She's a great writer," my friend said. "Maybe you two could collaborate on stuff."

❧ ❧ ❧ ❧

A month after the introduction to Sarah, I found myself in a canvas lawn chair, drinking wine from a plastic cup at an event called *Jazz in the Park*, which my colleagues had encouraged me, by way of friendly force, to attend arguing…*The reason you hate Milwaukee is that you never* do *anything in Milwaukee.*

Of course I did do things in Milwaukee. I taught, walked my dog, watched television and blogged. Sometimes, I rented a car and drove home to Chicago so I could tell friends and family, in person how much I hated Milwaukee.

Jazz, like Milwaukee bored me, so I drank wine

and clandestinely texted Sarah.

Sarah did not bore me in the least. She was matter-of-fact interesting, one of those rare types who hadn't spent much time considering how interesting she was. Without pretention, she'd offer anecdotes about that time she was on assignment in a Ugandan refugee camp or working security illegally at a housing project in Canada. Accustomed to people who crafted intrigue by aggressively drawing attention to their unorthodox philosophies, fanciful identities, sordid pasts, and fluency in esoteric subject matter, I'd sometimes laugh at Sarah's nonchalance. Hell, the last woman I loved was a tri-lingual, bi-sexual, former sex worker who painted pictures of floating chairs. I knew all of this within the first half hour of meeting her.

Sarah lived seventeen hundred miles away, in a place I could not fathom. After a week of incessant email exchanges, she suggested we talk on the phone. I hesitated. Worried she'd find me much less clever, and much more subdued than the voice in my blog posts, and as the composer of lengthy, candid emails.

Whoever we are in prose, in a Facebook status, in an email is but a palimpsest of the true self, only the best parts. Off the page, I was shy, moody, far less biting, and the phone call felt like an imminent unmasking.

"I might be more boring than my persona," I warned her.

She laughed and said, "she doubts that." Despite my trepidation, our first phone call lasted over three hours.

"Call again, if you're ever bored," I said.

"Or not bored," Sarah replied.

I laughed. "Yes. Or not bored."

I had no intention of falling in love, but as our phone calls became more frequent, I soon found myself unable to eat. I subsisted on black olives, coffee, and avocados I ate off the knife. On walks, I touched trees and flowers, anything that grew, my face lifting into a dumb smile. I let the worst ballads play themselves out on the car radio. Sometimes, I turned them up.

I was perpetually distracted.

I don't want to be like this, I lamented, as though love was a deformity, my heart, John Merrick.

After my second cup of chardonnay, I turned to my colleague, Lynne. "I've met someone."

Knowing I volleyed steadily between school and home, Lynne cocked her head, "Girl, please tell me it's not someone from the internet."

I shrugged, said nothing, but wanted to clarify, "It is someone from the internet, but it's not what you think."

I was open about my disinterest in dating, in romance. Had proudly declared I have better things to do with my life, and I didn't want anyone to think I had some clandestine OkCupid profile. I was a woman of my word, and I wanted Lynne to know that Sarah wasn't someone from the internet but an accident I had grown fond of. I'd grown attached to her clipped laughter, her sentence structure, and her knowledge of subjects ranging from Kudzu to Catholicism.

I wanted to clarify that something even more unprecedented than cancer had happened, and I felt a sudden, indescribable sense of wonder that might be love. My phone died mid Jazz and I felt suffocated. I left the event early saying, "The dog needs to go out," and once home, I frantically logged onto Facebook to message Sarah and explain that my battery died.

"I've had wine," I typed. Then, recklessly, I added, "*I might be falling in love with you.*" Though I despise text-speak, I followed the admission with a "lol."

The lol was an out. The confession that I'd drank wine was an escape. If I came across as foolish, if my feelings were unreciprocated, I could note the lol and the wine, as essential caveats.

❧ ❧ ❧ ❧

"You heard what happened to Dave, right?" My stylist asked as he shampooed my hair.

I admitted that, no, I did not hear what happened to Dave.

"He went to meet this guy he met online, like he flew all the way to Portland, and the guy never showed up at the airport," my stylist said.

I'd taken paid time off work, asked my neighbor to get the mail, left my dog with a coworker. Normally a story like this would elicit an eye-roll, a smug comment like flying to meet someone from the internet is fraught with risk. There were, after all, risks that were worth taking, like chemo, like moving out of state for a good job, and risks that were frivolous—like buying a plane ticket to visit someone you met in the anonymous wilds of the web.

I had no judgment left now. Instead, my mouth went dry. This was not gossip, but a cautionary tale. I could be Dave.

Nevertheless, the following morning, I boarded my flight, assuring myself, if nothing else, it will make a great story. This was a bit of self-comfort ahead of the hurt, the way they say you shouldn't wait for the pain to arrive before taking the pill.

On the plane as we neared Phoenix I studied the shadows cast by the clouds, feeling drowsy and proud of my own unpredictability. The entire situation was so completely out of character that I had shocked myself.

Prior to my departure, my best friend Kristine asked for Sarah's address. *Why?* I asked. *So you can send me a letter? I won't be gone that long. In case you end up in a shallow grave,* Kristine explained. *I want details for Dateline NBC.*

It was true that Sarah could be anyone, could be a stranger I had not anticipated, a thief, a fraud, an imposter, but I could be that stranger, too.

At the Sky Harbor baggage claim, I watched luggage clunk onto the carousel and a new panic filled my chest as I considered the limits of phone calls, email and photographs.

Sarah had only known me in fragments—what would she make of the pale, fearful whole? What would she make of this standard issue dyke, dressed more for a lecture than a romantic rendezvous, sweating through her blazer, dizzy and vulnerable.

I worried the back of my neck with a sweaty palm, until I saw her approaching in blue jeans and a fitted T-shirt. She was smaller and more attractive than I anticipated. She possessed an air of exoticism I had not noticed in the pictures she had shown me—her skin was a bit more olive, her eyes darker, a bit more upturned and bright.

I couldn't speak.

She said, "Come here," and pulled me in close as we waited, in silence, for my red suitcase to amble down the conveyer belt. We had logged countless hours on the phone, we had texted incessantly through our workdays, mailed one another books, music, long letters written out on sheets of yellow legal paper, and she once sent me a bucketful of succulents in adobe pots.

On one hand, she was entirely familiar. There was no reason for me to tremble as I was trembling. Here were all the revelations that could not be communicated digitally or via U.S. Postal Service. The way she smelled slightly of sweet corn, the sturdiness of her knuckled hands cool and roped with thick veins that made me think of blood draws, the way her teeth were so white they practically made me squint. The cracks in my imagination had been filled in.

"Are you disappointed?" I asked.

She seemed shocked. "No. Why? Are you?" She said.

"Of course not," I stammered. And this was true. I was not disappointed. I was stupefied.

She had shown up. She materialized. She was real.

❧ ❧ ❧ ❧

On the drive back to her apartment, we looked for a place where, like teenagers, we might park the car and fool around undetected. The roads had Old Western names like Stagecoach Lane, Horse Thief Basin Road. Saguaros, stout and old, stood like peculiar crucifixes in the red earth.

I had forsaken my attempts to understand what was happening, and allowed the unlikelihood of the moment to engulf me, driving through the desert with a beautiful woman I met online.

For three days, we would hardly leave her bed. We would make love, talk, take occasional breaks to gulp water and eat spoonfuls of almond butter from the jar. It felt odd to be naked around anyone without a medical degree. It felt foreign to be seen, undressed, in a way that was not diagnostic. But we joked about my missing nipple, the dash of absence created by cancer surgery…*Slightly used dyke—Missing a nipple. Probably won't need it.* She touched my scars, the old and the new, as though browsing a book collection, and asked for the particulars of their origins.

"This was when I was seven…and this when I was fourteen…and this when I was thirty-four." I said.

The first morning, while she slept, I traced words I could not say onto her back. When she awoke I propped myself up on one elbow and marveled at her. "Where did you come from?" I said.

She smiled, and without missing a beat answered, "I came from the internet."

That first afternoon together, giddy on the very reality of one another, eager to take advantage of being together without distance between us, we parked the car behind some brush, the sort of brush that men shoot at each other from in John Wayne movies. I breathed in the vanilla lotion on her skin, a scent that lingered on my clothes so that back in Milwaukee, when I opened my suitcase to unpack, a disarming gust of Sarah would breathe back at me.

As I clamored into the backseat, I was struck that though solid and strong, Sarah was very small. My glasses fogged in the heat of the air and our breath, and I felt clumsy, oafish.

"I don't want to hurt you," I mumbled.

The blazer I wore on the flight, sweat damp, was heaped on the front seat, a discarded and recent memory of someone I hardly know.

"You won't hurt me." Sarah assured.

I blindly accepted this because the slightest tap of logic against the surface of wonder can cause it to vanish. Whether we acknowledged it or not, somewhere in the desert, in the heat that visibly wobbled while we fumbled, muttered and laughed, was the actual truth. We could both hurt one another, terribly.

Despite this fact, or in honor of it, she reached for me and I reached back.

⁂

Back at Sky Harbor, I step into the TSA line, softly sobbing, and hand my driver's license to a security agent. A student stole my wallet, while I was in chemo, and my replacement license shows a sick, pissed off version of myself. Hair color BLD. The agent flicks her eyes at the picture and then at me—she likely thinks I'm crying because of cancer. She smiles sympathetically and calls me honey as she hands me back my identification.

I feel foolish for crying in public, but I am ushered quickly and politely through the security lines.

I gather myself together enough to purchase an overpriced chocolate milk shake at the burger chain near my gate. I text a picture of the shake to Sarah, "This is what misery looks like right now."

Once seated on the plane, I begin to cry again. It's futile to disguise my tears as sudden allergies, as something in my eye. I cannot keep brushing them away. They just keep falling. The large man next to me wears a Green Bay Packer's hoodie, reminding me of where I'm headed, where I do not want to be going. He plays solitaire on his iPad, and doesn't seem bothered by the weeping dyke. I fantasize that maybe the plane won't be able to take off, that no plane will ever be able to take off again and I'll have to stay in Arizona. I want to be stuck.

The following morning, quite under-slept, I'll teach my Composition course. I'll stand in a classroom in Milwaukee in front of seventeen students, who will not know their instructor's whole life has changed.

I will lead a discussion on Didion's "Goodbye to All That." I will say nothing about love or about Sarah even though love and Sarah occupy the whole of my mind. Midway through a tiresome thought about rhetoric, one I've had and stated countless times, I'll notice that red rock dust faintly marbles my black boots. This evidence will remind me of the walk we took in Sedona on the way back to the airport, when she took my hand and pointed to a field of small yellow flowers and called them *Allisons*. I'll notice the rust colored remnants of astonishment and lose all my familiar words.

Allison T. Gruber is an essayist and educator. Her book, You're Not Edith (George Braziller Inc., 2015) was a finalist for a Lambda Literary Award. Her work has appeared in Pithead Chapel, The Literary Review, Gravel Magazine, and Foliate Oak among many others. She lives with her wife in Flagstaff, Arizona.

Sweet Heart

By Kim Pritekel

Kinley Warner sat behind the wheel of the unfamiliar vehicle. She stared out the windshield, her hands running nervously on her denim-clad thighs.

❧ ❧ ❧ ❧

Six Months Earlier:

Kinley Warner's eyes were locked onto the magnificently huge structure they were pulling up to. Her seventeen-year-old nephew, Sam was giving her a ride to the place where she had a kitchen to use, the backseat of his beat up old Honda filled with bags of bought ingredients. After all, she had flown to Pueblo, Colorado from Georgia to bake Sam's mother, her sister, and Bethany's wedding cake.

"This place is friggin' massive," the teen next to her muttered.

"You're not kidding."

The house was aged red brick and stood four stories. The plethora of windows, were straddled by shutters painted white, as was the trim and Greek columns holding up the four-story portico. At initial count driving up to the house Kinley guessed there were at least nine fireplaces. Though intimidating and a bit cold she thought the place was gorgeous.

Bethany, who served on the Board of Trustees for Pueblo museums, had instructed that the front door would be open and gave her directions to get to the kitchen. The house should be vacant, all tours already run, so Kinley would be able to begin her work undisturbed.

"Whoa," she whispered, eyes wide as she took in the expansive entryway. It looked far more like something that belonged on a movie set than a home she was standing in. She eyed the elegant antique furniture that lined the huge foyer. What really caught her eye was the absolutely stunning grand staircase that led to the second floor. The balustrade was highly polished mahogany with hand carved detailing.

Tearing her eyes from it all, she weaved her way through the dark house, hesitant to turn on many lights as she already felt she was intruding. Finally, she reached the kitchen, which took her breath away.

If she were to dream up the perfect chef's kitchen, this would be it. The kitchen in the apartment she rented was nice—considering she conducted all her catering business out of it—but this place exceeded any and everything she'd ever need.

Considering the age of the house, it was obvious the kitchen had undergone extensive renovation within the past five to ten years.

"I'm in love," Kinley muttered, walking over to the island to unload her burden. She glanced over toward the first of two fridges, which was closest to the wall and noticed a small, narrow stairway, which she assumed belonged to the servants back in the day.

She let out a heavy sigh as she regarded her temporary kingdom. Continuing to unpack her bags of ingredients, she started when she thought she heard footsteps coming down the wooden stairs of what she assumed was the servant's staircase. Stilling her movements, she focused her attention for someone to appear. Utterly baffled when nobody did, she returned her attention to what she was doing.

Bethany's notes for ideas were loaded with requests for lemon. So, Kinley was making her an epic lemon cake with frosting lightly infused with raspberry, two flavors that were meant to be married together for a beautiful wedding cake.

Humming softly to herself as she performed her *mise en place*, she gathered all the things she'd need, which were hidden in the kitchen's amazing amount of storage.

Ready to start, she reached into the front pocket of her jeans and fished out the stretchy hair tie she'd dropped in there before leaving Bethany's house and gathered up her long, dark brown hair, tugging it into a tight ponytail before washing her hands and beginning the magic that was her passion.

It wasn't long before Kinley lost herself in her task on automatic pilot despite the love and care she was putting into this cake. Even so, she stopped. Suddenly, she had the feeling—yet again—that she was being watched.

Absently wiping her hands on a paper towel, she walked over to the servant's stairs. Standing at the bottom, she looked up into the dark, narrow depths, trying to make out anything, a figure, shadow, something that could explain her extreme feeling of unease.

"Hello?" she called, her voice sounding flat in the narrow stairway. Her heart was pounding. In truth she was afraid she'd get a response. When there was nothing forthcoming, as much as she wanted to turn around and ignore the feeling that crept up her spine, she found herself slowly taking one stair at a time, hands lightly patting on the curved walls on either side as she made her way deeper, all light and life behind her in the kitchen.

Stopping short, Kinley's hazel eyes opened wide, desperate to try and see in the darkness as she swore she heard noises further up the staircase.

"Hello?" she called again, slowly advancing.

Reaching the top of the winding staircase, she was relieved to see some light, which came through a large partially stained window in the wall to the left at the end of the long hallway. The old hardwood floors were painted with the greens, blues and reds coming in from the colored panes.

Stepping fully into the hallway she found it was similar to what she'd seen downstairs, beautiful and somewhat gaudy with old furnishings and antiques. The hallway was lined with rooms, all of which had lavish, carved wooden doors with elaborate oversized brass doorknobs. She could easily imagine the large brass keys needed for each.

Curiosity overriding her earlier fear, she headed down the hallway, though she was still all eyes and ears. At the end of the hall, she took a left at another long hall that ended in yet another staircase to lead to the third floor. The matching ornate wooden door that could lock the stairs off was slightly ajar.

The stairs squeaked slightly under her weight as she carefully made her way up, seeming to move from

1879 into a more futuristic world as she went. The silk wallpaper gave way to exposed brick, reminding her more of a Brooklyn apartment than a mansion in Denver.

She found herself in another hallway, though the walls were painted a medium gray on one side with the continued exposed brick on the other. Framed black and whites lined the walls —a gurgling stream in the mountains, pigeons scooping up the bread crumbs an old woman was tossing to them and the forever frozen laughter of children on a playground. Modern and basic furniture pieces were peppered here and there, all clean lines, black leather and chrome.

Moving further on, she found herself standing in front of a large rustic sliding door, which was partially open. Glancing over her shoulder to see that the way was clear, she slid inside. The exposed brick and gray walls extended into the huge space, but what caught her attention were voices she heard coming from the left, many voices.

She quietly made her way to find yet another sliding wood door, also partially open. Peeking inside, she gasped in surprise at the dark interior, only lit up by the ever-changing images from a huge bank of monitors, an entire wall of them from varying national and foreign news broadcasts to old episodes of *Loony Tunes.*

Beyond the monitors, the room was also filled with endless computer and electronic equipment. Kinley knew nothing about either, but had to guess there was at least a million dollars worth of equipment.

She turned, about to leave when she cried out in surprise and fear and suddenly she found herself pinned against the wall, arms clasped at the wrists and held against the wall over her head. She found herself looking into incredibly angry dark eyes.

"What are you doing in here?" the woman hissed, her voice deep and dangerous.

It was too dark and Kinley was too afraid to make out much of the woman who nearly had her entire body pressed against hers. She could feel her heaving breasts grazing the breasts of the woman holding her hostage.

"I'm sorry," she whispered, terrified. "I'm the cook, I mean the baker. I'm making the cake…"

She felt the woman lean in slightly, their bodies all but pressed together. She couldn't explain the strange little shiver that passed down her spine.

"Get out," the woman, said softly, though her tone firm, it wasn't as frightening as it had been. "Go back to your cake." With that, the woman turned and disappeared through the door, leaving Kinley trembling.

⁂

Ceremony over and reception in full swing, Kinley had cut the cake and most of the guests had grabbed a plate with a small slice upon it. She felt a bit exposed in the Maid of Honor dress she'd worn to stand up for Bethany. It was forest green satin, long and very fitted with a halter-top design that left her shoulders and cleavage embarrassingly exposed.

"This was excellent."

She looked up from where she'd been adjusting the bust of the dress to see a woman standing before her. She wore well-tailored black slacks and a women's cut fitted blouse, also black, unbuttoned perhaps just one too many. A peek of her cleavage was visible as well as two silver chains that gleamed at her neck, the pendants of each disappearing beneath the shirt.

At first glance, Kinley thought there was a tomboyish cute woman standing before her with short, dark brown hair and bangs that hung over one eye to give her an almost boyish, adorably innocent look. But, as she looked closer, she saw an absolutely beautiful woman behind what almost seemed to be bashful bangs. Her eyes were dark and beautifully shaped, her nose delicate and lips full. She had cheekbones that any model would die for and a proud jaw line.

Realizing she was staring, Kinley cleared her throat and gave the stranger a polite smile. "Thank you. I'm so pleased you enjoyed it."

"I did," the woman said, resting the empty plate down in the bin on a cart next to the cake table for that purpose. "I also say you look beautiful. So nice to see you in something other than your chef's whites."

"Excuse me?" Kinley asked, baffled. "Do I know you?"

The woman in black gave her a sheepish grin. "Sorry I scared the hell out of you the other day. I'm Castin Harlow at your service. "

Initially confused, but then, with a gasp and hand to her mouth, Kinley realized who she was talking to. Before she could speak, the woman glanced over her shoulder towards the live band, which had begun playing the Bangles', *Eternal Flame.*

"Come on," she said, reaching around the table to grab Kinley's hand. "Come dance with me."

Before Kinley could decline, she was nearly yanked out of her high heels and led to the dance floor where many of the other guests were already paired up and moving to the slow '80s song.

She was surprised yet again when her wrists were taken in gentle hands and brought up around this strange woman's neck. With a raised eyebrow, she said, "Isn't that a little forward?"

The woman grinned, showing beautiful teeth and adorable dimples. "Hey, it's better than being backwards."

Kinley shook her head, unable to respond as she smiled. "So, how did you know I've been in chef's whites for the past four days?" she asked instead.

"Because I've been watching you," the woman said simply, easily leading her in their dance.

Kinley looked into those dark eyes. "Do you have any idea how utterly creepy that could sound?" she challenged, for some reason feeling comfortable enough around this Castin Harlow woman to tease her. "But, weirdly, it doesn't coming from you."

"Yeah, well. When you possess as much charm as I do," Castin shrugged. "Everything just comes out right."

"So I saw," Kinley muttered dryly.

"Hey, I apologized. And, to make it up to you, I'd like to hire you to cater a fundraiser at the museum on Thursday night."

Shocked, Kinley stopped moving and stared up at the slightly taller woman. "I fly out tomorrow afternoon."

"Yes, I know. I'll pay all your travel expenses plus provide accommodations and one helluva generous compensation for your time and talents." Castin's hands fell from Kinley's waist to hook her thumbs in the front pockets of her slacks. " When Kinley said nothing, Castin gave her an adorable lopsided grin. "I'll make it worth your while."

⚶⚶⚶⚶

"You will be staying here," Castin said, pushing open a door to reveal a modest-sized room with a large bed, the room decorated in grays and blacks. There was also an attached bathroom. "Will this work?"

"Yeah, it's beautiful, thank you."

"Okay, well," Castin said, stepping into the room ahead of Kinley and leaving her roller-bag at the foot of the bed and her carry-on on the bed. "Well, take your time settling in then find me so we can talk about the event and the menu."

Left alone, Kinley looked around the room as she sat down on the comfy bed. "What have I gotten myself into?" she murmured.

⚶⚶⚶⚶

The fundraiser had been a success, she guessed. All her platters were empty. She was ashamed to admit that her attention had been captured by Castin Harlow all evening. While in her chef whites, the mistress of the house had been dressed in a fitted black dress which showed much skin, including an enticing amount of cleavage. Her short hair was smoothed back and her makeup was smoky and dangerous.

"The food was wonderful, dear."

An elderly woman, who was suddenly standing before her, usurped Kinley's attention. "Thank you, ma'am. So pleased you enjoyed it."

"Have you a business card? I have so many events every year and I've been looking for a good chef."

"Certainly." Kinley gave her a kind smile as she

reached into her pocket and produced a card for her catering company.

The evening came to an end and Kinley quickly began the long process of cleanup. She was used to having Ellis and the girls help her, but she was on her own. She could hear the group breaking up in the grand ballroom where the event had been held as she shrugged out of her chef's jacket to reveal a fitted tank top. She was hot, as was the kitchen, from hours of preparing the meals for the fundraiser.

She had just finished with the last pot when she heard someone enter the huge room. She wasn't entirely surprised to see Castin, but she was surprised to see how she was dressed. Obviously freshly showered, her damp hair hanging slightly in her face, which was scrubbed clean of makeup. She wore a black fitted tank top, very obviously no bra beneath as well as black and silver basketball shorts. What she found amusing was Marvin the Martian staring back at her from the front of the shirt. She looked absolutely adorable, bare feet and all.

She smiled then returned her attention to what she was doing.

"Everything went great tonight," Castin said, walking over to her and leaning her hip against the counter. "You did a great job and almost everyone here asked for your contact information." Castin grinned at her. "I think you're going to find yourself getting a whole lotta business in Colorado."

Kinley smirked. "Well, that might be a little tough since my kitchen is in Georgia."

"True facts," Castin conceded, reaching out to place a sealed envelope on the counter. "Here, this is for you."

Kinley glanced at it, noting her name scribbled across the front in neat, black letters. "Thank you."

She left the envelope where it was and tugged the dishtowel from where it was slung over her shoulder and dried her hands. Tossing the towel aside, she was startled to see Castin stood mere inches away. Before she could react, Castin leaned down and left a lingering kiss on Kinley's lips.

Kinley's eyes fluttered open as Castin stepped away. "Why did you do that?" she asked softly, more shocked than upset.

"I'm sorry," Castin replied just as softly. "I'll leave you to it."

Heart pounding, Kinley turned back to the counter, her hands resting on it as she tried to catch her breath. She gasped when suddenly her hand was grabbed and she was swung around to face the intensity in Castin's eyes. Though a thrill of fear and uncertainty passed through her, she realized the passion and connection she felt deep inside was looking down at her.

Without a moment to consider what was about to happen, Kinley found herself pushed back against one of the two fridges. Turning her brain off, she allowed her body and need to take over. Her hands came up and instantly and were buried in thick dark hair, pulling Castin as close as possible as the kiss deepened. She moaned when Castin's hands found her behind, pressing their hips together as the passion built.

She felt overwhelmed by the intensity of this beautiful woman who had captivated her from the start. She took fistfuls of the black tank top in her desperate need to be as close as possible. She'd never known need like this before.

❧❧❧❧❧

Kinley watched the tiny earth below pass by between the clouds. She rested her head against the window in the private jet she'd been loaded into. She could still hear Castin's last words echoing in her head. *I'm sorry I can't drive you, but I don't do good with goodbyes.* Castin had held her for a long moment before leaving a kiss to her lips and turning to head back into the house.

Her eyes slid closed as she recalled the feel of Castin's flesh against her own, the feel of a hot mouth and gentle, yet passionate hands and touch. The feel of her fingers inside of Kinley still sent a thrill of passion up her spine.

Despite the sudden arousal that gripped her, she couldn't keep the sadness she also felt at bay. As Colorado got further and further away, she felt as though part of herself was being left behind.

With a heavy sigh, she finally tore open the envelope Castin had given her and pulled out a check with two zeros added that wasn't part of the initial amount promised for her catering services.

For just a moment, she felt a bit slimy. Had she been used, paid for her other talents?

❧❧❧❧❧

"Ellis, can you grab that twenty-four pack of eggs, please?" Kinley asked from where she was carefully piping icing atop the order of cupcakes. "Damn it," she murmured, wiping her hands on a towel as she walked the short distance through her apartment to the front door when she heard a solid knock.

She was stunned when she came face-to-face with two-dozen red roses with legs.

"Can I help you?"

"Flowers for Kinley Warner," said a familiar voice. A moment later, Castin's adorable grin appeared around the bouquet. "It's been two weeks and I missed you," she said softly. She handed the stunned chef the flowers. "In fact," she continued, thumbs once again tucked into her tailored black slacks. "I can't stop thinking about you."

Kinley took the roses, unable to keep her pleased shock out of her eyes. "I missed you, too," she whispered.

Later that night, Kinley lay on her side with her head resting in an upturned palm. She looked down at the naked woman lying beside her. She felt satisfied and sated and smiled as Castin ran her fingers absently over Kinley's arm.

"So, what does all this mean?" she asked, bringing up a hand to run along Castin's jaw.

Castin's dark eyes met her own. "Dunno. I've never really been into the long distance thing, but I'm just not willing to let you go." She gave her a charming smile. "I told you, not good at the whole goodbye thing."

Kinley looked down into that beautiful face that she was quickly becoming addicted to. But, beyond that, she saw the heart hand soul of the woman behind it. She saw a woman capable of so much love and kindness, even as she hid behind dozens of computer monitors in her computer securities business. She saw—and felt—the tenderness of a very misunderstood woman, a woman that, in an extraordinarily short amount of time, she was losing herself and her heart to.

"What?" Castin asked, looking up into Kinley's face.

Kinley smiled and shook her head, not ready to give voice to her feelings and emotions. "Nothing."

"You keep your cards close to the vest, don't you?"

Kinley chuckled. "Yeah. Sometimes."

❧❧❧❧

"You're smiling."

Kinley glanced over at her employee and good friend. "You know what, concentrate on the damn chicken before I fire your ass."

Ellis burst into laughter, her rounded belly jiggling with the loud explosion. "I'm thinking you like this woman"

Kinley was quiet for a moment before nodding. "Yes."

"Well, she's adorable and, even I have to admit, a pretty sexy lady."

Kinley's grin widened, memories of their handful of nights together and endless phone call and texts over the past few months. "Yes, yes she is."

"Rich, too," Ellis pointed out, shutting the oven after she slid in the glass casserole pan with her chicken dish in it.

"That doesn't matter, Ellis," she said softly. Her voice just as soft and filled with all the emotions and feelings she felt towards the other woman, she continued, "Castin has such a beautiful heart and beautiful soul. She's unlike anyone I've ever known." She met kind brown eyes. "She's beautiful yes, but I can honestly say, never has my soul been as attracted to someone as I am Castin Harlow."

"You've fallen in love with her, haven't you?" Ellis asked, placing a hand on her boss' shoulder.

Kinley said nothing, though she knew she didn't have to.

❦❦❦❦

Chewing on the inside of her cheek, Kinley scrolled through various locations that showed up on a real estate site. It had been strange to input Colorado as the state of origin.

"That's cute," she murmured, checking out the specs on a location downtown for her bakery. The building was old and had all the lovely architecture features she loved from the 19th century. "How expensive are you?"

Scrolling further, she saw the name of the Realtor as well as the price. Grinning, she sat back against the back of the couch.

"I could afford that."

Suddenly she felt tears come to her eyes as the fear came. She slammed her laptop shut.

"What am I doing? I can't move across the country." Her head fell back against the couch as she stared up at the darkened ceiling. "What am I doing?"

❦❦❦❦

"Baby, are you okay?" Castin asked softly across the phone line.

Kinley wrapped in the oversized Superman T-shirt Castin had sent to her, knowing it was her favorite superhero, sat in her darkened bedroom, trying desperately to keep the emotion out of her voice. "Yeah," she muttered.

"Tell me the truth," Castin said gently.

"I miss you. It's really starting to get to me, the fact that I can't see you every day, can't share my day with you. I know we see each other as often as we can and talk every day on the phone, but ..."

"I know. I hate it, too." Castin sighed into the phone. "What do you want to do?"

Kinley reached up and swiped at a tear of frustration that was beginning to fall. "I don't know. You have your life and the estate there and I have my business here in Georgia." She squeezed her eyes shut, doing her damnedest to get her heart to stop hurting. "It's been almost six months now," she managed. "So often I worry we'll never get this together and it's all a dream, some kind of fantasy that I'm fooling myself with."

"Kinley, do you believe me when I tell you I want to be with you? That I want a future with you?"

Kinley wiped away more tears. "I'm trying to." She heard another sigh. "I'm sorry. I don't mean to be difficult, Castin. I just..." She bit her tongue, unable to say the words she'd so badly wanted to for months. "I just don't know."

❧ ❧ ❧ ❧

"So, let me get this straight," Ellis said, a slight edge to her voice and hands on rounded hips. "You're telling me you broke it off with this woman, this, oh, how did you put it? Love of your life, because you're afraid to leave."

"Ellis, please," Kinley sighed, kneading the dough she'd just made. "I don't need this."

"Yeah, yeah you do!"

The surprising raise and anger in her friend's voice got the chef's attention.

"Kinley, what are you afraid of?"

"I have a business here, Ellis," Kinley said, her own defensiveness rising to sound a lot like anger. "I can't just leave."

"Why not? We both know you've been saving forever to get your bakery. I know for a fact you've got the funds. Why are you dragging your feet on what could possibly be the best thing you've ever done?" She reached up to swipe at a tear. "You know I lost my Frank four years ago," she said softly. "On any given day, I'd give anything to have one more day with him, let alone a second chance with him." Saying nothing more, she turned her back, leaving Kinley to stare at her.

❧❧❧❧

Kinley sat behind the wheel of the unfamiliar vehicle. She stared out the windshield, her hands running nervously on her denim clad thighs.

"Last chance," she whispered, glancing over the building to her right. With a deep breath for courage, she reached for the keys and turned on the engine.

❧❧❧❧

Knowing the museum portion of the house was closed, Kinley walked to the side of the massive house where she knew Castin had her private entrance.

Reaching out, she felt faint as she pressed the buzzer. Her heart was racing and sweat began to gather between her shoulder blades and breasts. Finally, the large metal door was pushed open and Castin stood there, dressed in her typical fitted black slacks and black button up. The look on her beautiful face was less than welcoming.

"Hi," Kinley said softly, feeling utterly unsure of herself or what she'd done or was about to do. When Castin said nothing, she swallowed hard and buried her hands into the back pockets of her jeans. "How are you?"

"Confused," Castin said simply, arms crossing over her chest as she leaned a shoulder against the doorframe.

Kinley nodded. "I know. I'm sorry," she finally managed, meeting intense dark eyes. "I made a mistake. I've come to ask for forgiveness."

This time it was Castin's turn to keep her cards close to the vest. She nodded, looking out over the day. "How long are you staying?" she asked conversationally.

Kinley ran a nervous hand down the length of her ponytail. "Everything I own that didn't get sold is in that U-Haul parked at the curb."

"I thought you said you were afraid to leave Georgia, your business. Everything."

Kinley let out a heavy breath. "I was. I am." She met a carefully guarded gaze. "But, I'm not too afraid to follow my heart."

"You had your heart set on a bakery in Colorado, huh?" Castin asked with one of her trademark grins.

"Among other things," Kinley hedged, enjoying the playful tone in Castin's voice.

"You're sure? You're ready for this?"

Kinley stepped up to her and placed her hands on Castin's hips as she looked up into her eyes. "I've never been more sure about anything," she said, realizing she'd never meant seven words more in her life. But, she also realized she had three more she needed to say. "I love you."

Castin's grin was huge. She leaned down and placed a lingering kiss on Kinley's lips. "I love you, too. Let's do this."

"Let's do this."

"Is Ellis going to be pissed at me?" Castin murmured against Kinley's smile.

"Nope. She's coming to work for me once I get my bakery up and going. She wants to see if she can find herself a hot Colorado hunk."

Castin burst into laughter and pulled Kinley into her arms.

Kim Pritekel is an author of more than a dozen books and lives in beautiful Colorado. She can be reached at www.kimpritekel.com or www.facebook.com/WriterP

Ground That Sparkles

By Lindsey Wilson

We queers gathered to conference downtown, in my town, an occupation but not a takeover. We gathered to be seen and to see, to be heard and to hear, to be held and to hold—each other—in the last moments before the world changed orders. The streetlights stayed on even during the day, so grey and dark were the skies. We all knew a storm was breaking in a city just to our south, a storm that had been brewing for two months and probably three hundred years. A storm, that might end us all or might, in its destruction, wash us clean. Here in Philadelphia, we made our stand and drew our lines. We queers already knew how to fight. And we grabbed whomever we could in the days before the front lines opened on our front yards.

Thousands of beautiful people milled about, on sidewalks and in and out of coffee shops, and I arrived early to register, still broken from the losses I suffered earlier in the week, a partner and a friend, both with ultimatums hanging over their heads. Me or them. I was the me and the them, so I filled my pockets with stones, made precious by their memories of the ground. When I touched them I remembered dirt between my toes and scratches on my hands. Precious because their corners and facets reflected the light, what little could be seen on a day made dark by thick clouds of rain. So sick of watching my demise, of pressing stones into the cracks as they widened, I showed up distracted, wondering how to row my boat when I wasn't even sure I could find any water—my creek run dry. My tears run dry. Just numb dust covering my oars and throat, covering my fingers like guilt. I needed air.

So I trained and talked, stretched my limbs and my mind, looked and listened and opened my mouth with the boldness of a person with nothing left to lose. That's how I found her. We met the way people meet at these things, started talking—started wondering. I left my number at the end of the workshop she led that morning, an invitation. She was curious, too, and she reached out to spend some time with me in the afternoon.

It was only the second time we spoke, but she looked at me seriously and said, "I think we've been walking the same path for a long time, Lindsey." I thought of her lanky body in the forest, of her bare-feet on the earth, of us bounding through the woods together and singing with abandon. Hours before, I was struggling to find the blazes that marked my path forward, and then here she was…before we had language, people left piles of stones for one another in carefully balanced messages. My ancestors were stacking rocks to point in her direction. They were telling me to stop, look, and listen, to follow my instincts and look for the new path.

We didn't sleep the night we met. We were too busy learning each other, testing each other. We stood in the middle of a hotel room and threw each other down to the ground, carpet burning, scraping each other into the weave of our arms and legs. She was taller than me, stronger and bigger too, but we were both farmers, born women but no longer sure. On the night of the inauguration, we fucked and wrestled in a twenty-third floor hotel room. It was defiance, resistance, and a celebration. A seed, now planted, that would grow in any soil. Queer magic flowed through the air, and the raindrops must have felt it because they cleared the way for my journey home in the hours between night and day. I let my body get heavy on my bike, let the fatigue settle into my legs and arms, in my sinews and tendons, all stretched, all torn a little. All were aching for more, suddenly so aware of her absence.

The next afternoon we found ourselves in her hotel bed, fearing we'd miss out on the presentations, but fearing more we'd miss each other. She was just a visitor to this coast, headed home to California in a day's time, and I had deep roots in this city's grit. Some would have called our connection impossible, but we called it love and put our bodies together, built a temporary nest in our arms.

"This is my worry stone." She pulled a large orange stone from the bedside table. "I keep it around at times like this when I think that things might be really intense." We looked at the rock together, her hand held up to the light and my fingers tracing the lines of flesh and stone and all the places they joined. "It has this spot, which is really rough. And this side is smooth and flat. I like to feel the different textures when I'm upset." She traced her jawline with the rough side, then smooth side of the stone. "Here, put it against your face." She brought the stone to my lips, my cheeks, and I felt her body heat transmitted though the stone. All the worries went away, leaving just our intensity, just our need to be in this place, so sacred.

I took her home that night, making dinner

while she sang me songs so sweet my face hurt from all the smiling. We spent the night staring at each other, putting ourselves in all the lonely places, making apologies for all the past pains. Each scar was just another stone in our path to one another. Each freckle the reminder of harsh suns long past. She had a smattering on her shoulder, a constellation we were sure, and a sign from the sky. I wanted to trace them all, all those little brown dots, until I memorized her skin like braille on my fingertips. She wanted to make more freckles, tattoos of them, in patterns dancing across her body—shining with the lights of the stars.

The morning came before we were ready, but we pulled the last bits of sleep from our teeth and sucked each other's honey once more, proboscis probing, so animal in our instincts. It was time to say goodbye, but I wasn't ready, not even close. We kept talking, just trying to say all the things we could think of before our time ended. Before the universe kept spinning, having found its way to a grinding halt two days earlier. I could feel the acceleration coming, the vibrations already working through the ground. So I held tight to her hand, as we looked for a hallway, for one last chance to rub our bodies against one another. I saw a bench by a set of elevators and put down my backpack, sitting down. I started to slide to one side, but she shook her head, dropping to her knees in front of me.

"Stay right where you are, that's perfect." We pushed into each other's skin one last time, leaving thumbprints and small impressions, bruises that would fade—but slowly. "It's kind of strange," she whispered to my neck, "knowing that I found a part of myself this weekend." I wanted to reply, but the only way my tongue worked was against hers.

The elevator doors opened, and a few people got off on our floor. She stood. We moved together, fluid flowing with gravity, into the empty elevator shaft. We may have dropped or we may have flown, but as we kissed on the four-floor ride. I am sure my feet never touched the ground. We found ourselves across from the doors, and I, practicing my newly found restraint, leaned in for one last, long kiss. Then I turned, said goodbye, and let go of her hands, moving swiftly into the flow of humans exiting through the revolving doors. I walked the wrong way home, my sea legs disoriented, rocked by the flood of her body on mine, our bodies like the ground, like the rivers flowing on either side of this dirty city.

I had to work, had to go care for someone else's baby while my new baby boarded a plane and the wind swept her away on wings made of metal, so far removed from our earth. The hours drifted by, me fighting off sleep and watching a toddler, her hovering over the Midwest somewhere, moving farther away from me. I took the toddler outside to squish our boots in the mud, soil soaked by days of slow drizzle and mist. I pulled two rocks from the loam to send to the opposite coast. To show her how sacred, this land where we met. I must have fallen asleep, stretched out on the floor in a pile of crayons, her face suddenly before me again. My barriers had fallen, all my defenses were down, and in marched a warrior, a witch. *I'm a free witch*, she said in my dreams, *and I have no regrets*. I knew we would meet again. This meant too much to let go of, too much to let slip through our outstretched fingertips—we would grab hold of the ledge and cling to it, our hands strong and calloused.

On my way home from work I got a text. "So," it read, "my plane has been grounded on the runway for a few hours now. Crazy question…"

I didn't hesitate a moment to reply. "Do you need a place to stay tonight? Are you thinking about staying in Philly?"

"Wow, yeah, that's what I was going to ask. I think if I disembark now I can still book a return flight for tomorrow."

"Yes. You should totally do that. Let me know what you find out."

While she got off the plane, stretching her legs and breathing fresher air, I felt a surge of energy— her energy, beaming from the southern tip of the city, stretching across swamp and endless rows of houses to where I sat in a supermarket parking lot.

"I was able to get a ticket for 4:00 p.m. tomorrow. I'll start heading back to your place. I have your address in my bra."

"Yes, that's a great place to keep it, but I'll save you the trip on public. I'm on my way to the airport now!"

A half an hour later I arrived at the airport and there she was, walking back toward me in the same outfit I left her in, with the same grin across her face, the same eyes, the same skin and hair and teeth. Her same long braid was coiling from the short hair at the base of her neck around her collar and into the space between her collarbones, almost touching her breasts. We embraced and kissed and then searched each other's faces from the safety of our arms, smiling, basking in the serendipity—the strangeness. Our silence broke with peals of laughter, and I put her luggage in my car, heading back to the house where we'd shared the evening before. The universe, or some force within it, got a shout-out for the gift of a second chance to sleep in the same bed, tangled and touching and breathing together.

My ex-partner, now roommate, was home that night, so we tried to keep our bodies respectfully apart, but as we stood in the kitchen, after smoking a spliff on the cold patio slab, her hips shifted into mine. "Wait," I said, remembering the rocks I smuggled from the forest earlier in the day. I reached into my pocket and rubbed away the dried mud with my thumbs. "I was going to send these to you but now I'm really happy I can just give them to you. See, you weren't meant to leave Philly so soon!"

She reached out her palm and looked carefully at the two pebbles. One was smooth and rose tinted, quartz or something like it. The other was rough, flaky composed of a thousand thin sheets of mica, its crystal structure flat like a windowpane and colored like gold. The stone sparkled and shone, casting light all around her hand and onto her face.

"These are beautiful," she said, enraptured. "Can you tell me a little about them?"

"Well," I said, "these are the two rocks that are most common in the Wissahickon creek. There's a huge swath of protected forest on the edge of the city, and I like to go there to think about what this space is really, what it was before we flattened it and covered it with concrete and dug out soil to make room for condos. Sometimes when I'm in the woods because I feel sad, I take one of these," I picked up the sparkling stone, "from the river, and while it is wet and weak, I crumble it slowly into the water. They fall apart into flecks of glitter. Sometimes I need to remember that this city was built on ground that sparkles."

I swear something in her face changed then. Something in her voice changed, too. She got deeper, wider like the sea, and I felt her waves lapping at my shore, felt her currents pull me under. I wasn't afraid of drowning anymore. She could fill me, right my overturned bucket and fill me up, fill me to the point of spilling. I was pressed against the kitchen counter, a dark slab of granite wrested from the earth, polished and propped and still deadly, still alive with the glimmer of its minerals.

Her mouth opened to bathe me in beautiful words. "We queer folk have to heal our relationship with ourselves and insist that there is no trash—we are not trash. And we should not create trash in an attempt to celebrate our beauty."

Locked in her hold, her hips against my stomach, the counter pressing my low back, her hands on my waist, my face, my shoulders, I felt only bliss. I was not garbage. I was beauty itself, standing there in the reflection of her beauty. My ex started playing the chords that she strummed the night before, probably singing something sad, but all we heard were the sweet notes of those strings, stretched as tight as our muscles, which were tired from standing but never wanted to sit again. Eventually everyone went to bed.

We didn't even fuck that night, just held each other and whispered for hours. We talked about our families, about our dreams. We wanted to share everything but there were only a few hours left before dawn, and eventually we would need to sleep, need to come up for air.

With one of my bare legs between hers, her mouth inches from my nose, she stroked my short hair and said, "This feels really big, and also it's moving super fast, so that's kind of scary. I just wanted to put that out there."

"I agree. I definitely wasn't planning to fall in love with anyone this weekend, but here we are."

She laughed, reassured. "I know, right! Before I came to Philly, I made an offering to my ancestors and asked them to guide me to where I needed to be. Our ancestors were working hard for us this time. They were helping us."

I felt held, my spirit as well as my body, my whole self, held in her large, capable hands. They were tender, and I was tinder, waiting to be kindled, waiting for the spark that would let my flames hiss and moan, swelling under her careful supervision. This was a safe space, a space for love to grow as big and bold as it wanted. It was a space for magic to run loose and make the whole thing sparkle.

Dawn broke, cold and grey, and the makeshift drapes hastily pinned over the basement windows allowed just a thin stream of light to enter the makeshift bedroom where we spent our last night together. Rain poured from the clouds, splashing on oil covered streets and leaving big drops on windowpanes. We slept until we woke, finally resting, exhausted after three days of loving so fully.

"I could stay in the shower with you all day," she said after we finished washing each other, and ourselves "but we shouldn't waste that much water." I smiled and agreed, somewhat begrudgingly. I turned off the water and we patted each other dry with clean towels, and rubbed coconut oil all over each other's bodies. It was silly as much as sexy, and our laughter bubbled out of the small bathroom, filling the dark house with lightness and air. Even the houseplants perked their ears. We kissed the sweet oil, leaving mouth prints all over bodies. When we could take no more, we put our clothes on and drank coffee stretched lazily on my couch, with cats on either side. This could be life, this path we walked.

Under the light of a lamp, still so dark outside, I showed her relics—rocks and shards of tooth and bone, pieces of my home—that land of my past. These important parts of me, kept near to feel always the slow pull of the moon on the shores of Lake Michigan. Smooth stone and palms fused, all the temperatures adjusting, regulating our heat. She had to go. We wanted to stay. We wanted to leave, together, to start—finally start our lives. Our path cleared, widened in the wake of our meeting, and we would have barreled down it with childish glee had life not been so messy with stumps and undergrowth.

But there were bills to be paid and scores to be settled, flights to catch and lives to be packed. As I dropped her at the curb of the airport, I was already calculating my next move, figuring how I would get myself to her in the shortest time. When I next hopped a plane, it would be headed for California, for the ocean and her skin, for the salt and spray and honey, filling my senses again. I would fill my pockets with rocks and float, queer, magic, lighter than air because of our love, filling all the fissures between us with the glittering soil that shook from my boots by a wind that kept blowing me west.

Lindsey Wilson is a genderqueer AFAB farmer and emerging writer who fled rural Michigan for queer life on the East Coast. They write best when they are outside, scribbling heedlessly on scraps of paper, and recently received their first nonfiction publication in Storm Cellar Journal.

That Night in Bora Bora

By Lucy J. Madison

The distance between them was almost unbearable. A tangible heavy blanket of fog enveloped Natalie and the entire room. Natalie felt her chest tighten. The heaviness pressed against her making it difficult to breath. It was like someone had taken a giant suitcase filled with their worldly possessions and thrust it on top of her chest.

Natalie stared up at the ceiling her eyes following the single blade of a wide plantation fan as it slowly spun clockwise. Suddenly hot, she kicked a long leg out from underneath the white sheet and immediately felt the breeze from the fan against her recently sunburned leg. The sound of the ocean waves as they gently lapped against the beams to the overwater bungalow she lay in should have been soothing. Everything about this place should have been perfection but it all felt confined and incredibly uncomfortable for Natalie. Gone were the initial feelings of hope and positivity when she first arrived two days ago. She turned her head and stared at the clock that read 2:46 a.m. She threw back the starched white sheet and sat straight up in bed. *What the hell had she done?* The thought swirled around the room as if pushed by the ceiling fan above her.

Natalie wasn't normally a risk taker. She was

steady, stoic, and grounded. Her upper management job in Wesleyan University's college marketing department paid very well but the daily stress levels were hardly worth it. Her dream was to quit her job and become a full-time musician but the steady paycheck, medical insurance, and 401(k) were simply too valuable to walk away from. So, she cashed her paychecks and watched her savings account grow, and found moderate contentment playing guitar in an acoustic band with friends on weekends. On the surface, it was enough. She owned a house, a car, and a small boat that she puttered around Long Island Sound in. She was healthy and took care of herself. Her best friends lived nearby and filled her life with laughter. But something, or rather someone, had been missing for nearly three years, and that someone was Tasha.

Their relationship was complicated. They had been friends for nearly fifteen years, first meeting at a Wesleyan poetry reading. Back then, they shared ideas and thoughts on everything from Ericka Jong's poetry to politics to their combined love of music, and the lifelong dream to travel at least once to Bora Bora. Tasha was a visiting professor in African-American studies from Stanford. She was a one-of-a-kind California native who loved opera (especially Puccini), came from multiethnic family with six siblings, and drove a Harley. There was nothing soft about Tasha. She was firm, smart, and appealed to Natalie in a multitude of ways, including her masculine sexiness.

Natalie developed feelings for Tasha quickly but she hid them. Something deep inside her flashed red warning signals to keep her feelings under wraps. As their friendship progressed, Natalie found herself more and more at odds with those feelings. Somehow in the process of keeping her growing attraction to Tasha hidden, she increasingly turned inward, often becoming moody and quiet around Tasha when the urge to reach out and touch Tasha became particularly overwhelming.

"Why can't you just say what's on your mind?" Tasha asked, one moonlight spring night as they walked across campus. "I'd give anything to know what's going on in that head of yours. I can literally see the wheels spinning."

But instead of answering, Natalie remained silent. Every time Tasha pushed her to speak about her feelings over the next few weeks before the semester ended, Natalie remained silent. It wasn't as if Natalie didn't know what she was feeling. She did. She felt the intensity pulse from her toes to her scalp. She also knew that in a matter of weeks Tasha's position as a visiting professor would come to an end and she would return to Stanford.

Natalie's problem wasn't her lack of self-awareness. Her problem was fear in taking a risk. She was thirty-five years old and been so steady for so long the idea of risking anything for anyone, including herself, was so outside her comfort zone that she was paralyzed. No matter how hard she tried to make the pieces fit together in her mind, they just wouldn't. She would not leave her home in Connecticut, nor would she expect Tasha to ever relocate from her beloved California. They lived on opposite ends of the country, and while they agreed on many things, their lives and backgrounds were vastly different. Beyond that, Tasha was nearly ten years older than Natalie was. All that distance was just too much for Natalie to bridge all the jumbled thoughts buried deep inside her mind.

Her growing silence frustrated Tasha more and more until one rainy May Saturday, Tasha showed up to her house unannounced demanding answers.

"What the hell is wrong with you?" Tasha pressed, standing just inside Natalie's front door with water pouring off her clothes onto the hardwood floor. Natalie remained mute as she watched droplets of water slide down Tasha's honey colored cheeks. How she wished to lick them off with her tongue. Instead she stood there staring back at Tasha, blinking quickly as if Tasha was some apparition that would disappear as quickly as she had suddenly appeared.

"I don't know what to say," Natalie blurted out after a long, uncomfortable silence. She felt a red-hot rod of tension latch between her shoulder blades.

"Jesus, say anything! Anything would be an improvement to this thing between us that I don't even know what it is," pleaded Tasha.

"It's nothing," responded Natalie, her voice wavering on the edge of tears. Natalie took a deep breath and held it, her heart pounding so hard in her chest she swore Tasha could see it.

"I can't do this. I can't be friends, or whatever we might be, with someone who can't say what she wants to my face. I fly out tomorrow. Natalie, please." Tasha's eyes flashed with intensity.

Natalie started to speak, then stopped. She tried again. Her lips were dry to the point of nearly being glued together. Literally no sound came out. When Tasha turned her back on Natalie and reopened the front door, Natalie wanted to reach out and pull her back inside. She wanted to pull off her wet clothes and take her by the hand to her bedroom. She wanted to make love to her and show her with their bodies everything she was afraid to say out loud. But Natalie did none of those things. She simply stood in her own foyer like a stoic sentry guarding the feelings in her heart.

For a split second, the sweet, fragrant springtime air overwhelmed Natalie's senses. The spatter of the heavy rain hitting the front porch drowned out Natalie's internal dialogue. All she could do was stand there, listening to the rain slap against the porch as Tasha walked out of her house and out of her life.

Natalie wasn't sure how long she stood in the doorway listening to the rain. It might've been minutes or hours or days. None of it mattered anyway. She was silent when she should not have been. Long after Tasha walked down her front porch steps and out of sight, Natalie finally closed the front door and tried to figure out when she became a person afraid to take chances or unwilling live life to the fullest.

Now here she was literally halfway around the world at the ridiculously expensive Four Seasons Bora Bora, staring up at the ceiling of her bungalow suite wondering how the hell she could have ever thought this was a good idea.

In a totally uncharacteristic move, Natalie cashed in all the savings bonds her grandparents had given her ten years ago that she had been saving for a rainy day. She took three weeks off from work, stopped her mail and newspaper delivery and purchased two first class airfare tickets and a suite at the Four Seasons Bora Bora. She wrote a simple note to Tasha and sent it express mail with the airline ticket. The note read, "I'm ready to talk if you're still willing to listen."

Natalie's plan was simple. She arrived two full days before Tasha was even expected. This would give her time to settle in and calm her nerves. So far, that part of the plan hadn't worked particularly well. But Tasha was expected tomorrow if she decided to come at all. All Natalie could do was hope for the best and stick with the plan.

ง๒ง๒ง๒ง๒

After a fitful few hours of sleep, Natalie awoke to bright sunlight streaming through the open French doors that led out to the private deck and plunge pool directly over the clear turquoise lagoon. She rose naked, and walked out onto the deck, looking across the shimmering water at the castle-like Mount Otemanu as it pierced the sky above it. This place was magical, almost mystical. The energy was unlike anything she ever experienced in all her travels throughout Europe and the United States. She dove directly into her own personal plunge pool and let the cool, salty water strip away any of the residual doubt and uncertainty that she tried to let go of. Today was either going to be the best day of her life or the worst. There would be no in between. Either Tasha would show up and welcome what she had to say or she'd stand her up. Natalie hoped for the former. After a swim and a light room service breakfast, she dressed, packed a bag, and left the room, intent on seeing her plan to fruition.

Natalie sat in the hotel's expansive open-air lobby and waited patiently for the concierge to finish with another hotel guest. Her nerves were so on edge that every few moments, she found herself staring at the entrance hoping to see Tasha, but knowing if she did come at all, she wouldn't arrive for another hour or more.

"Ms. Mitchell, so sorry for the delay. How may I help you today?" The friendly concierge asked, jarring her out of her thoughts.

"I have a few things I'd like to set up with you for later today and this evening," Natalie responded, trying to steady her voice.

"Of course, how may I assist?"

"My friend, Tasha Reed, is expected to arrive in the next hour or so," Natalie began.

"Yes. That is correct. We are expecting Ms. Reed to arrive around noon," completed the concierge as he checked the computer screen.

"I'd like you to bring her to the room and please have a light lunch waiting for her upon arrival."

"Of course. Will lunch be for one or two people?" He asked.

"Just one. I'd like to give Tasha some time to settle in alone. I'd also like to schedule a private dinner on the beach for two this evening at seven. I don't want to deal with menus or a bill. To keep busy for the day, I'd also like to book a spa treatment and ask if I could have access to another room for the afternoon? I know it's an odd request."

"Ms. Mitchell, I understand. I will arrange a chef's tasting dinner for two on the beach that will be billed directly to your hotel account, and will ensure Ms. Reed arrives comfortably and has all she needs until dinner. If you'd like, we can have someone escort her to the beach for dinner?"

"Exactly. That would be perfect."

The concierge made notes in the computer. "Now let me see, we have one room available that you may use for the afternoon after your spa treatments. Let me just arrange that. We would normally charge for the room but I will waive that charge for you since I assume you will not be sleeping there?"

Natalie was thrown off guard a moment. "Um no, correct. I just need a place to relax for the afternoon, shower, and dress for dinner. I'd like to surprise Tasha at dinner."

"I understand. Is this a special occasion you are celebrating?"

Natalie hesitated. "Yes, I guess it is. It's the start of something incredible."

The concierge nodded and smiled broadly. "This is certainly some start! I won't book your spa treatment but I've let the spa know you are on your way and they promise to take good care of you with whatever treatments you'd like. Enjoy your day and don't worry, I'll make sure everything comes together perfectly."

"Thank you so much. I really appreciate it," said Natalie as she headed for the spa. One thing she knew for certain was that she needed a massage, and pronto.

❧❧❧❧

Six hours later, Natalie stood in front of a full-length mirror looking carefully back at her own reflection. Her skin had turned a golden tan already after just two days in the island sun. Her long, wavy blonde hair was tied back in a simple low ponytail. It was almost time. She was beginning to second-guess her choice in wearing white slacks and a navy silk V-neck tank top but she had no other options. This was all she brought with her from her room. Presuming Tasha was there now, there was no going back to swap clothes or bury herself under the covers and pretend she was not about to make the single biggest leap of her entire life. She finished applying charcoal eyeliner to her top eyelid, then mascara to her eyelashes. The Pacific sun and salt water had already begun to bleach out her hair and her eyelids were blonder than normal. She took a deep breath, grabbed her bag and headed for the door.

After a short canoe ride to a private beach and lagoon, Natalie sat alone at a private table for two on a narrow section of beach. She could smell the fragrant flowers on the table as the nearby palm trees swayed gently in the breeze. The sun was just setting over the horizon and cast this red and orange otherworldly glow on everything. The lush greens of the mountain created a scenic backdrop that somehow steadied Natalie as if she were moored on a ship looking toward shore. She waited for the server to open a bottle of champagne and pour her a glass, and twice resisted the urge of checking her watch before she finally gave into the need.

It was seven fifteen. The thread of worry that Tasha had not come at all began to weave its way around her mind and wrap tightly around her heart. *What if she doesn't come?* Natalie thought, the words circulating and undulating around her mouth, making the bubbly champagne taste sour on her palette. She leaned back in her chair and dug her bare feet and newly pink painted toenails further into the cool, white sand. Closing her eyes, she tried to pull together the strength from somewhere deep inside her to handle the fact that Tasha was not here. That she had not received her note with any modicum of interest. That she had moved on with her life in California and had no need to waste any more time on Natalie or her blasted silent treatments. Natalie rarely prayed, but in this moment in this magical place, she said a prayer to the creator or the giver of love, or both, and she asked for a second chance. Natalie held back the tears she felt pushing to the surface and resigned herself to a romantic dinner on the beach for one. She sat straighter in her chair and opened her eyes.

In that moment, as the sun barely peeked its red tip over the tropical postcard-perfect horizon, Natalie saw Tasha walking barefoot towards her, with her hair in a thick black braid and one hand casually holding a pair of sandals. Tasha wore a floral sundress that clung to the curves of her body making her look so exquisitely beautiful that Natalie felt all the air in her body escape in a loud sigh. She was instantly drawn to the sway of Tasha's hips like a bee to honey. Natalie could see the intensity in Tasha's eyes that were one hundred percent locked on her. Natalie rose from her chair and stood with one hand resting against the table to steady her from falling completely over. *She's here!* On the outside, Natalie tried to appear cool and nonchalant, but on the inside her heart flipped and danced and jumped around her chest in wild celebration.

Tasha stood face to face with Natalie. "You sure know how to get a girl's attention," said Tasha, her lips turned upward in the beginning of a smile.

"I was afraid you wouldn't come," admitted Natalie.

"How could I not come to Bora Bora? We only talked about this place a million times," said Tasha, her voice velvety smooth and so sexy. In that instant, Natalie could feel the twinge of her old habits like a scab itching to be scratched. In the past, she'd have shut down in the exact moment her feelings for Tasha overwhelmed her. But this time she let those emotions pass through her without paralyzing her. She pushed aside those old, useless habits that no longer served her and instead, she pulled Tasha into a full-body embrace. Tasha leaned into her with a force that surprised Natalie. Because in all her thinking and wondering, Natalie had never once really stopped to contemplate the strength of Tasha's feelings for her. In that moment, as she smelled coconut butter and spicy smell of Tasha's neck, she knew. All the pieces fell into place with a click. After what seemed like an eternity, Tasha broke free, her luminous brown eyes shining straight into Natalie's soul.

"You know you could have just called me, right?" Tasha asked, taking her seat opposite Natalie. "You didn't have to go to this extent."

"I wanted us to live a little. I wanted to close the distance between us. There's so much I want to say to you."

"Let's start at the beginning," suggested Tasha.

Natalie waited for the server to pour Tasha's champagne and deliver an array of *canapés* before she continued. She raised her glass and Tasha did the same.

"What are we toasting?" asked Tasha.

"Tasha. I brought you here to tell you what's been on my mind for so long." Natalie hesitated. Tasha leaned forward in her seat.

"I love you. I've loved you for so long. Tasha..." Natalie was unable to continue. Her voice was choked with emotion. She was afraid to make eye contact with Tasha, afraid that if Tasha didn't feel the same she would see it first in her eyes. But in that moment, she felt Tasha's fingertips underneath her chin, raising her head and her eyes up from the table. Their eyes locked and Tasha's eyes told her all she needed to know—she felt the same.

"You know I've been waiting for you to say that out loud to my face for a really, really long time," said Tasha as she sipped her champagne.

"You have?" Asked Natalie, surprise raising her voice an octave.

"Um hm. I could see you struggling with it whenever we were together. I didn't want to pressure you or make you feel like I was pushing you one way or the other. I knew you had to come to it on your own terms. So, I waited. But that day I came to your house and left in the rain, I didn't think I would ever see you again," Tasha explained, a calm confidence in her tone.

"I'm sorry it took me so long," said Natalie.

"Natalie, don't apologize. You did this. We're here together in this amazing place. Let's make the most of it." Tasha smiled and Natalie felt the butterflies swirl around her insides.

❧❧❧❧

Later that night after a long, leisurely and utterly romantic dinner by candlelight, where they both caught up on the last few years of their lives, Tasha and Natalie walked hand in hand down the winding wooden boardwalks to their overwater suite. Natalie immediately walked out to the deck and looked out at the water, inhaling the fragrant Pacific air. "Let's go for a swim," she suggested.

"Sure," agreed Tasha. "I'll get us towels." Tasha walked inside the suite. After a few moments, Natalie heard the seductive sounds of Nights in White Satin played Flamenco style on a guitar.

Natalie unbuttoned her white slacks and shook them off in one smooth motion. She pulled off her tank top and contemplated leaving on her underwear for a moment before deciding to ditch her bra and panties with the rest of her clothes. She slipped into the still warm water of the plunge pool and leaned against the side. Her body buzzed with anticipation.

Tasha reemerged with a white bath towel wrapped around her sturdy body. Without hesitation, she dropped the towel, standing naked in front of Natalie. Natalie devoured Tasha with her eyes, taking in every detail of her caramel colored skin as Tasha stepped into the pool. Natalie closed the distance between them with two full strokes. Natalie's lips connected with Tasha's in the same instant her hands connected with Tasha's body. Her hands glided up and down Tasha's strong midsection and hips underwater while above the water line, her tongue danced with Tasha's. Natalie broke from their kiss and pushed Tasha gently against the side of the plunge pool so Tasha could get her footing to hold them both in place. Natalie's lips trailed down her neck and up again as her fingertips ran over Tasha's full breasts and taut nipples. Her tongue circled Tasha's earlobe, drawing a slow moan of pleasure from Tasha that vibrated deep inside Natalie's core like a single guitar string connected to them both.

Natalie's knee pushed against Tasha's crotch, spreading her legs apart underwater. Tasha begin to grind herself against Natalie's knee, her arms wrapped tightly around Natalie's back. Natalie was no longer thinking. She let all her inhibitions go in this magical, mystical place over the ocean. In one swift movement, Tasha hoisted herself from the pool and rested her hips on the ledge of the pool, her legs swung over Natalie's shoulders. Natalie's tongue played and licked and flicked at Tasha's core with simultaneous patience and urgency. This was about pleasing Tasha. This was about telling Tasha everything she had been afraid to say, up until now. She would no longer be silent and she would use her mouth to speak to Tasha's body because this conversation was the most important of her entire life. Natalie felt Tasha's clitoris harden underneath her tongue as she continued to play Tasha's body the way she always dreamed of playing the guitar.

Tasha leaned back, her long black hair in a thick braid down the middle of her back, her hands holding up her body on the wooden deck surrounding the pool, water sliding down her body making it glisten as if oiled, by the light of the full moon. Natalie wrapped her arms around Tasha's legs, her tongue sliding in and out, over and under, through and over Tasha as she felt Tasha's body respond to her touch, as she felt Tasha's body rock back and forth in a steady motion.

"Oh, baby. Oh, Natalie don't stop. Please don't stop," whispered Tasha, her voice gravelly and thick. "I'm going to come in your mouth." An instant later, Tasha threw her head back and orgasmed hard. Natalie tasted her silken sweetness and looked up at Tasha, at her body tensed and arched with pleasure, at her eyes wide open to the full Bora Bora moon, the distance between them finally erased.

*Lucy J. Madison is a novelist, poet and screenwriter from Connecticut. She's the author of two contemporary lesbian romance novels entitled In the Direction of the Sun and Personal Foul as well as the collection of poetry I.V. Poems (Sapphire Books).
www.lucyjmadison.com Instagram, Twitter and Facebook @lucyjmadison*

Now that you've enjoyed Volume One in A Heart Well Traveled Anthology Series, be sure to pick up your copy of Volumes Two and Three.

Coming September 2017

A Heart Well Traveled
Volume Two
Tales of Erotica, Fantasy and Sci-Fi Love Affairs and Unlikely Outcomes.

Each unique short story in this supernatural anthology will transport you to a magical interpretation of romance as authors bring to life, uncommon love affairs and out of the ordinary long distance relationships. Escape into the realms of eroticism, fan fiction fables, intergalactic intimacies, lunar love, mythical fantasy, and past lives revisited.

Is it fate, is it destiny or is it one of those defining moments where the universe comes to a screeching halt as an epic love appears?

Coming December 2017

A Heart Well Traveled
Volume Three
Tales of International Love Affairs and Unlikely Outcomes.

Love stretches across international boundaries as Sapphire brings you a collection of unique stories of romance and intrigue across the continents.

Pack your bags and let your imagination run wild as you find yourself on romantic escapes to Africa, Australia, Bora Bora, Canada, Europe, the Middle East, South America and the United Kingdom.

This fast-paced anthology will leave you wondering if you could endure love with nothing but miles between you and your lover. Watch as the characters face countless impossibilities without ever losing sight of the one thing we all want, one true love.

www.ingramcontent.com/pod-product-compliance
Lightning Source LLC
Chambersburg PA
CBHW051642180726
48284CB00006B/1831

9 781943 353897